Sant m
D0924861

The Hummingbird House

By Donna Ball

Gift of the
John and Peggy Maximus Fund

Copyright 2013 by Donna Ball, Inc.
Cover art by www.bigstock.com

All rights reserved. No part of this book may be reproduced in any form without the express written permission of the author.

ISBN: 978-0985774837

This is a work of fiction. All characters, events, organizations and places in this book are either a product of the author's imagination or used fictitiously and no effort should be made to construe them as real. Any resemblance to any actual people, events or locations is purely coincidental

Published by Blue Merle Publishing
Drawer H
Mountain City Georgia 30562
www.bluemerlepublishing.com

Blue Merle Publishing

ONE

A comfortable old age is the reward of a well-spent youth.

Oscar Wilde

They all gathered around the hospital bed—those who were left, anyway—while the monitors beeped out the last moments of Annabelle Stephens's life. She had lived ninety-seven remarkable years, married one man and outlived him, given birth to three children and outlived two of them. She had attended the funerals of all her friends and most of her enemies, and if there was one thing she knew for certain it was that growing old was vastly overrated. It was time for her to go. She was ready.

The nurse came in on soft-soled shoes and walked over to check the IV drip. Annabelle's daughter Marion sniffled into a tissue, and her husband Jim, who was comfortably ensconced in the armchair by the window playing Angry Birds, glanced up from his phone. Two of the great-nieces, each of whom suspected the other of having tried to manipulate Annabelle's will and both of whom were right, moved closer to the bed, glancing at each other resentfully.

The nurse made a minute adjustment to the drip valve, checked one of the monitors, and gave them all a sympathetic smile. "It won't be much longer," she said softly. "You should say your good-byes now."

Marion smothered a sob, and the two great-nieces bent over the bed, each of them clutching one of Annabelle's thin, papery hands. Jim said, "How much longer, do you think?" And at his wife's horrified glance, he added defensively, "My tee time is at two. I need to know if I should cancel, or what."

Whatever his outraged wife might have replied was cut off by the whooshing open of the door. Their daughter Megan came in, her tight brunette curls wind-tossed, her skirt and jacket rumpled, her face streaked with anxiety. "Mama, I'm so sorry, my plane was delayed at Dulles and then we circled Dallas for over two hours. I came straight from the airport. Am I too late?"

"Oh, baby, I'm so glad you're here!" Marion opened her arms for her daughter but Megan's hug was perfunctory and her eyes never left the still, shrunken figure on the bed.

Megan pulled away from her mother's embrace and went to the bedside, edging around the two great-nieces for a seat on the bed. She smoothed away a wisp of iron gray hair from her grandmother's cool forehead and let her heart fill with memories of this extraordinary woman, this life lived so hugely and over too soon. If she had lived five hundred years it still would not have been long enough.

Some people, Megan knew, never got a chance to spend time with their grandparents as children beyond the occasional holiday visit, or to get to know them as adults at all. Megan could not imagine having missed out on the opportunity to be a part of the life that was now seeping out in slow stuttering breaths upon the hospital bed before her. At age sixty, Annabelle Stephens had won an amateur ballroom dancing competition. At age seventy-two, she had biked across Europe. She had taken Megan on her first zip line excursion less than five years ago and had earned her small-plane pilot's license when she was sixty-five. For Megan's thirteenth birthday, her grandmother had taken her to South Africa, and they spent two weeks traveling through unimaginable poverty and unbelievable beauty, staying in the villages and shopping in the open air markets. When she graduated from college, she and her grandmother had gone rafting down the Colorado River and spent ten days held in thrall by the vast, towering silence, the thousand shades of pink that sunrise could paint upon a canyon wall. Every day was an adventure to Annabelle Stephens, every moment a bright and sparkling gift that was to be overlooked or taken for granted at one's own peril. How could such a brilliant light fade so quickly? How could it even be contained, much less extinguished?

"Oh, Gram," she whispered, curling her fingers against the old woman's cheek. "Not yet. Please, not yet."

The beeping of the monitor grew slower, and then slower still. Marion sobbed and lurched toward the bed. Jim stood cautiously. The nurse stood by respectfully, ready to note the time for the death certificate. Megan's face melted into a pool of raw sorrow, and she brought her cheek to rest lightly beside her grandmother's on the pillow. "Oh, Gram. I'm not finished with you yet. I need you. Please don't go."

Her grandmother took a deep, shuddering breath, expelled it, and was still. No one in the room moved, or spoke, for several seconds. Even the monitor stopped beeping. It was as though, having waited for the moment they all had known was surely coming, now that it had arrived they did not know what to do.

The nurse stepped forward to turn off the monitor before it began shrilling its alarm, glanced at the screen, and hesitated. One of the great-nieces burst into tears. Marion cried, "Mama!" and surged forward.

Annabelle Stephens's eyes popped open and she looked around alertly. "Good heavens!" she exclaimed. "What's all this wailing and carrying on? It's enough to wake the dead!"

Half an hour later, Annabelle was sitting up in bed, sipping orange juice through a straw. The ribbon of her pink satin bed jacket was tied in a floppy bow at her neck, her hair was neatly brushed and finger-waved, and a sweep of powdered rouge expertly applied to each cheek. Her lipstick, a saucy shade called Pretty in Pink, brought back color to her face and a spark to her eyes. Everyone had been shooed away except Megan, who leaned against the closed door with her arms folded across her chest, regarding her grandmother with indulgent affection.

"They're all pretty mad at you, Gram."

Annabelle gave an impatient wave of her hand. "Let them be. Bunch of ghouls, anyway, just waiting for the body to grow cold." She tilted her head toward the door in a playful way and a mischievous glint came into her eyes as she added, "They all think I've got money. But shall I tell you a secret? Not a penny. Fooled them every one, all these years." She broke into a laugh that was so light and so easy Megan couldn't help grinning back.

"Well, it wasn't very nice," Megan said, trying her best to look disapproving. "You scared us half to death and almost made Daddy miss his tee time. Why on earth would you want to pretend to be on your death bed?"

Annabelle paused with the straw partway to her lips, looking surprised. "Good heavens, child, I wasn't pretending. At my age, what would be the point? No indeed, if those fine young doctors say I was breathing my last, then I suspect that is precisely what I was doing. Only ..." A thoughtful, puzzled look came over her face and she put the glass on the bed table. "I suppose I'm not quite as ready to go as

I had imagined. I had the dream again, and I think there's still something I need to do."

"What dream, Gram?"

Annabelle's hand was steady and sure as she pushed the swing-arm table to the side, and patted the place on the bed beside her. Megan came to sit beside her, and Annabelle watched her granddaughter with the smile of one who treasures deeply, loves long, and expects nothing beyond the moment of sweet, quiet watching. She wrapped her fingers around Megan's and gave them a squeeze.

"Sweet girl, I want you to do something for me."

Megan regarded her tenderly. "Grammy, you're the one who told me never to trust a man who bleaches his teeth. For that alone I'm your slave for life. You know you can count on me."

"I do know that for a fact." Annabelle gave a single decisive nod of her head and pursed her lips. As she glanced around the small room with its khaki-colored walls and narrow window and steel-and-vinyl furnishings, her expression turned to disdain. "What a place to spend the last moments of your life. It's a travesty, I tell you, a crime against God and nature. And ..." she sniffed the air and wrinkled her nose, "it smells like old people in here."

Megan laughed softly. "You're a card, Gram. Why do I have the feeling you're about to ask me to do something that will make your doctors very unhappy with me?"

"Oh, who cares what they think? A person has got the right to die where she wants to. But I'm not ready to die yet, and I don't need you to get me out of this jail cell. I can walk out on my own two good legs."

Her expression sobered somewhat and her eyes, a paler shade of her granddaughter's denim blue, turned introspective, carefully thoughtful, as though puzzling out a question phrase by phrase, turn by turn. "Sweet girl," she said, "I want you to help me find something."

"Okay, Gram. What did you lose?"

She replied slowly, "I'm not sure. But I know where I lost it."

Megan squeezed her grandmother's fingers in reassurance. "Okay. Where is it?"

Annabelle returned her gaze to her granddaughter but it was vague for a moment, as though her thoughts, travelling from such a long distance, needed time to catch up. Then she smiled. "That," she replied, "is what I want you to help me find."

She caught a corner of the sheet, tossed it aside, and swung her boney legs over the side of the bed. "Are you up for a road trip?"

OF VICE AND MEN

By Paul Slater

After twenty-three brilliant, flashy, and often outrageous years with you, Gentle Reader, the time has come for me to say good-bye to *In Style* and all it entails. We've laughed together, we've cried together. We survived mom jeans, Cuban heels, and Kim Kardashian together. But now the voice of adventure calls me in a different direction, and I know your best wishes for a safe passage are with me as I sally forth to boldly go where no self-respecting style guru has gone before.

The country.

It's been three months since I left the hustle and bustle of the big city for the bucolic pastimes of the Shenandoah Valley, and I'm often asked what I miss the most. The traffic jams on the Beltway? The gangland shootings that dominate the nightly news? The clever cocktail conversations of Washington's finest, those silver-tongued devils to whom we are eternally grateful for putting the hustle into the term "hustle and bustle"? Or perhaps simply the vastly underestimated delights of really reliable Internet service?

The answer, my friends, is none of the above.

Here in the country we watch the sunsets instead of musical theater. The musical stylings of the chickadees have replaced concerts in the park and we attend county fairs instead of the opera. Fusion cuisine may be a bit hard to find, but farm fresh produce is on every corner. The Manolo Blahnicks have been traded for gardening clogs and Fashion Week for the Founder's Day Parade, but life has never been richer.

"I certainly hope you don't expect to support us with that drivel," commented Derrick, reading the computer screen over Paul's shoulder. His arms were filled with folded towels—half aqua and half peach, six hundred thread count, finest quality Egyptian cotton—and his reading glasses had slipped down to the tip of his nose. He was, in fact, wearing gardening clogs.

Paul scowled at him briefly. "I'm experimenting with a new style."

"So I see. If you don't mind a suggestion …"

"I do."

Derrick lifted an eyebrow and used his index finger to push his glasses back onto the bridge of his nose. The tower of aqua and peach towels tilted precariously. Paul sprang up to help him. "Sorry," he said, transferring half the stack into his own arms. "I don't mean to be cranky."

"My suggestion was going to be," replied Derrick archly, "that you turn your considerable talent for the written word into producing advertising copy for our brochures. We're supposed to be running a business here, you know. By the way, the towels arrived. Gorgeous or not?"

"Gorgeous," agreed Paul, admiring them. "You didn't forget the white ones for the ladies to remove makeup, did you?"

"Shipping separately." Derrick nodded toward the cursor still blinking on the screen. "Where's the 'vice' part?"

Paul sighed. "Still looking for it."

"Aren't we all?" The muffled sound of a car door slamming reached them through the tall, wavy-paned window of the small office, and Derrick's face brightened. "That must be the girls. Bridget is bringing three dozen eggs and Cici promised to look at the leaky faucet. I ordered two cakes for tomorrow's brunch, too, and Lindsay is bringing another landscape. I'm going to try to get Bridget to help with the demi-glace for the pork loin while she's here. Come give us a hand, will you?"

Paul glanced thoughtfully back at the half-empty screen of the laptop. "Maybe I'll start a blog," he said.

"Boys!" a voice called from the kitchen door. "Are you here?"

"Be right there, sweeties!" Derrick paused at the doorway to glance back over his shoulder.

"Right," said Paul. "Coming."

But he lingered in the office as Derrick hurried away, gazing at the words on the screen. "What do I miss?" he muttered. "My life."

He used his elbow to close the laptop without bothering to save the document, then he went to put the towels away.

The lodge had begun its life, as far as anyone could tell, as a one-room way station for travelers in the days of rutted wagon roads and horse-drawn carriages, serving cold ale and hot stew, along with a straw mattress on the floor if you didn't mind sharing with six other men, for twenty-five cents. A bath was extra. Paul and Derrick had scoured the countryside antique shops for a tavern sign from the era, but the best they could do was a hand-painted wooden livery sign that harkened from a hundred years later, which they hung from the arch of the twig pergola that led to the herb garden.

When the Dry Creek gold mine opened in the 1830s, the lodge added a second story and another wing to accommodate the miners who flooded into the county to try their luck. A full course meal was offered every Saturday and Sunday night at the wide-board table in the dining room, and it became so popular that extra tables had to be set up on the porch in the summertime to accommodate the townspeople who drove out for the meal. The mine played out, and the lodge descended into the ignominy of a private home for a decade or two. Then came the Shenandoah Valley Railroad and the rooms were once again filled with the bustle of travelers and the aromas of good sturdy food. Derrick had salvaged a wooden bench from an old railroad station in Pennsylvania to commemorate the era, and it now welcomed modern day guests in the entry hall of the lodge.

The provenance of the lodge became muddled during the early part of the twentieth century, but there was a picture of it in the archives of the local paper when it opened its doors as the Blue View Motor Court in 1955 and again as the Heavenly Hash Diner in 1968. Paul had found a set of chrome stools with red vinyl seats from an old diner in Georgia, had had them beautifully restored by an acquaintance of his from Washington who just happened to own an auto-body repair shop, and had them bolted to the floor around the stainless steel island in the kitchen, almost as they might have been in the sixties.

The building was occupied by a group of lawyers in the eighties, stood empty in the nineties, and fell into disrepair until a private party undertook the task of restoration at the turn of the twenty-first century with the idea of turning it into a bed and breakfast. The result was a long rambling structure embraced by a wrap-around porch with peeled-log support posts, tall narrow windows, and a mixture of log and lap siding stained a nature-loving brown. There were seven airy guest suites, each with a door opening onto the shady porch, and each door was painted a different color—bright fuchsia, canary yellow, cobalt blue, emerald green, purple, tangerine, watermelon red. It sat in the midst of a tangle of wildflower gardens accented by twisted laurel arbors and colorful folk-art bird feeders, and was surrounded by the flowing vista of lavender blue mountains. It had functioned as the Mountain Laurel Bed and Breakfast for a mere six months before Paul and Derrick came to stay there with the idea of retiring in the Shenandoah Valley and building their dream house. They were immediately drawn in by the funky charm of the place, the quiet evenings, the lush gardens, the comic antics of the warrior hummingbirds, and grew enchanted with the life of ease and hospitality offered by life at the B&B. When the opportunity arose to purchase the property and become the permanent proprietors and gracious hosts of what was now known as The Hummingbird House, they did so without hesitation.

They were only now beginning to realize they had not entirely thought this through.

Of course there had been renovation and redecorating to do, and one could not accommodate paying guests while construction was going on. They had made a point of continuing to open for the Sunday brunch that had been popularized by the previous owner, and they always had a waiting list for reservations, but they both knew that was due mostly to the fact that their friend Bridget did the cooking. The art gallery that Derrick had established in the front of the house always saw a lot of traffic on Sundays, and their friend Lindsay, an amateur artist of considerable talent, helped keep the display interesting by rotating her own paintings through the collection each week in keeping with the current theme. The one thing they hadn't really given much thought to when they purchased the place was that older homes, particularly ones that are open to the public and required to meet certain health and building codes, demand a good bit of maintenance, and the only thing either one of them knew about maintaining property was how to dial the handyman's number. Fortunately, they now knew how to dial the number of their friend Cici, who had restored a hundred-year-old mansion practically single-handedly, and who knew more about nail guns and ratchets and pipe fittings than either of them was likely to learn in a lifetime.

If the truth be told, they never would have made it this far without the help of the girls, and that was why seeing them all gathered in the kitchen now with very determined looks on their faces filled both Paul and Derrick with an uneasy dismay. They didn't like to admit it, even to themselves, but they each had known this moment was coming for some time now.

Paul rubbed his hands together in false enthusiasm as he came into the kitchen, declaring, "Ladies, you've never looked more lovely! Lindsay, new shoes? Bridget, darling, love your hair! That shade is definitely you."

Lindsay glanced down in confusion at her worn, if freshly laundered, plaid sneakers, and Bridget gave him a skeptical look. "It should be," she said, touching her short platinum bob briefly. "It's the same color I've used for thirty years."

All three women had passed their first blush of youth decades ago, but all three still had legs that could wear shorts without embarrassment, and glitter polish on their toenails when the occasion called for it. The edge might have fallen off their fashion sense since they had abandoned the suburbs for the country, but they weren't exactly attending society parties every weekend, either. Even with their hair tied back against the warm midsummer day and their tee shirts less fresh than they might have been six hours ago, Paul's compliments were not entirely insincere.

Paul brushed a kiss across Cici's cheek. "Cici, you look—"

"I look like I spent the morning pulling weeds and the afternoon setting Japanese beetle traps in the orchard," she interrupted impatiently. "We need to talk."

"Will you look at these eggs?" Derrick put in cheerfully, trying to postpone the inevitable. He carefully transferred the eggs from their padded basket to a big yellow bowl on the countertop, fussing over them as he might a flower arrangement. "They're as pretty as Easter eggs. Brown and green and turquoise ... what do you call the green ones again, Bridget?"

Bridget forgot her stern demeanor and agreed happily, "They are pretty, aren't they? And the yolks are as bright as butter!" She started helping unpack the basket. "Now remember, fresh eggs don't have to be refrigerated, so these will do just fine until morning on the counter. In fact, if I were you ..."

Cici spoke over her. "Let's all sit down, shall we?"

Paul looked at Derrick. Derrick looked helplessly back. Like guilty children, they went to the table by the window where they took their family meals, held out a chair for each of the ladies, and then took their own seats. Cici took a breath.

"Boys, you know we love you," she began, "but we have to have a talk."

Derrick smothered a groan. "No good thing has ever happened to me after those words."

Paul gave Cici his most endearing smile. "Oh-oh. Have we over-imposed ourselves upon your good natures?"

"Oh, no, of course not!" Bridget exclaimed, but Lindsay silenced her with a sharp and meaningful look.

"The thing is," Lindsay said carefully, folding her hands atop the table, "we know it's hard getting settled into a new community, and that you never would have made the move if it hadn't been for us, and we love having you here, we really do. But—"

"But we can't keep running over here two and three times a day," Cici interrupted impatiently. "We're spending more time taking care of your place than we are our own. We have our hands full working to get the winery off the ground—"

"And I'm trying to open my own restaurant," Bridget put in.

"And I'm supposed to be planning my wedding," added Lindsay, "on top of everything else. It's not that we mind helping out—"

"Yes we do," Cici corrected her flatly, tossing her an exasperated look.

"It's just," continued Lindsay deliberately, "that we're worried that it's gone beyond helping, and is bordering on enabling."

Derrick looked at Paul with a touch of horrified embarrassment. "This is an intervention," he said.

Cici sat back and folded her arms. "Exactly."

A beat passed while they absorbed this. Then Paul glanced at Derrick uncertainly and said, "I don't suppose this would be a good time to mention the loose floorboard in the powder room."

Cici lifted her eyes to the heavens and blew out a breath that ruffled her bangs.

Bridget reached across the table and squeezed Derrick's hand, her gentle round face filled with compassion. "The Bed and Breakfast is yours now. You have to let it *be* yours. Take over, be in charge, make some decisions."

"We've made plenty of decisions," Paul objected. "We decided to completely redecorate the public rooms."

"*And* expand the art gallery," added Derrick.

"And enclose the side porch to enlarge the dining room."

"And you did a fine job with all of that," Bridget assured them. "Everyone loves the new glassed-in dining room."

"But who was over here every day helping you paint and strip wallpaper and move furniture?" Lindsay pointed out.

"And who was it who called the contractors and supervised the workers while you two were busy ordering Battenberg tablecloths and shopping for mismatched Havilland?" Cici put in.

Paul and Derrick exchanged a look that was both abashed and distressed. "They're right," Paul told his partner. "We've been fiends."

Derrick turned to Cici. "We used you outrageously. Can you ever forgive us?"

Cici shifted her gaze toward Lindsay in a mini-eye roll, but her lips quirked with repressed amusement. "You're not fiends," she admitted, "and you're forgiven. But …"

"But," Lindsay interrupted firmly, "it's time you started doing things for yourself. How can you make this place your own if you don't, well, own it?"

"And when are you going to open for business again?" Bridget added. "You're missing the height of the tourist season."

"We are open for business," Paul objected. "This is the most popular place in the county for Sunday brunch."

"It's the only place in the county for Sunday brunch," Bridget said. "And what I meant was, when are you going to start renting the rooms? That's what a bed and breakfast does, you know."

"A bed and breakfast also offers breakfast every morning," Paul said, "and I really only know how to make three things."

"Two," Derrick corrected, and Paul frowned a little. "Of course, I only know how to make two as well."

"One," Paul corrected.

They looked at each other for a moment, and then Derrick said, "We're not nearly ready to open to the public yet."

Paul added, "We haven't even started redecorating the guest rooms, and the entire second floor has to be remodeled …"

"Who knows what we'll even find when we get up there?" put in Derrick with a shudder. "We opened the door once and saw a spider the size of a puppy. Slammed the door closed and taped it shut."

"Not to mention the spa," Paul said, "which we haven't even started yet. Frankly, it's going to be rather more expensive than we'd planned, so it may take awhile."

"It would be a great deal more affordable without the Roman baths," Derrick pointed out smugly. "And I told you, one massage room is plenty if we intend to put in the steam room as well."

At Bridget's raised eyebrows, Paul explained, "Not Roman baths, just a simple hot tub. And I might have said something about a small waterfall."

Derrick looked self-satisfied, but said nothing.

Cici, Lindsay, and Bridget were also silent for a moment, but the look that passed between them spoke volumes. Finally Lindsay said, "You know, boys, considering the way your house-building project turned out, it might be a little too soon to take on a major construction project like a spa."

Derrick winced and Paul deliberately looked away. It was, in fact, too soon for them to even talk about that fiasco.

Lindsay said, "The guest rooms don't need redecorating. They're gorgeous. Everything is gorgeous."

"They're fine, I suppose," admitted Paul reluctantly, "if not entirely to our taste."

Bridget said gently, "Sometimes you can wait so long for everything to be perfect that nothing ever gets done."

Cici said, "Guys, I really don't know what the problem is. The place was in perfect operating condition when you bought it and it was full almost every weekend. It's the only really nice overnight accommodation within an hour's drive and it could be a gold mine for you. You just need to open."

Lindsay squeezed Derrick's hand. "All we want is for you to be happy. But how can you know if you're going to be happy here unless you actually try?"

Paul said worriedly, "I just don't think we're ready."

"Then get ready," exclaimed Cici, exasperated.

"We have plenty of towels," Derrick pointed out helpfully.

"We don't have a staff," Paul protested.

"All you need is a housekeeper," Lindsay said.

"And a cook," Bridget added quickly.

"Most people," Cici pointed out, "go into the bed-and-breakfast business because they want to do it themselves."

Paul looked at Derrick. "That's exactly why we wanted to do it," he agreed. "Only ..."

"Only," Derrick said, "I think we rather imagined ourselves more in the roles of genial hosts."

"*Patrons,*" agreed Paul. "Maître d'hôtel. Reminiscent of the grand houses of Europe."

The three women exchanged a look, the corners of their lips tightening in a mixture of resignation and repressed mirth. Bridget stood and kissed Derrick atop his head. "We love you. I'll put the cakes in the refrigerator. And," she added sternly, "hire a cook."

Cici dug a tool out of her pocket and handed it to Paul. "This," she told him, "is a wrench. It's used to fix leaky faucets. Come on, I'll show you how."

Paul meekly followed Cici from the kitchen and Lindsay turned to Derrick. Her tone was a little apologetic. "Are we still invited for brunch tomorrow?"

Derrick looked at her hopefully. "Do you know how to make a pork loin?"

On Ladybug Farm

"You know what the difference between men and women is?" declared Cici, flinging herself into the front porch rocking chair.

She was so distracted that she let the screen door bounce closed behind her, and Bridget, who followed with a tray of lemonade and cookies, caught it with her toe. "Well, for one thing, men usually hold the door."

"Oh, Bridge, I'm sorry." Cici leapt up again and held the door. There was a faint cloud of anxiety in her eyes as she added, "Do you think we were too hard on them?"

"Too hard on whom?" Lindsay came down the stairs, smelling of a delicate floral body wash and wearing a loose print maxi-dress with no bra, her hair pulled back and damp around the edges from her shower. The day was done, the chores were completed, they were at home with each other, and comfort was the order of the day. She grabbed a cookie from Bridget's tray before she took her own rocking chair, swinging her legs up onto the porch rail.

"The boys," Cici said. She moved some magazines off the white wicker table between the chairs to make room for the tray.

"I wasn't," Lindsay replied easily, biting into the cookie, "but you were, definitely. These are great, Bridget. Lemon drop, right?"

"I doubled the recipe," Bridget said, pouring the lemonade. "I'll take the boys a batch tomorrow."

"Good idea," said Cici. She handed a glass of lemonade to Lindsay, and took one for herself, along with two cookies. "I never knew of a problem a lemon drop cookie couldn't fix."

Lindsay tasted the lemonade. "Nice," she said. "Different."

Cici sipped and agreed, "It's a good day for lemonade."

Bridget poured herself a glass. "It is a nice change, isn't it? I used a fresh basil simple syrup."

The other two women tasted again and murmured their appreciation.

Sometimes it seemed like only yesterday that the three of them had shared a cul-de-sac in the suburbs of Baltimore and Paul and Derrick had been their neighbors. It had in fact been four years since they had stumbled upon the old brick mansion in the Shenandoah Valley and decided to try their hands at bringing it back to life. What they had imagined to be a quiet retirement clipping roses and drinking tea from patterned China cups in front of the fire had in fact turned out to consist of a dawn-to-dusk labor of love, replacing rotting timbers, pulling weeds, hauling fence posts, fighting potato bugs and planting a vineyard cutting by cutting. Now they shared not only a home, but a life, and Paul and Derrick—perhaps the most unlikely candidates imaginable for the rigors of rural living—were once again their neighbors.

A slow and lazy dusk settled over Ladybug Farm and the three women, as they had done every evening since they had moved into the old house, settled into their rocking chairs to watch the sun set and solve the problems of the world. Usually their refreshment of choice was wine, but after a hot day working in the vineyard they had decided the lemonade would be a refreshing break from the ordinary. A light breeze stirred the air beneath the shade of the wraparound porch, rustling the fronds of the ferns that hung in evenly spaced baskets around the porch and sending them to turning lazily. As the light took on the purplish shadows of evening across the wide expanse of meadow that stretched before them, the sheep huddled into their nighttime knots and the shoulders of the mountains that stood guard over them became muted with the deep greens and shadowy blues of another ending day. Through the open windows they could hear the sounds of Ida Mae, who had been taking care of the hundred-year-old house almost as long as it had been standing, rustling around in the kitchen, closing down the old day and preparing for a new one.

"So," said Bridget, settling into her chair with a cookie and a glass. "What's the difference between men and women?"

"This I've got to hear," murmured Lindsay.

Cici ignored her. "Men expect everything to be easy," she answered. "They're programmed that way from birth. All their lives they have some woman taking care of them, doing things for them …"

"That's because, most of the time, it's easier to do it ourselves," Bridget pointed out.

"Learned helplessness," said Lindsay, who had taught third grade for twenty-five years. "It's sweeping our society, like ADHD. Only you don't get it from Red Dye Number Seven or early childhood immunizations. You get it from well-meaning mothers."

Cici gave a decisive nod of agreement. "I'm not saying it's not our faults," she said. "I'm just saying men, as a gender, have an entirely different attitude about adversity than we do."

Bridget sniffed with laughter. "Anybody who's ever taken care of a man with a head cold can testify to that. A woman could go through twelve hours of labor while having both wisdom teeth extracted without making half as much fuss."

Lindsay and Cici raised their glasses in a toast to that.

"Women, on the other hand," Cici went on, "expect life to be difficult. We don't even bother to complain until things start approaching impossible."

"And we get it done anyway," said Bridget.

"Look what we took on with this house," Lindsay said.

"Broken plumbing, trees crashing through the sunroom …"

"Sheep storming the front porch, a sink hole in the backyard …"

"Rattlesnakes, fires, blizzards …"

"Not to mention the ordinary painting and refinishing and patching and rebuilding," Bridget said.

"The chicken coop, the goat house …"

"The winery," Lindsay added, and they all nodded, impressed with their accomplishments.

"And did we complain?" Cici demanded.

They thought about that for a moment, until Bridget finally admitted, "Well, maybe a little."

"All right, a little," Cici conceded. "But we never gave up."

"Talked about it a few times," Lindsay reminded them, and Cici frowned, annoyed.

"The point is," she began.

"The point is," Bridget spoke over her, "we got it done. Women always get it done."

"Right," said Cici.

Lindsay raised her glass. "To women who get it done."

The three clinked their goblets and sat back, sipping lemonade and munching cookies.

"Good lemonade," Cici said.

"Just tart enough," added Lindsay.

"Hits the spot," agreed Bridget.

They rocked for a moment, looking at their glasses.

"It's nice for a change," Lindsay said.

"Just the right amount of sugar," Cici said.

Bridget put aside her glass. "I'll get the wine," she said.

"I'll get the glasses." Cici followed her inside.

"The corkscrew's on the counter," Lindsay called after them.

Evening at Ladybug Farm had begun.

There was a stone patio in the back of the house between the herb garden and the wildflower garden that was furnished with laurel wood furniture made by a local craftsman. The laurel branches were soaked until malleable, twisted and woven together to shape chair backs and seats, and then mounted on sturdy tree-trunk legs. The chairs and love seats were decorated with comfortable cushions in a bright emerald flower garden print, and the occasional tables, also formed of laurel wood, were shellacked to a bright luster. Tall feathery stalks of dill and spiky rosemary bushes formed the living wall of the herb garden and perfumed the late afternoon air with their fragrance. Purple coneflower and bright pink dianthus competed with black-eyed Susans for the attention of the fat bumblebees that drifted from stem to stem. Above it all a colony of hummingbirds buzzed and darted from one red glass feeder to another, stopping along the way to sample the bright pink fuchsia that tumbled from the hanging baskets at the corners of the house or the trumpet vine that climbed along the back garden fence. There was nothing orderly or well managed about this garden at all; it was a riot of clashing colors and tangled vines, a veritable highway of busy activity for the birds and bees who called it their home, and it was without a doubt the most harmonious and relaxing corner of the entire property.

Brunch visitors liked to sit and chat and sip mimosas here on Sundays, gazing at the serene mountain view or laughing at the antics of the hummingbirds. Paul and Derrick made it a point to have cocktails here every afternoon, weather permitting, usually a nice sherry with a mild local cheese, or, if they were feeling experimental, an hors d'oeuvre from a recipe they'd found online. Paul brought the tray with sherry and cheese to the patio at six, just as Derrick came around the corner from the vegetable garden, lugging a wicker basket piled high with the largest tomatoes, zucchini, eggplants and yellow squash Paul had ever seen.

"Good lord," exclaimed Paul, setting the tray on one of the lacquered bark tables. "What are we, Lilliputians?"

Derrick set the basket on the patio and began to unpack it. A single tomato overflowed his hand, and there was an eggplant the size of a soccer ball. "Do you think they're edible? I've never seen vegetables this size. And so many of them! It's like Jack's beanstalk gone wild over there."

Paul balanced a green pepper the size of a small pumpkin on his palm. "Amazing. You could throw a vegetarian dinner party for sixteen on the contents of this basket alone. What do you suppose she did to make them grow this big?"

The previous owner had planted the vegetable garden in the spring, and they had enjoyed the fresh lettuces, spinach, and carrots when they first moved in. They continued to care for the garden according to the instructions Lindsay had given them, but they were quite sure even Lindsay had not expected a harvest like this.

"A better question," Derrick said, removing his floppy straw hat to dab at his damp brow with a folded handkerchief, "is what are we going to do with it all?"

"Take it to the girls, of course," Paul replied, "To make up for our beastly behavior of late."

Derrick regarded the bounty with a tilt of his head. "You do realize, of course, that they have a vegetable garden twice as large as ours?"

"True," Paul admitted. He picked up a tomato with both hands. "But their produce isn't nearly as grand as this."

Derrick said, "And this is just the beginning. It seems criminal to waste it all. Isn't there a way to preserve fresh produce?"

"Bridget would know."They looked at each other for a moment, but said nothing. Paul returned the tomato to the basket. Derrick poured the sherry. They took their chairs and watched the hummingbirds while the breezy late afternoon shadows shifted and danced across the stones.

Paul said, "I miss Fashion Week."

Derrick might have pointed out that since Fashion Week was in February and it was now only July, he had not yet had a chance to miss it. Instead, he sipped his sherry. "I miss Sotheby's."

Paul sighed. "I don't think this is turning out entirely the way we planned."

"I don't recall having a plan."

"That may be the problem." Paul watched the hummingbirds and sipped his sherry for a moment, his legs crossed, his free foot swinging restlessly. "But if we did have a plan, I suspect it would be for something a bit more significant than sitting in the sun on a Saturday evening watching the birds."

"Ah," agreed Derrick, inclining his head sagely, "a life of significance. The ultimate quest of every human being from Plato to Bon Jovi."

"Retirement," clarified Paul sourly, "an invention of the young to reduce the lives of their betters to rusty dreams and small ambitions. The devil of it is, they make it sound so damned alluring, anyone is likely to fall for it."

Derrick said quietly, "We were significant, you know. We had our moment. We were giants in our fields."

"Now we're just two old farts puttering around in the garden."

"Well, that's the way of things, isn't it?"

Paul glared at the sherry in his glass. "Why isn't this bourbon? I need a drink."

Derrick said unhappily, "You know what the worst of it is?"

Paul slammed back the sherry as though it was, indeed, bourbon, and poured himself another. "There's worse?"

Derrick looked at him. "The girls were right. We could do this if we wanted to."

Paul sipped his sherry, studiously avoiding his partner's gaze. "What if we fail?"

"What if we don't?"

"There's always mediocrity."

"Even worse than failure," Derrick admitted. "But why are those the only choices?"

Paul slid a glance his way. "Our dream house was swallowed up by our swimming pool," he reminded him. "We lost most of our life savings on carrara marble and imported statues we never saw. We don't exactly have the best track record with ventures of this sort. I think it's safer to take things slowly, think it through."

"You may be right." Derrick helped himself to a bit of the soft cheese, spreading it carefully on a toasted cracker. "There's no point in rushing. We're retired, after all."

Paul gazed out over the garden solemnly for a long moment before replying. "That," he agreed heavily, with a sigh, "we are."

TWO

The only things one never regrets are one's mistakes.

Oscar Wilde

His name was Joshua Whitman. He was named for a warrior and a poet, he was twenty-seven years old, and he had a degree—well, most of one, anyway— from Harvard. He had been on a waiting list for the most prestigious preschool in New York before he was even born. He'd been to Europe twice by the age of ten, attended one of the finest private schools in the country, and vacationed in Martha's Vineyard every summer until he was eighteen. Now he was standing outside a men's room at a truck stop in Las Vegas, waiting for a burly trucker who had smiled at him inside the diner. He had three dollars and twenty-seven cents in his pocket, and two of those dollars had been swiped from a tabletop on his way out of the diner.

It was three a.m., which meant nothing in places like this except the counter in the diner wasn't as crowded as it might have been a few hours earlier or later. Josh had spent a dollar he could ill afford on a cup of coffee and sat midway down the row of stools, scoping the place out. There was a loud, brassy haired blonde working the counter who looked at him like she knew he was trouble, but he gave her his baby-faced smile and she left him alone. A couple of truckers and a droopy-eyed businessman were eating eggs and bacon that smelled so good they made Josh light-headed. At the end of the counter a funny-looking bald man in plaid trousers was reading the newspaper, smiling and nodding to himself as he turned the pages.

The trucker a few seats down from Josh was slope-shouldered and scruffy-faced, and he kept sliding Josh looks as though he didn't know quite what to make of him. Josh kept his eyes to himself, but managed to see enough with his peripheral vision to note that when the trucker took out a bottle of aspirin and unscrewed the lid, the capsules inside were not sold over the counter. Josh figured there had to be a couple of hundred dollars worth of amphetamines inside, easy.

He watched the guy toss back a couple of the little eye-openers, and when the trucker saw him watching, Josh smiled at him. The other man deliberately replaced the cap on the bottle, tucked the bottle back into his jacket pocket, and then he smiled back. A few minutes later, he paid his bill and left. Josh watched through the big glass window as he went around the corner of the brightly lit building toward the showers and restrooms. He waited another thirty seconds, and then slid his fingers into his jeans pocket, touching the photograph there for courage. He got up and followed the man.

Now he stood with one shoulder leaning against the cool concrete wall where a half wall that hid the dumpsters offered a pool of shadow and a semblance of privacy, listening to the rumble of engines and breathing diesel fumes, his heart like a big pulsing lump in his throat. He watched as the man came out of the men's room, noticed him, and altered his course toward him. Josh smiled, and his hand tightened on the switchblade in the pocket of his windbreaker.

I am Joshua Whitman, he thought, *I was named for a warrior and a poet. This is not who I am.*

Nonetheless, he tilted his head in a friendly way toward the stranger and he said, "Hey man, you got an aspirin?"

The trucker came close, close enough that Josh could smell the old sweat that clung to his clothes and the piney soap he'd used to wash his hands. He had dead snake eyes that flicked Josh up and down without revealing anything. He said, "Yeah, I might." Close, and closer still, into the shadows. "What you got for me?"

Josh pulled out the knife. "This," he said, and that was when someone grabbed him from behind.

It all happened in a matter of seconds, of thundering heartbeats and flashing adrenaline. Josh didn't hear what was said. He was too busy calling himself every kind of fool for falling for the setup. There was laughter and somebody grunted something about "stupid punk kid" while the big man lunged at him and grabbed a hunk of Josh's hair, grinning a grin that showed two rotting front teeth. The other man twisted his arms behind him and the knife went clattering to the concrete floor.

Josh rolled his eyes back in his head let himself go limp, knees sagging to the floor. He felt the men's surprise. The first man let go of Josh's hair and the one who had his arms pinned shifted his weight to support him. It was enough to allow Josh to drive his elbow fiercely backward into his captor's gut; he heard the whoosh of air that left the other man's body even as Josh twisted and ducked and tore out of his jacket, swinging a roundhouse kick that smashed into the first man's kneecap and doubled him over. He ran.

Josh was small and lean, and he did not have a chance against the two men if they caught him. But he was also fast, and he had no intention of being caught. He slid between two trucks and made himself hold his breath, listening. Voices, angry, barely discernible above the growling hum of truck engines, but coming closer. He ducked under one of the trucks, pressing himself deep into the shadows beneath the wheel well, and watched a set of booted feet pass by, pause, and turn back. He made everything in his body go still. The boots stopped not six inches from his face. He didn't even blink. The boots moved on.

He waited, not breathing, until the boots were out of sight. Then he waited some more. He waited until he heard more footsteps, the cab door open, and the roar of the engine exploding to life. He barely rolled out of the way before eighteen wheels pressed him into the pavement.

Josh scrambled to the shadow of another truck and peeked cautiously around its edge toward the building. He saw the truck driver with another guy—probably the one who had pinned him from behind—and a cop. Maybe it wasn't a cop, maybe it was a security guard. It didn't matter. He knew the story they were telling, and the only thing he couldn't believe was that they had the balls to tell it. And in the end who would be believed, the truck drivers who made this a regular stop on their route and sprang for steak and eggs each time, or the kid in the run-down sneakers who could barely afford a cup of coffee?

Crouching low, he moved between the rows of vehicles. He tried the handle of a Subaru; it was locked. He checked out the bed of a pickup truck but there was nothing to hide under; he'd be spotted in an instant. When he glanced back toward the building, all three men were coming his way, moving with a determination that suggested they had seen something in the shadows that gave them reason to move in that direction. His throat went dry. He scurried around the corner of a battered tan and white Winnebago, circa 1970, and pressed himself flat against the door. To his very great surprise, the door gave a little with his weight, and when he turned the handle, it opened. He lifted himself inside and closed the door quietly behind himself.

The interior smelled like old socks and barbecue-flavored corn chips, which oddly enough made his stomach growl again. The shades were drawn over the tiny windows. That was good because no one could see in. It was bad because he barked his shin twice stumbling across the narrow floor space. As his eyes adjusted, he saw a small table and a built-in bench, some overhead cabinets, and a shelf-like bunk near the ceiling. He was about to check the cabinets for food—he really was starving—when the driver's side door abruptly opened. He dived to the floor, but not before he caught a glimpse of the driver in the brief illumination of the door lights. It was the weird little man in the plaid pants from the diner. With his bald head and big, funny-looking nose, he reminded Josh of a garden gnome.

He was humming an off-key tune as he climbed in and fastened his seat belt. He cranked up the engine and glanced in the rearview mirror. Josh stilled his breathing and tried to make himself invisible. Slowly the vehicle started to move, and when it made a turn, Josh took the opportunity to scrunch himself into a corner behind the table where, hopefully, even the flash of passing headlights wouldn't pick him up.

The vehicle creaked and groaned and shuddered its way through the gears, finally reaching a more or less steadily swaying speed that indicated they were on the highway. Traffic rumbled through the thin metal walls, dishes rattled in the cupboard, and highway lights danced on the floor. After a few moments, Josh peeked cautiously out from under the table, trying to assess his situation.

He met the eyes of the driver in the rearview mirror.

"So, young man," said the gnome cheerily, "where are you headed?"

After her second hip replacement at age ninety-two, Annabelle's daughter Marion had done everything but bring in a lawyer to try to get Annabelle out of the brick Tudor on the outskirts of Dallas in which she had lived for the past fifty years and into one of those nice, safe, gray-carpeted and wood-veneered assisted living units over at Magnolia View. Annabelle informed her loving daughter that if she was going to die anyway, she'd just as soon do it in a place where she knew where all the light switches were and could watch Pay-Per-View whenever she damn well pleased. Marion wept and wailed and stomped her foot and pleaded, but in the end Annabelle prevailed as she always did.

She did concede, however, that all those stairs were getting to be a bit much for her, so she remodeled the downstairs sitting room and adjoining bath to her bedroom suite, complete with cable TV and a newly converted walk-in closet, because being over ninety was no excuse for not dressing for the occasion. She'd closed off the upstairs and hadn't even missed the other half of her house ... until tonight.

It was almost four o'clock in the morning and after laboriously making her way up two flights of stairs, Annabelle felt she more than deserved the shot of well-aged bourbon from the bottle she had almost forgotten was stowed away at the back of a middle shelf in the closet next to the box she had come to retrieve. Her balance wasn't what it once had been, and a pair of dusty red stilettos and a painted tin box of costume jewelry clattered to the wood floor, making a noise like three devils fighting in a metal cage, before she reached what she wanted.

Less than five minutes later, Megan appeared at the doorway, looking rumpled and distressed in her pink polka dot boxer pajamas, her feet bare and her curly dark hair spilling out of its braid. "Gram!" Her voice was a mixture of relief and exasperation. "You scared me to death. I thought the place was haunted! What on earth are you doing up here?"

Annabelle examined her granddaughter critically. "You really could use a good haircut, sweetheart," she said, "and a few blonde highlights wouldn't hurt. The biggest mistake a woman can make is to let herself go the minute she turns forty. That's why there are so many divorces these days." She added innocently, "How is that nice young fellow of yours, anyway?"

"Not so young anymore," Megan replied, "like me." She came forward and knelt to scoop up the photographs that had spilled from the box on her grandmother's lap. "Now, what are you doing up this time of night? And didn't we talk about the stairs?"

Annabelle sipped bourbon from the Dixie cup she had found in the bathroom. "I've always liked him," she went on complacently. "There aren't many husbands who would let their wives just drop everything and fly across the country to keep an old woman company."

"Gram, this is the twenty-first century." But Megan studiously avoided her grandmother's eyes as she gathered up the photographs. "A woman doesn't need her husband's permission to do what she wants to do."

"We didn't need it in the twentieth century either," replied Annabelle, "but it's always polite to ask."

Megan gazed for a moment at the handful of photographs she held without seeing them. Then she said, "Nick and I are separated."

Her grandmother said nothing, but the compassion Megan could feel in her gaze made it difficult to look at her, even for a moment. She managed one quick glance as she added quietly, "Six weeks ago." She swallowed hard. "Mother doesn't know. No one does, really. I'm okay with it." She swallowed again. "Really."

"Do you want to tell me what happened?"

Megan shook her head as she stood to return the photographs to the box. "Not yet." Her voice was hoarse.

"Well then," said Annabelle briskly, lifting the cup again, "it's a good thing I didn't die. Now you have something to occupy your time while you think things through. It's amazing how things work out when you live right and work hard. "

Megan chuckled. Her grandmother had always been able to pull her out of her pain, whether that pain was from a scraped knee or a broken heart. "What do you know about living right?" She brushed a kiss across Annabelle's cheek as she moved toward the adjacent bathroom. "You're the crazy person who climbed up two flights of stairs in the middle of the night when you know perfectly well how dangerous that is." She returned with a paper cup and poured a measure of bourbon into it from the bottle at her grandmother's feet. "What if you'd fallen?"

"I'd never do anything so inconsiderate. That would have ruined our big adventure."

Megan looked around the dusty, nearly barren room until she found a footstool in the corner, and dragged it close to her grandmothers chair. She sat and took a sip of the bourbon. "If your idea of a big adventure is sitting in an empty room looking at old photographs, I'm starting to regret springing you from the hospital."

"Well, we can hardly start our adventure until we find the first clue, can we?"

"The clue to what?" Megan reached forward and scooped a handful of photos from the box. "Is this a scavenger hunt?"

"In a way, I suppose."

Megan began to sort through the photos. "What are we looking for?"

"We are looking," replied Annabelle with more than a hint of the dramatic in her tone, "for a place to begin."

Megan fixed a dry look upon her. "Don't make me sorry I agreed to help you with this."

A smile twitched at Annabelle's lips and she took another sip of the whiskey. "When I was six years old," she said, "a very, very long time ago, my mother and I went on a trip together. A birthday trip. It was the happiest summer of my life. " Her eyes clouded for a moment, and her brow furrowed with the struggle for memory. "What we are looking for ... what I need to remember, is where we went." She smiled. "In a way, I suppose, I am looking for my happy place."

Megan looked up at her grandmother. "Do you have any idea where to start?"

"Not really. But I remember there's a photograph of us on that trip. My mother used to keep it in a silver frame on her bedroom dresser, and whenever she looked at it her smile would grow kind of sad. Eventually the frame broke, but I kept it in this box, with all the other family photos from the old days."

"Wow, some of these are really old." Megan looked through the photographs slowly. "Is this World War Two?"

Annabelle glanced at the faded 3x3 snapshot of a young man in uniform she held up. "That's your grandfather. And the picture we're looking for is older than that." She chuckled. "The camera was still a new-fangled invention back then. It's a wonder in this world that it even held a picture after all these years. "

"You really should preserve these somehow."

"I've preserved them for sixty-eight years, and I think that's long enough. But you're welcome to give it a try, if you've a mind to."

They sipped and sorted for a time in leisure, occasionally taking a foray down memory lane when Megan held up a studio portrait of a baby or a bride, a boy with a new wagon or a girl on a pony. The farther toward the bottom of the box they went, the stiffer and more faded the photographs became, the edges of the paper crumbling like moth wings to the touch. Megan looked up with a smile to inquire about the children posed in front of a very old-fashioned Christmas tree, and realized that her grandmother had gone very still. She was staring at the photograph she held.

"Mission accomplished," she said softly.

"You found it?" Megan got up and came around her grandmother's chair, bending down to look over her shoulder.

The snapshot was of a young woman in a flapper-era bob and pleated skirt with a short jacket and gloves standing at the side of the road in front of a sign of some sort. A young girl with curly blond hair in a sailor dress with a big white collar and white stockings stood between them, squinting into the camera and looking impatient with it all. Megan could not prevent a wash of pure awe to realize that the woman who now sat gazing into the past, as faded and as fragile as the photograph she held, had once been that blonde-haired child in itchy crinolines and cotton stockings so eager to have the photograph finished so that she could get on with living the almost one hundred years that awaited her. Stealing a quick glance at her grandmother's melancholy face, she wondered if she was thinking the same thing, and if she had known everything that those years before her would hold, whether she would have been quite so anxious to get on with them way back then.

Megan looked back at the photograph. There were mountains in the background, and lots of trees. It might have been taken at a roadway overlook, or a national park.

"Where is this?" she asked.

"I have no idea." Annabelle gave a satisfied nod. "But this is it. This is where it all started. Look." She pointed with a thin, wavering finger to a corner of the photograph. "See that mountain in the background, the way the shadows fall? It looks like a T-Rex."

Megan giggled, astonished at the trick of nature, or of photography, that had captured a prehistoric creature on film from the nineteen twenties. "It does!"

"When we find this place, we'll be well on our way to solving the mystery."

"But …" Megan took the photograph carefully from her grandmother's hands and studied it closely. "Gram, a lot can change in eighty-odd years. Trees grow, landscapes change, roads close, high-rises are built … even mountains get strip-mined. How are we going to figure out where this place is? You're standing in front of the sign."

Annabelle smiled complacently and sipped her whiskey. "My dear," she said, "that's what makes it a mystery."

Josh weighed his options for a brief moment, then made his way cautiously forward. As far as he could tell, he only had two weapons: his wit and his charm. He hoped one of them was still working.

"Hey," he said, and gave the gnome his most disingenuous smile as he slid into the cracked leather passenger seat. "Thanks for not freaking out. I didn't mean to stow away. The thing is, my brother's RV looks just like this, and it was so late, and I was so tired, I guess I didn't notice I was in the wrong one. I must've dozed off, and when I woke up we were already moving. I should've said something, but I was afraid you'd shoot me."

It was the lamest story even Josh had ever heard, but the gnome didn't appear to spot the flaws. He replied cheerfully, "Not much chance of that."

Josh held on to his smile. "Well, I appreciate that. You can just drop me off at the next exit, if it's not too much trouble. I can call my brother to come get me." He forced a rueful laugh. "He'll be telling this story at family dinners for the next ten years, you can bet on that."

The old man just nodded pleasantly and kept his eyes on the road. "I like driving at night, don't you? You've got the road to yourself, no sun in your eyes, and I'm afraid the air-conditioning in this old baby isn't what she used to be, so it's a blessing to be out of the heat of the day." He reached forward to pat the battered dashboard affectionately. "There's a campground in the foothills I like to stop at. Quiet, lots of shade, easy to sleep through the day. We ought to get there right after sunup."

Josh's smile faded. "I said you could let me off at the next exit."

"Now why in the world would you want me to do that?" the man replied cheerfully. "You wouldn't be a bit better off than you were. At least this way, you're going somewhere."

Josh's fingers dug into the armrest and his voice lost its charm. "Listen, you crazy old pervert, I don't know what you've got in mind but it's not going to happen. And if you try anything, you need to know I've got a knife."

The gnome chuckled. "I don't think so. I think you lost it to that fellow you tried to rob back at the truck stop. And I'm not a pervert." He sounded a little hurt. "You really mustn't think the worst of everyone you meet."

Josh swallowed hard, cursing himself, the old man, the thugs at the truck stop, and his own stupidity. A green exit sign flashed past the window, and then nothing but highway.

"So what are you going to do?" he said. "Call the cops on me?"

He darted a quick astonished look at Josh. "For what? There was no harm done, was there? Besides, how in heaven's name would I call the police even if I wanted to? I'm driving down the highway."

Josh blinked and stared at him in disbelief. "Wait a minute. Don't you have a phone?"

"Why, no." He sounded mildly surprised. "Do you?"

Josh stared straight ahead, every muscle in his body tensed for the flight that was not going to happen because there was no place to go. He was trapped in this rolling tin can with one of the seven dwarves until sunrise and there was not a thing he could do about it. "If I did I'd use to it report a kidnapping."

"Oh?" He looked interested. "Whose?"

"Mine."

Again the man laughed. "Oh my, you are an amusing young man. This is going to be an entertaining trip. Do you like music?"

"No."

The man turned a knob on the dashboard and Frank Sinatra was singing "My Way." For a moment Josh was flooded with memories, and each memory was a sensation—the flicker of candlelight tingled in his throat, the smell of perfume burned his eyes, the brush of a woman's silk dress as it swayed past him smothered his breath—until the pain threatened to explode in his gut and he reached forward and snapped the radio off. The driver appeared not to notice, or care.

"My name's Artemis," he said. "People call me Artie. What's yours?"

"Joshua," replied Josh before he could think to tell a lie.

"Ah. You were named for a warrior."

Josh shot him a sharp, suspicious look.

"I'm headed for Memphis, myself," he went on easily, "to pay my respects to the King. Where did you say you were bound again?"

"London, to see the queen," Josh returned irritably.

The man called Artie chuckled again. He was very easily amused. "Well, you've got a long trip ahead of you. If you're hungry, I've got some cookies in that cabinet behind the driver's seat. I could use one myself."

That was the first thing the gnome had said that got Josh's full attention. He got up and, holding on to the seats for balance, made his way back to the overhead cabinet.

Artie said, "Be careful when you open it—" just as Josh twisted the lock and the door sprang open, raining packages of cookies, potato chips, crackers, and dried soup over his head. He swore and batted them away as Artie finished, "Because things can fall out."

Josh glared at the back of the Artie's head as the last mini-box of raisin bran bounced to the floor, and he knelt to start picking things up. He tossed a bag of chips and two candy bars, along with the entire package of cookies, into the passenger seat, and stuffed four more candy bars into his pockets. He was gathering up the cereal and soup when he noticed a leather pouch that did not appear to contain food mixed in with the boxes and bags. In the flickering dimness it was hard to tell, but it looked like a bank bag. He glanced furtively at the driver's seat, but Artie's eyes were on the road. He unzipped the bag, and sure enough, it was filled with cash.

"I've got some sodas in the fridge underneath the table," Artie added without looking around. "Help yourself."

"Thanks," said Josh, He stuffed the bank pouch under his shirt, and stood to replace the groceries in the cabinet. "I will."

Things were looking up.

Brunch at the Hummingbird House began at 11:00 a.m., but the preparations started hours earlier with wildflowers in cobalt glass vases on each table, linen napkins starched and folded just so, china and sterling—fashionably mismatched of course—artfully arranged at each place setting. The menu of the day was printed on heavy vellum paper in flowing script and folded to stand in the center of each table beside the flower vase, and a small basket of dainty nibbles—usually miniature scones and cheese biscuits from Bridget—was placed on each table.

In the foyer, a platter of goat cheese and water crackers greeted guests, along with small crystal glasses—barely more than a sip, really—of an appropriately priced wine. Paul and Derrick wanted to be hospitable, but they were not complete fools, and they barely made a profit on brunch as it was. The surround sound stereo system, which had been one of their first additions to the ambiance of the B&B, was adjusted until the volume of the classical music that wafted from the front foyer, through the art gallery back to the dining room and even into the back garden, was precisely right to be heard over the clatter of dishware and the murmur of voices, but not so loud that it distracted from civilized conversation.

In the kitchen, the big urn would be filled with coffee, and Derrick would be fussing over the sugar bowls and cream pitchers while Paul mixed the drink of the day—this Sunday it was bright mint grasshoppers made with mint crushed fresh from the garden only minutes earlier—and whatever entrée Bridget had brought over the day before filled the kitchen with delectable aromas. Foil-covered sides would be heating in the warming oven and fragrant sauces simmering on the burners.

On most Sundays.

On this particular Sunday, Derrick opened the oven door and stared in dismay at the beautifully tied, prepped, and completely raw pork loin that should have by now been a lovely, moist golden brown main dish.

Paul said, "When Bridget said to start it in a cold oven, I don't think this is what she meant."

Derrick reached into the oven and lifted out the roasting pan with his bare hands. "We forgot to turn the oven on," he announced in the flat, expressionless tone of someone who is still in a state of shock. "How could we forget to turn the oven on?"

"Well," Paul said, "we had to chop all those vegetables for the country salad …"

"And then I had to make the vinaigrette …"

"Which wouldn't have taken half as long if the Internet hadn't been down so we couldn't find the recipe …"

"And then I had to puree the yams, and salt the eggplant for the casserole …"

"And I had to boil the eggs for the garnish …"

They looked at each other. "Preparing a brunch by ourselves is a good deal more complex than we anticipated," Derrick admitted. "We have twenty-five people coming for brunch in fifteen minutes and we have nothing to serve them but pureed yams and chopped vegetables in vinaigrette."

Paul rubbed his hands together briskly. "Don't despair. We've been in worse spots than this. Remember the time I almost seated the editor of the *New York Times* Book Review next to that porn star?"

"She wasn't a porn star," Derrick reminded him patiently, "she only wrote porn."

"Precisely. But disaster averted, and we'll do it again." He looked around the kitchen alertly. "We have eggs, we have fontina, we have escarole we can pretend is spinach … I can make omelets."

"You're going to charge thirty-five dollars a head for an omelet?" Derrick was incredulous. "In the *country?*"

Paul frowned a little. "We have some dried porcini mushrooms, don't we? We'll shave them on top and tell people they're truffles."

Derrick's eyes grew even bigger. "You're going to *lie?*"

Paul grabbed the bowl of eggs and took them over to the stove. "First I'm going to serve free drinks."

"But what about the eggplant? And all those lovely pureed yams? And—"

"Y'all looking for a cook?"

A young woman in faded jeans and a tee shirt decorated with glitter-enhanced dancing poodles stood at the entry to the kitchen, chewing gum and looking around, assessing. She had a freckled nose and a brown ponytail that swung when she tilted her head, and she carried a big patchwork purse slung over one shoulder. Both Paul and Derrick stared at her for a moment, and then Derrick said, "Excuse me?"

She held her ground at the doorway. "My name is Purline Williams. I need a half day off Wednesdays and an hour and a half Sunday mornings off for church. Otherwise I work seven to three weekdays so I can pick up my kids from school. I do cleaning, laundry, windows, and cooking."

Paul looked at Derrick, confusion gradually widening his eyes into delight. "Bridget!' he said.

"Of course!" Derrick turned to the girl happily. "Did Bridget send you?"

She frowned. "Bridget who?"

"It doesn't matter." Derrick rushed to take her purse and pull her into the room. "Can you make a roast loin of pork in fifteen minutes?"

Three hours and twenty-five servings of pan-roasted medallions of pork served with herb gravy, curried sweet potatoes, and sliced eggplant later, the hosts of the Hummingbird House Sunday brunch joined their three lady friends at their table on the sun porch. Lindsay beamed at them.

"You see?" she said. "I knew you could do it!"

"It was quite good," admitted Bridget. She dipped the tines of her fork into the smudge of gravy that was left on her plate and licked it off with an air of casual discernment. "Personally, I would have added just a smidge of port wine to the sauce. And maybe a whisk of sour cream. But otherwise, it was really … quite nice." She seemed both surprised and reluctantly impressed.

Cici grinned and lifted her glass to them. "I'm proud of you! You took charge, you found yourself a cook, you pulled it off. And this is just the beginning! The only thing I can't figure out is what took you so long."

Paul gazed around the dining porch with an air of cautious satisfaction. Only a few diners lingered over coffee with ice cream and fresh berries, and Purline had cleared the tables—centerpieces, tablecloths, and all—as soon as they had emptied. Paul made a mental note to ask her to wait until brunch was over to strip the tables in the future, but otherwise he thought things had gone remarkably well. "Everyone did seem to enjoy it, didn't they?" He tried not to sound too anxious for reassurance.

"Everyone always enjoys your brunches," Cici said. "It's the only chance we get to dress up and pretend to be elegant for a few hours."

"And the food was good?" insisted Derrick, making no attempt whatsoever to hide his anxiety. "You're not just saying that to be polite?"

"Didn't you taste it?"

"Heavens no, I was far too nervous to eat."

"You could charge a hundred dollars a person in the city," Lindsay assured him.

Paul looked at Derrick thoughtfully. "We'd have to serve better wine."

"Seriously?" Derrick looked alarmed. "All our profit goes to booze now."

"So where did you find this girl, again?" Bridget asked. "What's her name?"

"We told you, she just walked in. I thought you'd sent her."

"Heaven sent her," declared Derrick extravagantly. "She is an angel."

At that moment, the angel in question appeared and whisked the three plates away, despite the fact that Cici was still savoring her last bite of sweet potato, her fork in midair.

"Williams," said the girl, snatching up silverware and glasses. "My name's Purline Williams. P-u-r-l-i-n-e. Y'all about done here?"

Lindsay grabbed her glass, which still had a little wine left in it, before it was snatched away, and Derrick quickly introduced the three of them to Purline. Purline regarded the ladies with narrowed eyes for a moment before announcing, "I know who you all are. You bought the old Blackwell place a few years back. Everybody round here said you were crazy."

"I'm not too sure they were wrong," Cici agreed wryly.

"We've known the girls for years," Paul explained. "In fact, they're the reason we moved here."

"It's a pleasure to meet you, Purline." Bridget smiled warmly, and extended her hand across the table.

Purline regarded the offered hand for a moment, then shifted the stack of dishes to the other arm, wiped her hand on her jeans, and gave Bridget's hand a firm, military shake. "Likewise."

"The meal was delicious," added Lindsay.

"But perhaps," Paul pointed out tactfully, "you might clear the tables with a little less alacrity next time."

Purline stared at him, snapped her gum, and said, "Alacrity, huh?" She thought about that for another moment, then turned and walked away, her jeaned hips and ponytail swinging in counterpoint to each other.

Paul's smile was just a trace uneasy. "Charming, am I right? The very salt of the Appalachian earth. Exactly what this place needs."

"She seems delightful," Bridget assured him.

"And she can cook," Lindsay added.

"And if she can help you keep the place in order," Cici said, "what more do you need?"

Derrick looked torn. "I don't know. It's just that we had pictured someone a little more ..."

"Mature," supplied Paul.

"Sophisticated," suggested Derrick.

"Reserved," said Paul.

Derrick said helplessly, "The gum, really. Can we live with that?"

"Are you going to talk to her about it?"

"I do think given half the chance she would have stripped our guests bare and tossed their clothing in the laundry with the tablecloths."

"There is such a thing as being too efficient," Paul agreed.

Derrick looked at him. "Did we make a mistake?"

Lindsay rolled her eyes, Bridget sighed, and Cici placed her balled up napkin on the table. The three of them rose. "Good-bye, boys. Thank you for brunch. It was absolutely perfect."

"Perfect," repeated Bridget with emphasis, and kissed Paul's cheek.

"Don't be idiots," Lindsay advised. "You know what they say about gift horses."

"I know what the Trojans said," Paul replied, escorting them out. Derrick spotted a customer who was about to leave and excused himself to say good-bye. They prided themselves on taking a moment to chat with all the customers when they were seated and before they departed.

Cici said, "Oh, for heaven's sake, relax, will you? For once, everything is going well. Enjoy it."

"Stop by this week for some cherry wine jam," Bridget invited. "I just put up a new batch, and if Purline is any kind of cook at all she'll know what to do with it."

"And I want to show you the new swatches for the table decorations for the reception," Lindsay added. "I'm thinking onyx and dove gray."

"For a vineyard wedding?" Paul stopped dead in his tracks, staring at her. "I'll throw myself in front of a train first. I'll throw *you* in front of a train. I'll be over first thing in the morning. Clearly there's no time to waste."

Lindsay opened her mouth to protest, but they all turned at the sound of Derrick's voice. He had an odd, strained smile on his face as he came toward them, a man in a blue suit at his side.

"Um, Paul," Derrick said, "this gentleman has a question."

A look of slow and carefully restrained dread came over Paul's face which was quickly disguised by a gracious smile. "Everything was all right with the meal, I hope?"

The man's expression was unreadable as he reached into his jacket pocket and brought out a small leather wallet. One of the ladies gasped when he opened it to reveal a badge. "My name is Reginald Styles from the Virginia Department of Alcoholic Beverage Control. I just need to take a look at your liquor license, if I may."

The smile faded from Paul's face. He looked at Derrick. Derrick's eyes widened in a silent helpless message, which Paul received with the blank expression of absolute shock. He looked back at Reginald Styles.

"What liquor license?" he said weakly.

THREE

Every saint has a past, and every sinner has a future.

Oscar Wilde

"I suppose," Derrick said thoughtfully, "we could always go back to Washington." He polished a smudge off of one of the cobalt bud vases before carefully placing it in the breakfront with its charmingly mismatched companions. "I've always wanted to open a dog grooming parlor."

"We can't go back to Washington," Paul groaned as he sank into one of the empty dining room chairs and dropped his forehead to his hands. "I can never show my face in public again. I'm a criminal." And then he glanced up at Derrick, distracted. "Dog grooming parlor? You hate dogs."

"I do not hate them." Derrick plucked the wilting wildflowers from another vase centerpiece and tossed them into the garbage bag he carried from table to table. "I'm just not entirely comfortable around them. But I'm sure I could learn. And there's no time like the present to get started."

"If you two ain't the most pathetic excuses for businessmen I ever did see," Purline declared, spraying disinfectant on the table and attacking it with a sponge. "Everybody knows you can't sell liquor without a license. *Everybody*."

"Except, apparently," replied Paul with a dark look at Derrick, "the person whose job it was to apply for one."

"You're the writer," Derrick returned, chin held high, "you're accustomed to dealing with paperwork." He focused determinedly on polishing the bud vase. "I'm an artist. I deal in concepts, not details."

Purline rolled her eyes and moved to the next table.

"Class One Misdemeanor," Paul said, pressing his forehead into his hands again. "Do you know what that means?"

"A $2500 fine, according to the gentleman with the badge."

"And up to a year in jail and a hundred hours community service."

"Well, I can't go to jail," Derrick informed him flatly, holding the newly polished bud vase up to the window light and squinting for fingerprints. "I'm much too pretty. And I have no intention of missing the next season of *Downton Abbey*."

"It goes on your permanent record," Paul informed him darkly. "I looked it up."

"Which certainly will not look good the next time I try to purchase a firearm."

"I had a cousin that went to jail once," Purline volunteered, scrubbing hard. "He couldn't even get a job butchering meat after that."

Paul raised his head from his hands to look at her steadily. "Well, I suppose the one saving grace in this whole sordid affair is the fact that, of all the dreams that have been crushed today, my ambition to get a job butchering meat was not among them."

Purline snapped her gum. "It's a lot easier than grooming dogs, I'll tell you that much. I had a neighbor that got bit by a rat terrier. Ended up with the rabies. They cut out his brain."

Paul and Derrick exchanged a cautious look, neither one of them quite willing to ask. "The neighbor?" Derrick said finally, when he couldn't contain his curiosity any longer.

She gave him a disgusted look. "The dog. That's how they knew it had the rabies." Then she added thoughtfully, "I knew a man with a hole in his brain once, though. Of course, that was from a bullet. He walked around with it just fine for thirty-eight years, then one day fell over dead. Y'all've got pork chops and gravy for your supper, with some eggplant casserole and sliced tomatoes, and I whipped you up a blackberry cobbler for dessert. You know if you don't pick those berries they'll attract bears, don't you? And your bushes are just about bent to the ground." She walked over to Paul and held out her hand. "I'll take my day's wages, if you don't mind."

Paul's mind raced between bears, berries, bullets, and rabid dogs, but when he saw Derrick open his mouth to question, he was forced to focus. "Thank you, Purline," he said quickly, reaching for his wallet. "Will cash be all right? You've been a lifesaver today. I'm sorry it didn't work out."

She frowned at him. "What didn't work out? You don't like my work, you need to speak up and I'll fix it tomorrow."

"Tomorrow?" Paul fumbled for words, surprised. "Well, that's fine, that's good news, it's just with all the fuss ..."

"And since they closed down the restaurant ..." Derrick added.

"And since we talked about a weekly salary ..."

"We just assumed you'd decided not to stay," Derrick finished, and Paul nodded.

Purline looked from one to the other of them with a stubborn jut of her jaw. "You've still got to have somebody to cook and clean for you, don't you? That's what you hired me for, didn't you?"

"Well, yes, but—"

"Then that's what I aim to do. You got a problem with that?"

"No, no problem at all. We're delighted, really."

"So you're coming back in the morning?"

"Right after I drop the kids off at school." She held out her hand again. "Cash is just fine. I've got to make a car payment."

Paul passed the bills to her, looking uncertain as he explained, "I'm afraid it's not enough for a car payment."

She counted the money. "You haven't seen my car." She tucked the money into the back pocket of her jeans and added, "Don't you ruin my pork chops in the microwave. Put them in a slow oven for twenty-five minutes until the gravy simmers. And how about picking some of those tomatoes that're about to rot on the vine? I'll bring over some jars and start putting them up tomorrow. How in God's green acres did you grow them so big, anyhow?"

And, without waiting for a reply, she sauntered back into the kitchen, slung her purse strap over her shoulder, and left by the back door.

Derrick waited until they heard her car start up before venturing uncertainly, "It's a good thing that she's coming back, right?"

Paul shook his head slowly. "Bears, rabies, liquor licenses ..." He looked at Derrick with a touch of hesitance and a healthy portion of dismay. "Did it ever occur to you that we might not be cut out for this?"

Derrick gave a philosophical lift of his shoulders. "The good news is that, according to the latest government reports, both bears and rabies are in short supply in jail."

Paul glared at him. "Bullets in the head, however, are not. Why aren't you taking this seriously?"

Derrick smiled and patted his shoulder on his way into the kitchen. "Because, dear heart, while you were busy looking up the penalty for a Class One Misdemeanor, I was on the phone with Harrington."

Paul looked interested as he followed him into the kitchen. "Our lawyer?"

"No, Harrington the Lionhearted." But it didn't even take a glance to assure him that Paul was in no mood for jokes, so Derrick went on quickly, "Harrington assures me that you can only go to jail for a misdemeanor if you're convicted. He's putting together the necessary paperwork to keep that from happening as we speak."

"Along with the application for our liquor license, I hope."

"I shouldn't be a bit surprised."

Paul's expression sank into glumness again. "Meanwhile, our livelihood is slowly circling the drain. What are we supposed to do with ourselves now?"

Derrick dropped the trash bag into the container and suggested helpfully, "Go antiquing?"

Paul opened a glass-fronted cabinet door and took out two sherry glasses. Derrick rearranged one of the lemons that sat in the carved wooden dough bowl on the countertop, and casually folded a bright yellow napkin next to it, making a mental note to remind Purline about the importance of staging. Paul poured the sherry.

"Maybe this is a sign," Paul said. Though his tone was neutral, his expression was shadowed and he was careful not to look at Derrick. "Maybe we should just cut our losses and move on."

"And open a dog grooming parlor?" Derrick opened the refrigerator and took out a wedge of havarti and a bunch of grapes, handing both to Paul over his shoulder. "This eggplant casserole looks divine, by the way. I'm glad we didn't make dinner plans."

Paul unwrapped the cheese and arranged it on the wooden board with a cheese knife and the grapes. "How many times in our lives have we been able to say that?"

"Goodness me, you are Miss Deborah Downer today." Derrick searched for cocktail napkins, which Purline had apparently removed to the utility drawer for reasons known only to herself. He arranged two napkins on the cheese board and placed the remainder in the accessories drawer, where they belonged. "Wasn't that the point of moving to the country? To escape the rat race?"

"I personally never thought of our friends as rats. Not the majority of them, anyway." Paul took the grape snips from a hook on the pegboard—made with cork salvaged from an old schoolhouse that still boasted faded scraps of original graffiti—and placed them on the cheese board. "And it would be nice to occasionally—just occasionally, mind you—have plans for dinner. Or even cocktails."

"We've only been here a few months," Derrick reminded him. But even he looked a little wistful as he arranged the two sherry glasses on a tray. "It takes time to fit in to a new place."

Paul picked up the cheese tray. "We need to face the fact," he replied soberly, "that we may never fit in here."

Derrick frowned, searching for a reply, but he couldn't find one. They headed for the back hall and the garden door.

"And," Paul added, "who knows how long the restaurant will be closed down? Every week we don't open we're losing money."

"We need a plan," Derrick admitted. He shifted the tray with the sherry to one hand while he nudged open the leaded glass French door, which always stuck. Today the humidity made it more stubborn than usual, and Paul reached around to give him a hand. The door rattled when he shoved the handle, but didn't move.

"What we need," Paul said, putting his shoulder to the job, "is a miracle."

"Then this is your lucky day," came an amused contralto voice behind them, "because I just happen to be in the miracle business."

On Ladybug Farm

"We should have stayed," Bridget said, worried. "You don't just run out on friends when they're in trouble."

"We stayed for over an hour," Cici reminded her. "We offered to go to court with them. And we tried to explain to that agent about the mix-up."

The three of them were gathered around the work island in the big brick-floored kitchen of Ladybug Farm, snapping green beans from the overflowing bushel basket at their feet into a big porcelain tub. Two pots of sweet vinegar pickling brine and a five-gallon canner simmered on the stove, steaming up the already heated kitchen, which the two fans that were aimed directly at them did very little to dissipate. Ida Mae, who refused to work on Sunday, sat in a rocking chair in the corner, fanning herself with a church bulletin and supervising.

"It really wasn't their fault," Lindsay said, blotting her sweaty forehead with the back of her arm. They had all changed from the dressy brunch clothes into shorts and sleeveless cotton tops, tied back their hair, and kicked off their shoes. The windows were open to the still green late afternoon, as was the back door. But there was no such thing as a comfortable kitchen during canning season, so all they could do was make the best of it. She added, "What I mean is, not entirely. I mean, you can see how they might have thought that the license the last owner had was transferrable with the property."

Cici regarded her with lifted eyebrow. "Seriously?"

"Face it," Bridget said with a sigh. "No one has ever been better at self-sabotage than those two. Ever."

The quart jars they were sterilizing in the canner began to rattle, and Ida Mae pointed out from her rocking chair, "Y'all're gonna break them jars if you don't turn down the heat. You can't put up beans in chipped jars. You won't get a seal."

Bridget got up and turned down the burners, commenting as she passed, "I don't see how you can dress like that on a day like this, Ida Mae. Aren't you sweltering?"

Ida Mae, whose sense of style favored steel-toed boots and work pants worn under cotton dresses and baggy sweaters, appeared perfectly comfortable in her Sunday-afternoon outfit of black tights and a quilted satin housecoat worn over a print polyester muumuu. She sniffed in reply. "I ain't foolish enough to put up beans in the middle of the day, am I? That's a job you do before sunup. And you *don't* do it on a Sunday," she added, rocking faster in disapproval. "I'll be very much surprised if every one of them jars don't bust."

"I'm with you on that, Ida Mae," Lindsay said, wiping another trickle of sweat from her cheek with her shoulder. "It's way too hot for this."

"Well, we couldn't let them go to waste," Bridget said, scooping up another bowl full of beans as she resumed her seat. "After the boys went to all that trouble to pick them for us."

"Because we don't have enough to do with our own garden," Cici said, and then added quickly, "Not that it wasn't sweet of them."

"What I don't understand," Lindsay said, "is how two completely incompetent gardeners who know absolutely nothing about anything related to growing things could have produced a crop like theirs. Did you see the size of those tomatoes?"

"They need to be in some kind of record book," Bridget said. "Thank heaven we talked them out of giving us some. We would have been up all night canning tomatoes."

"It ain't them," said Ida Mae, "it's the place. Some places've got nourishment in their bones. Some places you can't grow rocks."

Cici plopped a handful of beans into the porcelain tub. "Makes sense, I suppose. Like that place in Alaska that grows pumpkins the size of trucks. They say it's the volcanic soil."

"It ain't the soil," insisted Ida Mae, rocking and fanning, "it's the place."

They all knew better than to argue details with Ida Mae.

"What *I* don't understand," said Bridget, returning to the topic at hand, "is how two perfectly competent, incredibly successful businessmen could have made such a stupid mistake in the first place. It's not like they're a couple of boobs at their first pony ride, you know."

"Although they're certainly acting like it," Cici put in.

"Paul is an award-winning writer," Bridget went on, "and Derrick has run his own business for twenty-six years."

"And not one penny went out of that gallery that he didn't account for, let me promise you that," Lindsay said. "You don't hold your own in Washington, DC by being an idiot with money." She thought about that for a moment and qualified, "Well, not unless you're in Congress,"

"It's not like this is the first time they've reinvented themselves, either," Cici pointed out. "Remember when they first decided it would be a kick to move to the suburbs? We didn't think they'd last a year. Next thing you know, Paul is hosting progressive dinners and putting out the neighborhood newsletter, Derrick is running the Community Beautification League and heading two charity drives, and they both have more friends than we do."

"Of course, the suburbs of Baltimore are a little different from the middle of the Shenandoah Valley," Bridget said.

"Do you know what I think?" Lindsay dropped another handful of snapped beans into the tub. "I think they're scared."

Bridget nodded. "Sure. I remember how I felt when we first moved here. It was such a big step. What if I didn't like it? What if I didn't fit in? We'd pretty much burned our bridges, just like they have. What if it turned out to be the biggest mistake of our lives?"

The other two nodded, remembering. Cici added, "It's even more than that, you know. When you reinvent yourself, sometimes you're not sure you're going to like the person you've become. I think that's the scariest part of all. What if you don't even like yourself, after you've changed everything to fit into your new life?"

Bridget nodded thoughtfully. "I think you're right. They're just afraid, that's all. Afraid it won't work out."

Ida Mae gave a snort of derision. "That ain't it," she said, and, planting her feet firmly on the floor, pushed herself up from the rocker. "They're afraid it *will.*" She marched over to the stove and lifted the lid on the simmering brine. "You put plenty of vinegar in this, didn't you? Otherwise you're all gonna die of the botulism."

She dipped a spoon into the hot mixture, tasted it cautiously and wrinkled up her nose, although whether that was a sign of approval or disapproval none of them could tell. "Well, come on then, get them beans over here," she commanded. "You gonna take all night about it? I swear to Goshen, sometimes it'd just be easier to do it all myself."

Josh woke up on the narrow vinyl bench that served as a bed in a pool of his own sweat, gummy-mouthed and groggy. The generator chugged a mighty roar and the air conditioner spit forth a feeble stream of tepid air overhead. The first thing he did, with a lurch of alarm, was grab for the bank pouch he'd hidden under his shirt. His pulse returned to normal when he found it was still there. Next he touched the photograph in his pocket, just to make sure it was still there, too, and when it was his world was right again. He sat up, swinging his feet to the floor, rubbing his face with his hands. He needed a shower. Bad.

He hadn't intended to fall asleep, but there had been nothing he could do until the weird little man called Artie pulled into his campsite for the day. He had stretched out on the bed to rest his eyes and to avoid conversation with his host, but before he knew it the sound of the road and the sway of the vehicle put him out. Now the vehicle was parked, Artie was nowhere to be seen, and judging by the feeble slant of sun that was visible through the crack between the windowsill and the tattered brown curtain that covered it, the afternoon was mostly gone. With luck, ol' Artie was sacked out somewhere and Josh could stroll away unnoticed. He would hitch a ride to the nearest town and with the cash he had in hand he could buy a plane ticket and be in Kansas City by this time tomorrow. After that, he didn't know and it didn't matter. He was going to make it to Kansas City, and just knowing that put an easiness in his mind that he hadn't felt in so long he had almost forgotten what it felt like.

He eased open the cabin door and was greeted by the aroma of charcoal smoke and sizzling meat. His mouth filled with saliva. The air was fresh and green, and easily ten degrees cooler than it had been inside the camper. Above the sound of the chugging generator he could hear the background whine of a country radio station from a nearby campsite, and somewhere a kid squealed, the way kids do. They never laughed or talked or even cried the way regular people did; they always squealed, usually at the precise decibel level known to pierce the human eardrum. For some reason that made him smile, not on the outside, but inside where no one could see. His mother used to call that a heart smile. *Joshua,* she would say when he was trying not to show how pleased he was with something she had said or done by hiding his smile, *is that a heart smile I see? Because it sure looks like one from here.* It had been a long time since he'd felt his heart smile. And even longer since he'd heard a little kid squeal.

He looked around cautiously, the way he had recently learned to do, before coming out. For a campground, it wasn't half bad. There were trees surrounding the concrete parking pad, and beyond them he thought he saw a glint of water. He heard more childish laughter accompanied by what surely must be a splash, and he figured there was a lake nearby. Some kind of national park? A hammock was strung between two trees, and by the tangle of bed sheets that drooped from it, he guessed that was where Artie had slept away the day. Artie himself was bent over a park grill with a set of barbecue tongs, flipping a huge piece of meat and waving away the smoke that flared up from the juices. There were a couple of foil packets roasting near the meat, and at the back of the grill an aluminum pan filled with what looked to be canned baked beans bubbled away. Artie grinned when he saw Josh, and gave an inviting wave of the barbecue tongs.

"There you are, sleepyhead," he declared. "I thought I was going to have to eat this steak all by myself."

Josh stepped down from the camper and saw that the meat was in fact a T-bone, 20 ounces at least. He tried to remember the last time he had had steak. That one was big enough to feed a family of four with leftovers, and he could've eaten the whole thing at one sitting. He approached the grill against his better judgment.

"Smells good," he admitted.

"Hope you like it medium rare. I've got some corn on the cob and a couple of baked potatoes going on here, and beans in the pot. My mama used to put a little ketchup and brown sugar in hers along with a dash of Tabasco, freshens them right up." He glanced at Josh convivially. "What about yours?"

Josh stared at him, mouth watering. "My what?"

"Your mama. She ever make barbeque beans?"

Josh felt something inside him shut down. "Listen," he said abruptly, "I've got to shove off. Thanks for the ride, I guess."

Artie lifted the big steak onto a plastic platter that was splashed with faded psychedelic blue and green flowers. "Well now, that's a shame." The meat settled into a delicious looking puddle of its own juices, and Josh could not stop looking at it.

"Where're you off to that it can't wait until you eat a bite?"

Josh tried to think of an answer but it was hard to think about anything while watching Artie transfer the steaming foil packets to the platter beside the dripping steak. He scowled. "Where are we, anyway?"

"Arizona. A place called Cold Creek." He paused and looked around appreciatively. "Gorgeous country, isn't it? Reminds me of a place Kit Carson liked to stop when he went through this part of the country."

"Is there a town close by?"

"I imagine. There usually is these days." He turned back to the grill and wrapped a towel around the handle of the bean pot, lifting it off. "Now there was an interesting fellow, that Kit," he went on. "One of the smartest men you'd ever want to meet, but couldn't read or write a lick. Said book learning cluttered up the brain. Have you ever heard such a thing? On the other hand, you take a college educated man today and put him up against Kit in the middle of the wilderness and only one of them is coming out alive, so maybe he had a point."

Josh watched as Artie carried the platter and the pot over to a camp table. He said, to distract himself from the succulent smells, "Are you talking about Kit Carson, the Indian fighter?"

"Oh, Kit did a lot more than fight Indians. In fact, if you want to know the truth, I think toward the end of his life he came to regret some of the events he was involved in regarding the Native American population. But, as I tried to explain, everyone has a role to play in history, and regretting yours is pointless."

Josh blinked. "You explained that. To Kit Carson."

Artie smiled at him as he set the dishes on the center of the table next to a foil packet of buttered bread. "Sure you won't change your mind?"

It occurred to Josh that the other man was probably a little nuts. But he couldn't take his eyes off that table. It was covered with a red checked table cloth and set for two with heavy-duty paper plates and big yellow plastic cups. The foil packets were brown on the outside with the escaped sugar from the corn. The steak glistened. The pot of beans was still bubbling.

Sometimes, as a kid, Josh would go on picnics in Central Park, near the lake. His mother always packed a red checked tablecloth.

Josh's stomach growled loudly enough to be heard at the next campsite. He dragged his eyes away from the feast and frowned again, trying for sarcasm. "Are you making s'mores later?"

Artie's eyes twinkled as he sank into one of the folding chairs and picked up a knife and fork. "We could."

He sliced the big steak in half and plopped one piece on each plate. By that time Josh was already seated and slathering butter on a cob of corn. Artie poured tea from a clear plastic pitcher and they ate in silence for a time, Josh shoveling the steak into his mouth as fast as he could chew it. He wasn't sure if he had ever tasted anything as good, not in his entire life.

When the steak was half gone and nothing was left on the cob, Josh dug into the foil-wrapped potato, slowing down a little. Artie settled back in his canvas camp chair, enjoying his meal more slowly, taking in his surroundings with easy appreciation. "Nothing like the taste of a good charcoal grilled steak," he said. "Unless maybe it's my campfire coffee. Something about the way the wood smoke gets into the flavor, you can't beat it. I'll be brewing up a pot later for the road." He chuckled. "Maybe we'll make those s'mores after all, now that you've got me thinking about them. You do much camping as a kid, Josh?"

Josh shook his head, scraping the flesh from the potato skin. Replete and very nearly content, he forgot for a moment to be cautious. "My dad wasn't exactly the camping type." And the minute he said it, he was sorry. He added with a frown, "Anyway, he wasn't my dad. He was my stepdad."

But all Artie said was, "Too bad. You missed out on one of life's great pleasures. Where're you from, Josh?"

"Back east." Josh focused on the potato, spearing another forkful. "New York."

"Is that right? How'd you end up out here? "

Josh shrugged, digging into the beans. Artie asked far too many questions for his own good. What did it matter to him, anyway? He needed to just mind his own business.

"Well, that's okay," Artie replied to his silence. His tone was relaxed and genial. "Like Kit used to say, a land as big as this is good for swallowing up a man's secrets. And if you don't mind my saying so, it looks to me like you've got a few."

"Yeah, well, who doesn't?" Josh shoveled another bite of steak into his mouth, chewed and swallowed, and washed it down with a gulp of sweet iced tea.

"That can be a lonely thing, holding onto secrets," Artie observed, just as though someone had asked him. "Like Kit used to say, if they don't get swallowed up, they will for sure swallow you up. I'll bet your folks sure would love to hear from you long about now."

Josh could feel his forehead knotting, and his stomach. "I'm not a kid. I'm twenty-seven years old. Anyway, my mom's dead."

"What about your dad?"

Josh looked at Artie coldly. "He's the one who killed her."

He waited for a reaction, but all he got was another nod. Interested, polite. Like Josh had said, "It's going to be a warm night," or "Good steak." Just a nod.

Josh got up from the table abruptly. "Is there a check-in station or a welcome center around here? Somebody's got to know how to get to the nearest town."

Artie said, "Sure. Down the road a half mile or so. They're open until nine. They've got all kinds of pamphlets on local attractions, and a payphone too. I'm sure somebody can help you out. But I'll be happy to drop you off at the next town, if that's where you want to go."

Josh was acutely aware of the leather money pouch, sweaty against his now-bulging stomach. "That's okay," he mumbled. "I need to get going."

Artie returned another one of those understanding nods and what looked very much like a wink. "It sounds like you've got somebody waiting for you."

"Yeah," said Josh, and was surprised at how good it felt to actually say it out loud. "Yeah I do."

"A girl?"

Josh felt another one of those heart smiles start to melt something deep inside him, and the melting felt oddly like a stream of backed-up tears. He swallowed hard. "Yeah," he said, his voice a little hoarse. "A girl."

"Well then." Artie sat back in his chair and spread his hands benevolently. "You'd better not keep her waiting. One thing I know for sure is that pretty girls and fresh fish don't keep." He cackled at his own witticism and pushed up from the chair, gathering up the paper plates. "You're going to need some traveling money," he said. "I've got some put by in that cupboard where the cookies are."

Josh felt his heart stop beating. "What?"

"Take what you need to get where you're going." Artie scraped the few leftover beans onto a paper plate and balled up the empty tin foil. "You can pay me back when you get a chance."

Josh's heart started again with a lurch. Sweat broke out on the back of his neck. "What, are you kidding me?" His voice sounded tight and odd, although he tried to look amused. "You'd give money to a perfect stranger?"

"Why not?" Artie tossed the trash into the trashcan at the edge of the campsite. "I do it every day. Grocery clerks, gas station attendants ... why, just the other day, I gave a perfect stranger twenty bucks and he gave me this great-looking shirt." He grinned and plucked the corners of his tee shirt at the chest. "That's what money is for, right? To give it away. And most of the time you end up giving it to strangers."

The guy was clearly crazy. And why was Josh arguing with him? Josh said cautiously, "What if I can't pay you back? I mean, I won't even know where to find you."

Artie just smiled. "You'll find me." He took the aluminum coffee pot and filled it with water from a jug on the table. "Go on, now, get going. It'll be getting dark soon."

Josh's brows tented sharply. "Why are you doing this? You don't even know me."

Artie's eyes twinkled. "If the cause is love, never let it be said that Artie Bullwinkle failed to rise to the occasion." He tilted his head, gazing at Josh. "It is for love, right?"

Josh swallowed another sudden lump in his throat. The leather pouch burned against his belly. "Yeah," he said, softly. "Love."

"Then what can go wrong?" Artie's smile was benevolent, and he began scooping coffee grounds into the pot. "Say, while you're in the cookie cabinet, see if I've got any graham crackers, will you? I know I've got chocolate in the cooler, and the marshmallows are right here—sometimes I like to melt one in my coffee—but you can't make s'mores without graham crackers."

Josh turned toward the camper, moving slowly and keeping his eye on the other man, the way a person would do if he were trying to back away from a rattlesnake. But the little gnome-faced man was not a snake. He was just crazy. Crazier than an outhouse rat, as they said out here. Crazier than a one-eyed tennis player. Just plain-assed crazy.

Josh mumbled something like, "Yeah, okay." And went inside the camper.

By then the weight of the leather pouch was practically blistering his stomach. He yanked it out of his belt and stared at it, all faded and sweat-stained, feeling the shape of the stack of bills inside. There was more than enough for a plane ticket. There might even be enough for a cheap used car. The guy was crazy. He deserved to lose it all. He shouldn't even be allowed out around normal people.

Maybe if he just took a couple of hundred. Enough for bus fare maybe. Or bus fare and a cheap throw-away cell phone. He'd said to take what he needed, hadn't he?

The problem was, what Josh needed was not in that leather pouch.

His hand went to his pocket; he pulled out the photograph. When he entered the trailer, he'd been breathing fast, but now, looking at it, his breath slowed. *You deserve this,* he thought. *Whatever it takes, you're worth it.*

And because that was true, he knew what he had to do.

"Damn it," he whispered, staring at the pouch. And then, more fiercely, "*Damn it.*"

He opened the cabinet, thrust the pouch inside, and slammed the door again abruptly. He returned the photograph to his pocket and was out of the camper and headed out of the camp site before another three seconds passed.

"Keep your money," he told Artie shortly as he strode past. "And be more careful about who you pick up on the road."

Artie straightened up from the coffee and started to say something, but Josh didn't break stride. "You're out of graham crackers," he added gruffly, and in another two steps he was beyond the camper, out of the camp site, feet crunching on the gravel road. Even then he could feel Artie's gaze following him, and something about the kind, thoroughly unsurprised smile in them haunted him all the way down the road.

The woman with the amazing voice was afloat in swirling chiffon scarves and an extravagance of bleached-blond curls. She had the bosom of Mae West and the eyes of Betty Davis, and that smoky voice that came straight out of a French bistro in the twenties. Unfortunately, she also had the face of a sixty-year-old circus clown, from which the slash of bright fuchsia lipstick and dangling, six-inch peacock feather earrings were, admittedly, a distraction. She wore a purple paisley silk caftan beneath the flutter of multi-colored scarves, and bright pink suede ankle boots. Her arm jingled with a dozen or more bangle bracelets as she extended a graceful, well-manicured hand, offering a card.

"Harmony Haven," she introduced herself grandly, "spiritualist to the stars. I have a reservation."

For a moment, both Paul and Derrick found themselves completely bereft of savoir faire. They, who had chatted with ambassadors and attended press parties for movie stars—then made catty remarks about the couture the moment they were out of earshot, of course—could not, for an awful endless moment, think of a single thing to say between them.

They both moved at once. The sherry tray tilted dangerously and the cheese slid into the grapes as they both reached for the business card that dangled from the tips of her glittered fuchsia nails. Paul won the prize, and Derrick read over his shoulder. In flowing white script against a bold pink, indigo, and purple background, it read: *Harmony Haven* Spiritual Advisor* Psychic* Manicurist* Animal Communicator* Yoga Instructor* Licensed Massage Therapist* Dog Training by Appointment.*

Derrick looked up at her with interest. "You're a licensed massage therapist?"

Paul elbowed him not-very-discreetly in the ribs and sherry splashed out of one of the glasses.

"I'm sorry," Paul told her politely, offering the card. "We're not open for business."

"Don't be silly." She waved away the card he tried to return. "I've had this reservation for eighteen months. I've been coming here every summer for years, you know. I always stay in the fuchsia room." And she smiled at them, fluffing her curls. "That's my signature color. It balances all the blue in my aura."

Her smile was like the whisper of a cashmere blanket settling against the skin on a crisp autumn day. Like silk against ermine. Like sunshine on water. It was so utterly out of place on her face that for a moment both men were once again entranced into speechlessness.

Paul made a physical effort to break the spell, and glanced down at her card again. "What stars, exactly, were you spiritual advisor to?"

"My dear," she replied, lowering her tone confidentially, "who exactly do you think told Nicole to leave Tom Cruise? The spirits were very specific about that. There was something terribly wrong there from the beginning."

"I know!" agreed Paul, forgetting himself for a moment. "What *was* that?"

"Well, of course I'm bound by confidentiality. But I've offered major spiritual advice to everyone from Billy Joel to Kate Middleton. I told her she was having a boy before she even knew she was pregnant."

"Well, the chances were fifty-fifty," Paul felt compelled to point out, and this time Derrick elbowed him.

Harmony appeared not to notice. "Now," she declared, folding her arms across her ample chest beneficently, "the important question is how I can help you. It's simple really. This is a sacred space, and until you allow it to live up to its full potential you will have nothing but misfortune."

Derrick looked around uneasily. "Did the spirits tell you that?"

"All homes are sacred spaces," she replied. She tilted her head and drew in a deep breath, as though inhaling the essence of the place and extracting from it the molecules of truth only she could discern. "This one more so than others," she murmured, her eyes half-closed. "It yearns to fulfill its destiny." She opened her eyes and looked at them with a decisive nod, then helped herself to a glass of sherry from Paul's tray. "You are going to have a grand opening," she declared. "And not just any grand opening, a *celebrity* grand opening."

Paul's interest was piqued, even as curiosity warred with skepticism. "Did the spirits tell you *that*?"

"Of course not, darling. I was director of marketing for Nissan for twenty-two years. Anyone can see your problem is branding." She sipped the sherry, raised an appreciative eyebrow, and held the glass out to admire it. Then she looked back at them, her tone brisk and businesslike. "B&Bs in the Shenandoah Valley are a dime a dozen," she said, "and yours is twenty miles off the interstate. That's probably why the last owner couldn't make it. This needs to become a *destination*. A resort of distinction. You'll establish that with a celebrity grand opening, get written up in all the trades, and watch the reservations pile up from there." She lifted her glass and took another healthy swallow. "Success, my darlings, is yours."

Paul looked at Derrick, the wheels of his mind turning with speed and precision. "You know," he said, careful not to sound too excited, "that's not an entirely ridiculous idea."

"I still have my client list from the gallery," Derrick said. His eyes took on a spark. "Everyone who's anyone in Washington bought art from me. Senators, lobbyists, decorators of corporate jets ..." He turned eagerly to Harmony. "Could you get Nicole Kidman?"

She just smiled and sipped her sherry.

Paul said, "I know one of Oprah's producers. I don't like her," he admitted, "but I know her."

Derrick's eyes flew wide with delight. "Oh my God!" he exclaimed, gripping Paul's wrist. "I have Johnny Depp's manager's business card!"

"And Lester Carson!"

"The travel editor for the *Times*? Of course! One word from him—"

"And he totally owes me a favor after that dreadful Christmas party of his I salvaged."

"Who do we know at Hearst? They publish every lifestyle magazine worth reading."

"Remember that intern from *Vogue*?"

Derrick grimaced. "What a bitch."

"Yes, but he was in love with Eric Schwartz, who was related to Missy Hampton, whose son went to school with—"

"Bette Midler's daughter," breathed Derrick, and sank back in silence to contemplate the possibilities.

Paul looked at him in cautious wonder. "We could do this," he said.

Derrick agreed, big-eyed, "We totally could."

Harmony placed her empty glass on the tray with a clack and swung open the sticky French door effortlessly, sweeping out into the garden in a trail of fluttering chiffon and lavender scent. "Bring the bottle, boys," she called over her shoulder, "we'll work out the details. You can take my things to my room later."

Paul drew a breath to reply, debated with himself, and seemed to come to an uneasy conclusion. He looked at Derrick anxiously, whispering, "Are there sheets on the bed in the fuchsia room?"

Derrick looked insulted. "Of course there are!" Then he frowned a little. "But they're pink. We were going to go with bone-on-bone stripe. And I hate that rose scented bath salts in the bathroom. It utterly clashes with the aqua towels."

"We can't let her stay," Paul said uneasily.

"Of course not."

"We're not open for business."

"You told her that."

"We don't even have mints for the pillow."

Derrick's brows knit briefly. "I wonder how she knew."

"Knew what?"

"That we were having problems with the business."

"She must have overheard us talking." But it was his turn to frown as he glanced back down the hallway.

"I suppose. It's just that ... we weren't really talking about the B&B when she came in."

Paul glanced toward the garden door and lowered his voice. "Oh my God, did you see those earrings? And can that possibly be her real name?"

"Of course not."

"Stripper?"

"Porn star?"

"Drag queen?"

They looked at each other for a moment and then agreed as one, "Impossible."

Derrick added, shifting his eyes meaningfully toward the garden and its occupant. "I have to ask …"

"Forty-six Double F, easily," replied Paul without hesitation.

Derrick lifted his eyebrows. "I didn't know they made Double Fs."

Paul gave a dismissive flick of his wrist. "Please. It's the twenty-first century. Keep up."

Through the open door, Harmony called sweetly, "Fellows? Sherry?"

Derrick looked worried. "Are we allowed to serve her alcohol? She's a paying customer."

"She hasn't paid us anything yet," Paul pointed out.

"And I have a fabulous idea for your logo!" she called from the garden. "Did I mention I used to be a graphic designer?"

Derrick looked at Paul thoughtfully. "The Hummingbird House Bed and Breakfast," he murmured. "A Destination of Distinction."

"Audubon," said Paul. "We'll send out invitations to the grand opening printed on Audubon prints of birds."

"In boxes with tiny candies shaped liked eggs nestled in a bird's nest," added Derrick.

"Perhaps a bit much," suggested Paul. "But," he added before Derrick could act hurt, "definitely a destination of distinction."

Derrick inclined his head in a gesture of forgiveness. "Just one more question."

"Which is?"

"Are we open for business?"

Paul hesitated, then sighed. "I'll get the sherry," he said.

FOUR

An idea that is not dangerous is unworthy of being called an idea at all.

Oscar Wilde

If there was one thing Paul knew, it was how to throw a party. And if there was one thing Derrick knew, it was how to be a good host. Until Harmony Haven moved into the B&B, they could never have imagined a time that those two things could be in conflict.

"What you need, darlings," Harmony explained patiently as they sat down to dinner on her third night of residence, "is a theme. It has to be a grand theme. As grand as your grand opening."

Derrick sailed in at that moment with a platter of country pot roast and vegetables that Purline had left simmering on the stove before she left. Sensing a tense moment in the making, he exclaimed, "Don't you look lovely tonight, Harmony? Is that gown vintage?"

Harmony liked to dress for dinner—even though, when they looked back, neither Paul nor Derrick could remember ever inviting her to dinner in the first place—which meant trading her flowing caftans and colorful scarves for floor length lace gowns and costume jewelry. This habit had inspired the gentlemen to rise to the occasion as well, observing a regular dinner hour and setting one of the dining room tables with candles and a tablecloth each evening rather than dining at the kitchen table whenever the mood struck them. Tonight she wore a black 1920's style gown with a midnight blue lace over-blouse which was no doubt supposed to imitate a Worth design from that era, complemented by three strands of pearls. Her mad cascade of blond curls had been tamed into an upsweep that must have taken hours to accomplish.

She smiled and inclined her head at Derrick's compliment. "Thank you, dear heart. It's just like one I wore on the *Queen Mary* in my former life as the Duchess of Extonbury. What a crossing that was, may I live to tell you!" She reached for the serving utensils and helped herself to a generous portion of the beef from the platter Derrick set before her, along with a more than adequate portion of vegetables. "Is that gravy, my love? And I do believe I'll have just a wee smidgen of that bread."

Paul refused to be distracted, even as he watched half the contents of the gravy boat disappear onto Harmony's plate.

"We have a theme," he replied, equally as patiently, although anyone who knew him could tell the patience had an edge to it. "It's artisanal elegance. It's our credo, it's our specialty, it's our raison d'être. Very now. Very locavore. Very us."

Derrick passed the platter to Paul. "The beef practically falls off the fork," he said. "That Purline is a wonder. I swear she must have studied in Ida Mae's kitchen."

Paul gave him a mildly accusing look as he took the roast beef platter. "You know you shouldn't be eating red meat. I thought Purline was going to start serving more fish."

Derrick tried not to look annoyed. "We had fish only last week."

"It was fried and served with hushpuppies."

Derrick smiled and sliced his beef. "It was heavenly."

Paul stabbed a carrot. "We'll just see how heavenly Dr. Fredericks thinks it is. Your physical is coming up in two weeks, you know."

"How could I forget? You programmed a countdown into my BlackBerry." And with a look of defiance, Derrick bit down on one of Purline's angel biscuits.

Harmony spread her smile over the two of them. "Don't you worry, darling, your heart is just fine, and it has been for months. Your cardiologist will be amazed, but that's because he doesn't understand that healing must first take place on the inside."

Derrick stopped in mid-bite, staring at her. "I never told you about my heart. How did you know Dr. Fredericks was a cardiologist?"

Paul's look held a stern warning. They had talked about not encouraging Harmony. "It's hardly a secret," he pointed out.

Harmony just held up her empty wine glass, which Derrick was quick to refill. "The spirits know all," she said.

It was with a very great effort that Paul restrained himself from making a comment about the spirits that lived in the bottom of a wine bottle. Derrick caught the struggle in his eyes and it was his turn to issue a warning look.

"Now," declared Harmony, taking a generous sip from her glass before attacking her beef with a knife and fork, "about your theme. What you're looking for is something specific, something unique. Something memorable. Something with …" she put down her fork just long enough to kiss her fingers to the air, *"je ne sais quoi."*

Paul drew a sharp breath for a reply, but Derrick interrupted quickly, "Harmony was telling me the most fascinating story about Walter Cronkite this afternoon. Can you imagine? She actually saved his wife from being struck by a car!"

Needing very little encouragement, Harmony added, "This was back in the sixties, not long before the Cuban missile crisis, if I recall—of course, I was barely a girl then, you understand, but my special gifts were already beginning to show and …"

The truth was that Harmony's stories were captivating, and what they might have lacked in factuality they more than made up for in flair. It was impossible not to enjoy her company when she was at her best, but she was definitely an acquired taste.

Midway through the second bottle of wine, Harmony declared, "I have it! Your theme has been revealed to me!" She set down her wine glass with a flourish and framed the air in front of her. "The Seasons of Man. *That* is your theme. We'll have progressive displays of the evolution of man and at each station there will be a delicacy appropriate to the era. Roast venison, Roman bread …"

"This is not a university lecture series," Paul objected, trying to mute his horror.

And even Derrick put in, "I'm not entirely sure posters of Cro-Magnon man are appropriate at a B&B."

"Clocks," replied Harmony, tossing back a gulp of wine. Her eyes were bright and focused on the future. "Dozens and dozens of clocks to represent the seasons."

"*Calendars,*" Paul said, setting his teeth. "Calendars represent the seasons."

She gasped with delight. "Our invitations will be shaped like clocks!"

"Our?" Paul eyebrows shot high. "*Our*?"

"Round envelopes," Derrick worried. "They'll take forever to design and print."

"Leave it to me," Harmony assured him airily, finishing off her wine. "I can find anything. This is going to be the most memorable event in the history of Virginia. Virginia!" She gasped again, touching her throat. "We must have a tribute to Thomas Jefferson. Or the Mayflower!"

"The Mayflower landed at Plymouth Rock," Derrick said, confused.

"We're not having a tribute to Thomas Jefferson," Paul said firmly, picking up his own glass.

"You must excuse me, gentlemen," Harmony said, fluttering to her feet. "I must go meditate on this while the spirits are with me. And take notes. Don't you worry, I'll make plenty of notes. "

"Or clocks!" Paul called after her. "We're not having clocks!"

She did not appear to hear.

Derrick got to his feet, his lips set in a thin line, and began to clear the table.

"What?" Paul insisted. He picked up his own plate and followed him into the kitchen.

"That," said Derrick, stacking the dishes neatly in the sink, "was rude."

"It was not rude, it was self-defense. You can't possibly seriously be considering clocks and Neanderthals."

"You never make a guest in your home feel uncomfortable," Derrick replied shortly, "no matter how stupid her ideas. It's rude. Anyone who was raised in the South learned that at his mother's knee."

Paul, who had been born in New Jersey, had nothing to reply to that. Derrick returned to the table for the remainder of the dishes and Paul began to rinse the ones in the sink before transferring them to the dishwasher.

"I suppose," Paul conceded by way of apology when Derrick returned, "with all things considered, we certainly could have done worse for our first guest."

"She didn't even blink at the room rate," agreed Derrick.

"And she's very entertaining."

"Hardly ever in the way."

"Well ..." Paul hesitated over that. "Not according to Purline."

Their one guest persisted on annoying their only staff member by sleeping until ten, meditating in her room until two, and then requesting tea in the garden while she worked on her watercolors which, according to Purline, were nothing more than wet splotches of color on paper.

"Of course, it's nice to have the company," Paul added carefully, "particularly at mealtime."

Derrick took over the loading of the dishwasher while Paul rinsed. "But she does drink a bit much."

"Like a fish. And," added Paul flatly, "there is no Duchess of Extonbury."

Derrick sighed. "I know. And let's not even *talk* about that former life on the *Titanic.*"

"*Queen Mary,*" corrected Paul. He met Derrick's gaze with a raised eyebrow. "Certifiable?"

"One hundred percent," agreed Derrick without hesitation.

"So no Cro-Magnon men at our grand opening."

"Of course not. By tomorrow she will have completely forgotten the evolutionary theme and have moved on to something else." Derrick added thoughtfully, "I do have to wonder what a Cro-Magnon era delicacy would taste like, though."

"Frozen wooly mammoth?" suggested Paul.

"Prehistoric shark sushi?" offered Derrick, unable to hold back a grin.

"Oh, boys, I almost forgot."

They quickly smothered their amusement and put on studiously pleasant faces as Harmony came through the swinging door to the kitchen, waving a piece of paper. "Just a few names for your guest list."

Derrick dried his hands and took the paper from her, scanning it politely. He caught his breath with an audible sound. "This is *not* Keith Richards's home address." His eyes bulged as he looked at her.

She waved her hand. "Of course not. Which home would you send it to? That's his business manager, but he'll see Keith gets it. Of course, he probably won't come, but wouldn't it be lovely if he did?"

Paul grabbed a dishtowel and read over Derrick's shoulder. "Lindsay Lohan, Ryan Seacrest … Nancy Reagan?"

Harmony pointed with a long purple fingernail at the address. "Of course, she doesn't get around much these days, but we've known the Reagans for years, and I know she'll come if she's able. I'll write a note."

Paul said, a little hoarsely, "That would be …" he cleared his throat. "That will be lovely. Thank you."

"Which reminds me," she went on, "all of your invitations should be handwritten. You'll have a printed cover card, of course, but the enclosure should be a personal, requests-the-pleasure-of-your-company sort of thing. It adds to the atmosphere of elegance and exclusivity."

"Yes," said Derrick, clutching the list. "We'd planned to."

"I've already ordered the vellum," Paul put in quickly. "It's being overnighted."

"Perfect." She favored them with the brilliance of her smile. "Now I must be off and see what else the spirits have to say to me. Good night, my darlings."

"Good night," they echoed in unison.

Paul lifted a hand weakly and called after her, "Mention my name."

She turned and blew them a kiss, leaving the door swinging in her wake.

"Well," said Derrick.

"Well," said Paul.

Derrick looked at the paper in his hand. He cleared his throat. "You know, there was that scandal during the Reagan administration about the first lady consulting a spiritualist."

"I'm sure it wasn't the same one," Paul said.

Derrick said, "I'm sure it wasn't."

"She could be making the entire thing up."

Derrick looked at him. "What if she's not?"

Paul blew out a slow, thoughtful breath. "I think," he said, tossing aside the dishtowel, "I will go research the proper protocol for entertaining a former First Lady of the United States."

It was strange, the phases one went through when the foundation of one's life began to crumble. At first she had been addicted to Nick's voice messages. *Megan, we can't leave it like this. Megan, call*

me back. Megan, I know I was wrong but you were too. I was hurt, and angry. I should have listened to you. We need to talk. Megan, I don't know how I can understand what's going on with you if you won't talk to me. And finally, *Meg, I'm starting to wonder if there's anything left to save.* She never returned his calls. She always wanted to. She would sit staring at her phone, finger poised over his number, for endless agonizing moments, but in the end, at the last moment, she would always lose her courage. She didn't know what to say. And eventually the messages stopped coming.

For a while she had been addicted to listening to the saved messages, sometimes just to hear the sound of his voice, sometimes fantasizing that it was not, after all, too late to call him back, to come up with the magic words that would make everything all right, to erase from her memory the look of hurt and disappointment in her husband's eyes and to erase from his what she had done to put it there. But there were no words.

Now she was addicted to not listening to the messages, to scrolling through her missed calls, to fighting back tears when the number she was looking for was never among them. Today there were three missed calls and two voice mails from her mother. There was nothing from Nick.

She heard her grandmother's step in the hallway and tucked the phone back into the pocket of her purse, rubbed both palms over her face just in case a stray tear lingered, and went to check the coffee cake in the oven. She always baked when she was stressed, and it was nice to have someone besides the squirrels to share her bounty with.

"Raspberry cream coffee cake," declared Annabelle from the doorway. "Now there's a reason to get out of bed in the morning if I ever smelled one."

"With streusel topping," added Megan, wrapping her hands in a kitchen towel to remove the pan from the oven. "We're going to be very naughty and have cake for breakfast. I figured you wouldn't mind."

"Being naughty is my favorite way to start the day."

Megan brought the cake to the breakfast table, which was already set with a bright yellow tablecloth, two glasses of orange juice, and two mugs of coffee. Annabelle, dressed in a lime green track suit and silver high-tops, lowered herself to her chair and snapped open her napkin.

"I could boil some eggs," volunteered Megan, feeling a little guilty for not being more conscientious about her grandmother's nutrition. "Or make oatmeal."

"I'm quite sure you could, my dear," replied Annabelle, "but you're a pastry chef, not a short order cook. Always go with your strength, I say."

Megan smiled, but it was a tired thing, like an old party dress that had been forced into service one too many times. "I'm not a pastry chef," she reminded her grandmother. "I'm a bookkeeper."

"In your heart, you're a pastry chef. What you do for a living is immaterial. Is there any butter?"

Megan brought the butter dish to the table along with the serving knife and two breakfast plates. She knew exactly what her grandmother would say if she reminded her of the doctor's advice about watching her cholesterol—*I didn't get to be this old by listening to that fool* – so she tried another approach. "A real chef would be insulted by that."

"There's no such thing as too much salt or too much butter," replied her grandmother, stirring cream into her coffee complacently. "And you and I have been trying to improve on each other's recipes since you were five years old."

Megan sat down across from her grandmother and sliced into the cake, releasing a waft of sweet-smelling steam and a gooey ooze of the rich raspberry sauce in the middle. "This is one of yours, you know—or it's based on it, anyway. Remember that apple-cinnamon lava cake you used to make?"

"Well, don't forget my royalties when you open your bakery." She sipped her coffee, watching Megan slide a perfect wedge of cake onto the plate and let the bright red sauce that was left on the knife drizzle artfully over the top. "I can't imagine how that restaurant of yours will manage while you're gone. The entire business structure is likely to come tumbling down, and it will be all my fault for taking you away."

"It's not my restaurant. I just keep the books."

"Indeed? I always thought it was a good deal more than that."

Megan cut another, smaller slice for herself and unfolded her napkin. "You always saw me as so much more than I am," she told her softly. "You know that, don't you? Cooking is only one of the things I learned to do because you told me I could. That was a beautiful gift."

"For all the good it did." Annabelle sliced into the cake with the edge of her fork. "I always wanted you to be a jet pilot. Besides, you know perfectly well you learned to cook in self-defense. Your mother, God bless her, has many wonderful qualities, but cooking is not one of them." She tasted the cake, made an appreciative sound in the back of her throat, and added casually, "Indulge a nosy old woman, my dear, but why was it you never went to cooking school? I remember a time when that was all you wanted to do."

Megan smashed together a few crumbs of coffee cake on her plate, absorbed in the pattern the raspberry filling made on the white surface. "Oh, I don't know. There never seemed to be enough time, or money ..."

"Or ambition?"

Megan didn't even bother to challenge that, and as much as she knew her lack of spirit would disappoint her grandmother, she couldn't help it. She lifted a shoulder, not looking up. "Probably. You get into a routine, you know. After a while it seemed like everything depended on me just doing my job and, well, it didn't seem fair."

Her grandmother's eyes were, it seemed, unusually piercing. "Was that what Nick said?"

Megan immediately protested, "No, of course not! Nick would have supported whatever I wanted to do. I just ..." She dropped her eyes again. "I guess I was afraid. After all, we had one star in the family already." Her smile was strained. "Why rock the boat, right?"

Her grandmother's gaze was thoughtful and a little too perceptive, making Megan wonder suddenly whether the innocent questions had been designed to uncover more than they suggested, and whether she had not, in fact, revealed more than she had intended. But Annabelle merely took another bite of cake and said mildly, "Couldn't agree with you more, my dear. People who rock the boat generally end up standing on shore, soaking wet in their underwear while everyone else parties on."

An unexpected and completely unpreventable laugh bubbled up in Megan's throat. "You're in rare form today, Gram. What put you in such a good mood?"

"Besides this marvelous cake?" She tasted it, and made a circle with her thumb and forefinger in approval. Then she dabbed her lips with her napkin, sipped her coffee, and leaned back in her chair, smiling. "Today," she said, "we begin our big adventure. My bag is all packed, and first thing after breakfast we'll gas up the car and head out. By my calculation, we can make a hundred miles before lunch."

Megan paused with a forkful of cake halfway to her mouth. "Wait," she said. "Are you serious? Are we really going to do this?"

Annabelle looked surprised and mildly offended. "Well, that was the whole point of my coming back from the dead, wasn't it?"

Megan returned the forkful of cake to her plate untasted. "You did not come back from the dead, you—" But she stopped herself from the distraction of a tangent with an impatient shake of her head. "Anyway, where will we go? We can't just drive around at random looking for … what *are* we looking for, anyway?"

"The mountains," replied Annabelle promptly. She reached into the pocket of her velour jacket and brought out the photograph of the two women and the child standing in front of the sign. "The *Blue Ridge* Mountains," she specified, pointing to the hazy undulation of mountains in the background of the photo. "We're heading east, my girl. Back to the beginning."

Megan regarded her grandmother with a mixture of patience and suspicion. "I just came from the east," she pointed out.

"What a coincidence."

"Six hours on a plane. Now the plan is to turn around and *drive* back? Gram, you know I love you, but …" She looked at her grandmother narrowly. "This wouldn't by chance be your way of getting me back home to Nick, would it? Because …"

Annabelle interrupted her with a regal, dismissive wave of her hand. "My dear girl, I'm dying. I have much more immediate things to worry about than your marriage. As much as I like the fellow, you'll get on just fine without him, if it comes to that. You may not think so now, but you will. I, on the other hand, have a limited amount of time to accomplish my mission, so let's focus on what's important, shall we?"

Megan released an exasperated half-laugh. "Fine. But would you at least tell me what this mission of yours is?"

"Of course, my dear. But first, get your bag packed and help me load the car."

"I'll load the car," Megan assured her quickly, having no doubt that her grandmother would be dragging suitcases to the garage if she decided the preparations were moving too slowly. She stood and began clearing the table. "My bag is still packed from the trip out here. It'll only take me a minute. You just sit and enjoy your coffee."

The way Annabelle smiled and settled back assured Megan that had been her intention all along. She picked up her fork again. "Don't forget to cancel the newspaper, and call Mr. Harmond next door and ask him to keep an eye on the place." She took a bite of cake and savored it. "And wrap up some of this lovely cake for the trip, won't you?" She smiled sweetly at Megan. "Who knows how long we'll be gone, and it would be a shame to waste it."

"How about September 6?" suggested Paul.

Derrick shook his head. "Labor Day weekend. Everyone is closing up their summer houses."

"September 14?"

"That's Lindsay's wedding weekend."

"Oh no, she changed it to the twenty-first."

At Derrick's questioning look, Paul returned a "Don't ask" roll of his eyes. So far the date had been changed six times, and she had only been engaged three weeks.

The two men were comfortably settled across from one another at the big partners' desk in their newly refurbished office off the main reception area. Deep indigo walls were accented by warm mahogany bookshelves lined with books in colorful dust jackets, and a primitive oak dry sink served as a display area for a vase of wildflowers and a copper tube and funnel that had come from an old moonshine still. There was a small, ancient fireplace faced with time-worn pebbles over which Derrick had hung a large boldly colored folk art painting of a bonneted woman hanging laundry while stick-figure children played nearby. Derrick's chair was a high-backed, old world tapestry pattern while Paul's was worn tufted leather. The carpet that covered the ancient pine floor was an exquisitely faded, hand-knotted, red-and-blue Persian. And it all came together beautifully, of course.

Each partner had his own computer, and on this bright summer morning each had an identical calendar program open on his screen. In the background, the hum of the vacuum cleaner blessedly drowned out Purline's off-key singing of "Rock of Ages." The house smelled of lemon polish and baking bread, and for that and other reasons Paul and Derrick had decided to tolerate the singing.

Paul scrolled down his calendar. "How about the twenty-sixth then?"

Derrick shook his head. "Rosh Hashanah." And when Paul stared at him he added, "Do you know how many people on our A-list are Jewish?"

Paul considered this for a moment and agreed. He tapped a key. "We're into October then."

"Look no further, gentlemen, I have it!"

Harmony Haven exploded into the room like a rainbow cloudburst, a swirl of yellow and blue and pink and electric with confidence. Paul had to remove his glasses and blink several times to clear his vision before he could look at her.

As Derrick had predicted, Harmony had abandoned the idea of the Evolution of Man for the grand opening by the next morning—something about a dispute between the spirits—and had instead turned her attentions to cleansing the environs of astral negativity with chunks of burning sage and tiny tinkling bells. The entire house had smelled like a college dorm, and Purline had given them suspicious looks for days afterward. But for the sake of Nancy Reagan, they had kept their complaints to a minimum.

Harmony carried a fuchsia-bound notebook in her hand and a pen decorated with a bright pink feather, which she used to tap an open page of the book importantly. "August fifteenth," she declared. "The first night of the new moon—perfect for beginning new projects! Mercury is in Cancer, trining Venus and Mars, and Jupiter is in the sixth house of successful partnerships, not to mention the sun in its native sign—my darlings, you couldn't order a more auspicious date to launch your enterprise!"

Paul repeated carefully, "Mercury in Cancer?"

"The sign of home and harmony," she assured him.

"Everyone knows that," Derrick added smugly.

Paul gave him a mild warning look. "We can't possibly put together an event like this by August fifteenth," he explained to Harmony. "That's only three weeks away."

"Nonsense." Harmony's filmy sleeve rippled a kaleidoscope of colors as she waved away the objection as though it were a bad odor. "When the stars are aligned anything is possible. By the way, we're out of TP in the public bathroom, and the flowers on the reception desk are looking a little droopy. You should tell your girl."

Paul drew back his shoulders, his expression annoyed. "Purline is not our 'girl.' She's a valuable member of our staff and—"

"We'll take care of it," Derrick interrupted with a quick smile. "Thank you, Harmony."

She consulted the small glittered notebook in her hand. "Now, I'm thinking a wine and cheese reception in the garden for thirty-five on Friday night, followed by a sit-down banquet on the sun porch—"

"How can we do that? Derrick objected, horrified. "The law has closed us down!"

"It's a private party," Harmony explained patiently. "You're not charging a dime, you're entertaining guests."

"We'll line the garden paths with votives," Paul said, forgetting his annoyance as his imagination came to life. "Thousands of them. And thousands more all around the porch."

"We'll hang white gauze curtains and put the votives behind them," added Derrick. "They'll look like fireflies."

"We'll have to use electric candles, then."

"Only behind the curtains. And fountains!" exclaimed Derrick excitedly. "We'll bring in fountains for each corner and a big one for the garden."

"Fire and water," agreed Harmony happily. "What about earth?"

Paul, who was still trying to figure out what Derrick meant about "bringing in" fountains, said, "We'll have three long tables with white tablecloths, and the centerpieces will be low runners made of wildflowers and vines."

"Perfect!" Harmony clapped her hands. "We have fire, earth, water … what about air?"

They all were thoughtful for a time. Then Derrick suggested, "Ceiling fans?"

Harmony nodded her approval. "Now, you see? You're catching on."

Paul said uncertainly, "Well, at least they don't have to be brought in. They're already installed."

"You can accommodate seven couples overnight," Harmony went on, "but *only* from your A-list. We'll set up a tent for couples massages, hire limos for tours …"

"What are they going to tour?" Paul wondered.

"Oh, please," Derrick insisted. "These people never even get to see grass. We'll take them to the vineyard, a historic site or two …"

"What historic site?"

"There's got to be a historic site around here somewhere," Derrick replied dismissively. "It's the country, for heaven's sake." And then his eyes flew wide with the onset of an idea. "Horses!" he exclaimed. "We'll rent horses!"

"For what?" objected Paul.

"Riding! This is horse country, don't you read the papers? And celebrities love to ride." He gave a satisfied nod. "Definitely horses."

Harmony spread her bountiful smile over them like a blessing. "Now you see how beautifully it's all coming together? I'll start making out our to-do list, you get started on the invitations. Chop-chop, fellows. August fifteenth is just around the corner."

Paul said, "Seriously, we can't begin to pull this together by August."

"We couldn't possibly get a caterer by then," added Derrick.

"Not to mention design the invitations, order the wine …"

"Refine the guest list …"

"And the indigo room still has those hideous drapes …"

"We have to have entertainment," Paul pointed out, "and the best chamber quartets are booked months in advance."

Derrick tapped a couple of more keys on his computer. "Maybe we should start looking in November."

"The holidays. Everyone is booked." Paul scrolled down several pages. "January?"

"Too risky. The weather is foul."

"August fifteenth," repeated Harmony firmly. "It's written in the stars." She turned on her heel and sailed grandly out, leaving a trail of color and scent in her wake.

Paul put his glasses back on and looked across at Derrick, lowering his voice. "You know," he said, "having a celebrity launch party was a fabulous idea..."

"A lot of her ideas are fabulous," agreed Derrick, but he looked a trifle uneasy as he glanced at the door through which she had departed. "Others ... not so much."

"It's not that I don't appreciate all her support..."

"And the idea for the hummingbird logo was wonderful," Derrick added, "or it will be, once Lindsay refines it."

"It's just ..." Paul lowered his voice another fraction, leaning close over the desk, "do you remember how she told us she had had this reservation for eighteen months? Well, I was looking through some of the old registers yesterday and it turns out this place wasn't even open eighteen months ago!"

Derrick took off his glasses and leaned across the desk, too, casting a surreptitious glance over his shoulder toward the door. "I'll tell you something else," he said, practically whispering. "She's been here a week and hasn't said a thing about when she's leaving ... or settling her bill."

Paul looked worried. "We have her credit card info."

"I know, but our policy is to charge on check-out. I don't think we can change it now." Now Derrick glanced guiltily toward the door. "Can we?"

"Have you asked her when she's leaving?"

"Well, that would be rude." Derrick look offended at the thought. "But," he admitted, "I have tried to bring the subject up in a more delicate fashion."

"And?"

"And she always just says something about the stars, or the spirits, or angels."

"That's because she's a nut," Purline said flatly, striding through the door with a dust cloth and a bottle of lemon polish in her hand. "You all know that, don't you?"

Both men started guiltily at the sound of her voice and sat back, trying to look busy. Paul said, a little pompously, "There's no need to be unkind, Purline."

Purline gave a disdainful snort. "She's got no more pull with Ryan Seacrest than I do, and if you ask me the only stars she ever advised were the ones spinning around in her head."

She started to squirt lemon polish on the dry sink and Derrick leapt from his chair, taking the bottle from her. "Please, my dear! Dry cloth only, remember?"

Purline gave him a sour look and retrieved the bottle of polish, turning to the bookshelves. "She's eating you out of house and home, too. I thought this was supposed to be a Bed and Breakfast, not a Bed and Three-Squares. I hope you're charging extra for that."

Paul and Derrick shared an uneasy look. They were a house divided about the entire meal situation. Derrick declared that having a guest in the house had improved their own dining experience considerably, beginning with Purline's baked apples, homemade waffles and hash-brown scramble in the morning and ending with chicken fried steak and mashed potatoes with garden-fresh vegetables at night. Paul worried about what the three calorie-rich meals a day were doing to Derrick's cholesterol—not to mention his own waistline—and was constantly arguing with Purline about it behind Derrick's back. On the other hand, the one thing they both agreed on was that it was pleasant to have company for dinner again. Harmony was a never ending source of fascinating stories, and half the fun of listening to them was trying to discern which, if any, parts might be true. They had missed putting down a tablecloth, lighting candles, and being the gracious hosts they naturally were. For that alone, they could tolerate a great deal.

On yet another hand, neither of them had ever seen a woman put away quite as much wine as she did without showing a single ill effect. They had quickly learned the value of keeping several bottles of inexpensive table wine within reach while cellaring anything priced over 9.99. They were running a business, after all.

With this in mind, Derrick pointed out, "Actually, we can't charge her anything at all. The restaurant is supposed to be closed, remember?"

"That reminds me," Purline said, pulling a handful of envelopes out of her back pocket, "here's your mail."

They knew Purline too well by now to question how a discussion of meals should remind her of mail, so Derrick took the envelopes with murmured thanks and set them in his in-box—a beautifully refinished nineteenth century wooden tackle box with traces of the original faded blue paint still intact.

"By the way," Purline said, liberally squirting furniture polish over the bookshelves, "I don't cook for parties, in case that's what you were thinking. I've got my own family to take care of. But if you need a singer, I might be able to help you out."

Paul's jaw dropped in horror at the very thought, and Derrick said quickly, "Thank you, Purline, that's sweet of you. We'll keep that in mind."

Paul added, "We'll probably bring a caterer for the party."

Purline scrubbed at the bookshelves with the cloth. "Good idea. You shouldn't have any trouble a'tall getting somebody out here in August. August is dead as a doornail, don't know why. Seems like everybody's kind of tired of summer by then, they've all done whatever they set out to do, nothing much going on. Anyhow, if you're looking for somebody, I recommend Smokey's Barbecue. He did my sister's wedding and everybody just raved. He makes a cornbread casserole that's to die for. Of course," she admitted, "the cake was a little strange. The icing tasted like bacon."

While the men tried to absorb that picture, she gave a final squirt of the lemon polish across the covers of the books. Derrick smothered a gasp of horror and started to lurch from his chair. Paul reached across the desk and grabbed his arm."That's a fabulous idea, Purline," he said. "Thank you."

Derrick widened his eyes until Paul thought they might very well pop out of his head.

Purline gave a final swipe across the bookshelf with her cloth and turned to go. "Mention my name to Smokey," she told them, "he'll give you a good deal." And she swaggered out of the room, hips swinging in tight denim shorts, humming an old Kenny Rogers tune that was so off-key even Paul winced.

Derrick rushed to the bookshelf with a wad of tissues, scrubbing at the oil dampened covers. "This is an Agatha Christie first edition!" he moaned. And he turned on Paul accusingly. "Why did you let her get away with that?"

"We're in the middle of a grand opening," he replied, "we can't afford to lose our only staff member now." His expression grew thoughtful. "Besides, she had a good point."

Derrick's expression changed from dismay to indignation. "We are *not* serving barbecue at our grand opening!"

"No," agreed Paul, smiling in a very self-satisfied way, "but we might serve pork belly, prepared by one of the most exclusive chefs in DC … in August, when absolutely nothing else is going on."

Derrick looked at him for a moment, comprehension slowly dawning, and then he sank back into his chair, his hand over his heart. "Oh. My. God," he said. "You're right." He blinked. "Purline is right. *Nobody* does anything in August. How many times have we simply *died* of ennui in the city for the entire month?"

"Wishing we had somewhere to go, something to do?"

"Because if you don't make your reservations in April—"

"And nobody who's anybody has time to do that."

"Then you're left high and dry in August!"

Derrick raised his palm for a high five, a habit which had become more than a little annoying of late, and Paul said, "Seriously. Don't do that."

Derrick frowned and dropped his hand, but brightened almost immediately, stretching out his arms with palms upraised as though receiving a gift from the heavens. "Harvest time in the country," he announced grandly. "The perfect showcase for artisanal elegance." He hesitated. "August *is* harvest time, isn't it?"

Paul's eyes shone. "The invitations will be printed on brown paper."

"In gold!"

"And delivered with a box of …" He cast around in his mind. "What's in season?"

"Everything is in season!"

"Blackberries?"

Derrick shook his head adamantly. "Too fragile. They'll arrive as a box of blackberry jam."

"Cherries!"

"Pits."

"Zucchini?"

"We'll think of something."

Paul scrambled in his desk drawer for a pen. "We'll use antique candlesticks as place cards …"

"Local wines in every room."

"We'll send out fifty invitations."

"We only have seven rooms."

"Celebrities stay overnight. Press are accommodated elsewhere."

"Brilliant."

"We'll have to provide cars. You know how the press corps drinks. Do you have a pen? I need to make notes."

Derrick took a pen from one of the cubbies in his in-box and passed it to Paul, disturbing the collection of mail in the process. One of the envelopes caught his eye and he used his embossed sterling letter opener to slit it open.

"We can get the invitations printed overnight," Paul said, scribbling madly, "but it'll cost the moon. Oh well, one does what one must." He gasped with sudden delight and exclaimed, "Heidi Klum! Our new top-of-the-list. Even if she doesn't come, although why she wouldn't I can't imagine because I've certainly written enough checks to her charities to float an armada, just having her on the list is bound to—"

He broke off at the expression on Derrick's face as he studied the sheet of paper in his hand. "What?" he demanded. "What are you reading?"

Derrick swallowed hard and passed the paper to Paul. "Whatever we're going to do, we'd better do it fast," he said. "We're due to appear in court next Wednesday."

On Ladybug Farm

"I don't know about you girls," Cici said unhappily, "but I feel responsible for this." She kicked off her shoes and sank into her rocking chair, a glass of white wine in hand.

A late afternoon rain storm had left the air sweet smelling and misty, and the green twilight that drifted in from the mountains brought on its breath the memory of cool autumn evenings to come. The heads of the pink and purple hydrangeas that surrounded the big oak tree in the front yard nodded drunkenly in the breeze, sate with the unexpected downpour. In the distance, the vineyard rows hugged the hillside like an extravagantly dressed lady greeting her lover, and closer to home a chickadee tapped on the bird feeder that hung from the eaves of the porch.

"After all," Lindsay agreed, taking a sip of her own wine, "we were the ones who told them to hire some help and open for business."

"Oh, for heaven's sake, girls," Bridget said tartly, "we didn't take them to raise. They're great big grown-up boys who make their own decisions." But at the look of astonishment from both women—after all, she was usually the first one to leap to the defense of the helpless and the incompetent—she frowned uncomfortably into her glass and admitted, "Although I'm not completely crazy about that Purline, if you want to know the truth. How old do you think she is? Eighteen?"

"Paul said she wasn't old enough to drink," Cici confided.

"Impossible. She has school-age children."

Cici shrugged. "They get married young around here."

Bridget pursed her lips in disapproval. "A teenager for a housekeeper. Surely they can do better."

Lindsay raised her glass to her lips to hide her smile. "You're just jealous because they aren't calling you up every day begging for a recipe or hinting about how much they'd love one of your cakes. Face it, Purline is almost as good a cook as you are."

"She's okay, I suppose," replied Bridget with studied negligence, "for a country cook. But the way she dresses ..." She suppressed a shudder.

"I don't think her short shorts and tank tops are going to endanger either Paul's or Derrick's morals," Lindsay pointed out with a quirk of her lips.

"That may be. But it's unprofessional."

"Which is so important in a maid," replied Lindsay with a modified eye roll.

"Purline is fine." Cici dismissed the debate with a wave of her hand. "But that woman ... what's her name? Chastity? Peace?"

"Harmony," supplied Lindsay.

Cici gave a small dismayed shake of her head. "Who names their baby Harmony?"

"Who names their baby Blanket?" Bridget said. "Or Apple?"

Lindsay said, "Michael Jackson and Gwyneth Paltrow."

Bridget looked surprised, and Lindsay explained, "I read the same tabloid article."

Bridget sipped her wine. "That's the whole problem, you know. America's obsession with celebrity."

"It's not just America," Cici said. "Look at the British and their Cinderella fantasy about the royal family."

"Well, in that case it's justified," said Lindsay. "I've been wild about Harry since he was in diapers."

Cici glanced at her. "The fact that you can remember when he was in diapers should tell you exactly what's wrong with that picture."

Lindsay refused to dignify that with a reply, but sipped her wine in a superior silence.

"Anyway," Bridget said, "you have to realize that it's not just modern culture that deifies celebrities … humans have elevated other humans since the beginning of time. Most of the Roman gods started out as regular men—Icarus trying to fly with a pair of homemade wings, Hercules the strong man—and what about the 'ton' of eighteenth-century Britain and the railroad barons of nineteenth-century America? They were the celebrities of their own eras."

Bridget could always be counted upon to contribute a scrap or two of arcane knowledge to any conversation, and Lindsay and Cici gave this one the consideration it was due. "I think," Cici said, "the whole purpose of celebrity is to give the rest of us something to think about besides ourselves."

"I think it's to give the common man—or woman—something to aspire to," Lindsay said.

Bridget said, "Good heavens, who would want to be a celebrity? I've got enough problems as it is."

They all murmured agreement to that, and rocked in silence for a time, idly watching the path made by a small bunny through the tall grass at the edge of the lawn. Without so much as a bark of warning, the border collie who had been sleeping under the porch streaked across the lawn after it, tail cartwheeling for balance, and within the next blink of an eye both bunny and collie disappeared into the woods.

"I just don't understand why they couldn't just hang an 'open' sign on the door and update their website," Cici said. "Why does it have to be such a big deal?"

"Well, you know Paul," said Bridget. "Everything with him has to be over the top."

"And Derrick is just like a crow when he sees something shiny," Lindsay said. "He can't resist picking it up."

Cici slid her a skeptical glance. "I assume you're referring to that Heavenly person."

"Who?"

"Harmony," Bridget supplied.

"Right," said Cici. "I lay full responsibility for this whole thing at her door. I mean, what is she, a paying guest, or a business consultant?"

"Spiritual consultant," corrected Bridget.

"Oh, please." Cici did not bother to disguise the roll of her eyes. "I have the distinct impression that this entire thing was her idea."

"It's going to end up costing them the earth," Bridget said.

Lindsay shrugged. "They can afford it." She frowned a little. "I just hope Paul doesn't get so caught up in this crazy scheme he doesn't have time to help with the wedding."

Cici glanced at her. "So when is the big day, now?"

Lindsay had changed the date so many times that Bridget and Cici had stopped marking it on their calendars. As Lindsay explained, her last wedding, almost twenty-five years ago, had been as unremarkable as the short-lived marriage it symbolized, and she wanted this one to be perfect. Getting married in mid-life was a huge deal, and she had every intention of taking her time with the details.

Lindsay tilted her head thoughtfully. "Well, it depends a lot on when this party is scheduled. But I've always loved the idea of a Christmas wedding. Red roses and white lace, twinkly lights everywhere ... we could put evergreen boughs on the floor and hang them from the ceiling so it would look like a bower. I saw that in a magazine."

"You try that and Ida Mae will kill you," Bridget warned. "I'll help her. We'd be sweeping up pine needles for the next two years."

Lindsay shrugged. "On the other hand, Dominic is pretty set on having it in the vineyard, and I suppose he's right. That's what brought us together, after all."

Then she grinned. "Wouldn't it be cool if Johnny Depp really did come?"

Cici lifted her eyebrows. "To your wedding?"

"No, silly, to the grand opening."

Cici sipped her wine. "I wouldn't get my hopes up."

"Derrick says they're inviting Nancy Reagan. Apparently Harmony is a friend of the family."

Cici's answer was a skeptical grunt.

Lindsay said thoughtfully, "Do you suppose they're homesick? It just seems to me they're trying a little too hard to bring the city to the country."

"And it's never going to work," Cici pointed out.

Bridget agreed, "It never works. If you're going to be someplace, you have to be one hundred percent there. You can't live in between."

Lindsay nodded her head thoughtfully. "Sometimes having too many options is not a good thing."

"On the other hand," said Cici, "if anybody in this world could pull off a celebrity party in the middle of nowhere, it would be Paul."

"And if anybody could convince celebrities and movie stars to actually come to the middle of nowhere," Bridget added, "it would be Derrick."

"You know," said Lindsay, sipping her wine, "it's entirely possible they just might be onto something here. The Hummingbird House B&B could actually put this little corner of the Shenandoah Valley on the map."

The women considered this for a time. Then Lindsay looked at Cici. Cici looked at Bridget. Bridget looked at both of them. As one, they shook their heads.

"Nah," said Cici.

"No way," agreed Lindsay.

"Not in a million years," added Bridget.

In their quiet corner of the valley, a tree frog began to trill, and dusk cast its purple shadows over the faces of the hydrangea blossoms. A light came on in the house behind them. They sat and finished their wine in the sweet evening air and listened to the peace, happy to be living in the middle of nowhere.

FIVE

Morality, like art, means drawing the line somewhere.

Oscar Wilde

The postmaster at the Blue Valley, Virginia, post office talked for weeks about the custom-designed, Express Mail, caligraphied packages he had sent out to exotic, prestigious addresses in zip codes like 90210, 10010, and 20007. And while postal ethics prevented him from revealing the exact names or addresses to which the packages were directed, he concluded every telling of the story with a low whistle and a shake of his head, observing that the new owners of that B&B over on the highway surely did have some high-class friends. Things were changing around this little town, he always liked to add, and that was a fact.

And so the invitations to the Hummingbird House Grand Opening, beautifully inscribed and accompanied by hand-woven baskets of home-grown Hummingbird House blueberries still dewy from the garden, sped across the country in a dozen different directions by jet, by truck and by postal carrier until they arrived at their destination, where they came to an abrupt and screeching halt. There they were X-rayed, opened, scrutinized, photographed, background checked, tasted, and approved by as many as four security guards, household managers, and assistants before being carefully rewrapped and hand-delivered to the social director or personal assistant of the person for whom the invitation was intended. That person would check the name of the sender against a list of known acquaintances, rank the invitation by priority, and deliver it accordingly. The blueberries, however, were enjoyed by all.

Lester Carson, travel editor for the *New York Times*, received his invitation the day after he arrived home from Beijing, although by then it had already been sitting on his desk for four days. Lester kept a strikingly neat home office in the loft area of his midtown apartment: all chrome and glass and white lacquer, books precisely arranged on shelves amidst carefully chosen souvenirs of his travels—a mask from Africa, a geode from Madagascar, a small carving of a fertility goddess from India—and everything was dusted, polished, and put back exactly where it belonged twice a week by his housekeeper. The wide glass desk held a computer monitor, a chrome box for mail, and a framed photograph. He sorted through and disposed of his mail on a daily basis; it made him uneasy to see the chrome box full.

And it filled him with sorrow to see the box empty, because he never found inside it what he was hoping for.

Mrs. Goddard, his secretary—who liked to be called an administrative assistant—had been with him since the days he had kept a haphazard, randomly cluttered office in the corner of an apartment that had been, more often than not, in a constant state of happy chaos. Novels had been placed on shelves between works of non-fiction, manila folders packed with notes and research material had been stashed between bound atlases, and crayon drawings and test papers had been proudly displayed on a corkboard behind his desk. But that was before the light had gone out of the world and everything had grown cold, ordered, and sharp-edged.

Mrs. Goddard had been trained to extract order from chaos, and she knew how to keep his in-box clean, so that even after half a month away it rarely took more than ten minutes to deal with what awaited him there. That was why he was so disappointed to find the invitation to yet another event he had no intention of attending, much less covering, lying atop other, far more important, papers. He tossed it aside.

"Oh, for God's sake, Mrs. Goddard, how did this get in here? I think you must be slipping."

Mrs. Goddard was not much older than he was and still an attractive woman, but they had agreed long ago on an atmosphere of formality at work—a construct that not only made the long hours together in often intimate surroundings much more comfortable for both of them, but which also gave her husband of twenty-five years a certain amount of reassurance as well. She turned from unpacking his briefcase to notice the heavy vellum paper he had discarded.

"Actually, sir, I marked it for your attention. It's from Paul Slater."

He frowned a little. "Who?" Then his brow cleared, though he still didn't look happy. "Oh. Right." There had been a Christmas party some years back that he'd felt obligated to give even though it was the last thing he wanted to do. He'd gotten drunk, the whole thing had been on the verge of being headlined on Page Six the next morning, and Paul had stepped in to diffuse things. That had been decent of him; Lester hoped he had sent him a bottle of wine as a thank you but he really couldn't remember. He didn't like to think about those days.

"He's opening up a B&B in Virginia," Mrs. Goddard went on, "did you know that? It actually sounds quite delightful. I thought you might enjoy the getaway."

"Virginia? Good God, I can't think of anything more tiresome." He picked up a contract from a publisher for whom he had agreed to write a book at some time in the undetermined future and began to glance through it.

"It's shaping up to be quite the gala," went on his secretary, transferring some papers from his briefcase into their proper file in the lacquered credenza. "He's called a couple of times. A good many people you know will be there. Also, the invitation was accompanied by the most extraordinary basket of blueberries. I hope you don't mind, but they were about to spoil so I took them home."

"Hmm." He did not look up. "Hate blueberries." He snapped closed the pages of the contract and tossed it on his desk. "Call my agent. Tell him we agreed on a thirty-five percent bonus for the first week on the *Times* list and six percent increments for every week thereafter and that's non-negotiable. Regrets to Slater."

Mrs. Goddard made a few quick notes on her iPad and picked up the contract, but hesitated with his last sentence. Her look was so pointed that he was forced to ask, "What?"

"The invitation was personalized and handwritten," she said. "At the very least, it requires a response from your personal e-mail account."

"Oh, for Christ's sake," he muttered, swallowing a groan. "All right, all right. I'll get around to it."

"The deadline for RSVP is in two weeks," she said, but he was no longer listening.

His attention was fixed upon the photograph in the silver frame, and as it always did at such times a weight seemed to fall upon his shoulders that aged him twenty years. His eyes appeared sunken, his face haggard. One could almost imagine that, if the shell of the man could be peeled away in search of the soul, there would be nothing there. Nothing at all.

He said in a low tone, without looking up, "I don't suppose..."

Her silence was his answer. She had long ago lost the will to say the words.

In a moment he straightened his shoulders and gave himself a small, almost imperceptible shake, as though tossing off the weight of an uncomfortable cloak. He said simply, Well, then."

"I'm praying for you, you know," she said softly.

He turned back to his inbox and took up another handful of papers. His tone was brusque. "You are wasting your time, Mrs. Goddard. I have it on very good authority that there is no God."

She just smiled, and turned toward the door. Then she turned back. "Oh, and a Mr. Halligan called this morning before you were up. He said it wasn't urgent, but you should call him back when you had a chance. Shall I get him for you?"

A faint, almost undetectable transformation came over Lester's face, although his tone remained calm. "Thank you, Mrs. Goddard, but I have it. That will be all for now."

He waited until she had descended the stairs to her own office in the back of the apartment before he took out his cell phone and punched the numbers. His voice was low and fierce when the man on the other end of the call answered.

"You have my cell," he said shortly, "why did you call my home number?"

"Cell wasn't working," said the other man. "I guess you were out of range."

Lester's heart was pounding; it always was when he talked to this man. "I told you I want to know the minute you find something. What do you have?"

"I'm sorry, Mr. Carson," said the private detective. "It's not good news."

Lester Carson sank to a chair, pushed up his glasses and pressed his fingers to his eyes, trying not to cry as he heard the report.

There was an abandoned gas station on the outskirts of Winter Lake, Idaho, where the indigent, the homeless and the just plain down-on-their-luck gathered every morning before dawn hoping for day labor. Every town had a place like that. The trucks would come by, pick out the healthiest and biggest looking, and drive off, leaving those left behind to hope for better days. Josh, who wasn't the healthiest or biggest by any means but who happened to be one of the few men who looked sober on that particular Monday morning, picked up two days' worth of work unloading landscaping timbers into some rich person's yard, and earned a hundred fifty dollars. He spent six dollars on a box of protein bars, two of which he consumed on the spot, and three dollars on a roll of duck tape. Another thirty went to a cell phone with twenty-five minutes worth of free airtime. After he cleaned up a little in the Wal-Mart bathroom, the girl at the electronics counter even activated it for him.

He found a plastic patio chair outside in the garden department, behind a hedge of wilted tropical plants, and took out the phone. There he hesitated, staring at the keypad. There were two numbers he knew by heart. If he dialed one of them, the person on the other end would deny him nothing. Money, airline tickets, a car. All he had to do was ask. Dial the number.

Ask.

He set his jaw, and dialed the other number.

It rang. Once, twice, three times … "Come on, Leda," he muttered, hand tightening on the phone. "Come on …"

Four times, and then, "We're sorry, the number you have dialed is no longer in service …"

He removed the phone from his face and stared at it in disbelief. He punched "end call" and tried again, his fingers a little unsteady this time. It rang only twice before the message came again. "We're sorry, the number you have dialed is no longer in service. Please check the number and try again."

"Damn it!" he whispered, because his throat was too dry to make a louder sound. He disconnected the call and tightened his fist around the phone, thinking for a moment about tossing it across the parking lot. Instead, after a long and helpless moment, he put the phone in his pocket. His fingers brushed the photograph there, and he couldn't help himself: he had to take it out, and look at it one more time. It was all sweaty and wrinkled and starting to fade, but it was like a drug to him. Better than a drug, because one hit could keep him going all day and there wasn't any crash afterward. He looked at it, and his heart smiled.

Carefully, he put the photograph away. The guy with the landscaping timbers had told him he'd have more work for him in a day or two. God knew there were worse places to sleep at night than a Wal-Mart parking lot, and he'd learned that if he was lucky and smart he could sometimes cop a night inside in the AC, as long as he avoided the security cameras. But staying here was wasting time. Staying here was too far away from where he needed to be. He had four protein bars and a hundred dollars, and six hundred miles left to go.

He took the roll of duct tape from the plastic bag and wound it around his shoe to keep the sole from flapping. He'd found a thrift store that had let him have a clean pair of jeans and a tee shirt for a dollar, but they hadn't had any shoes in his size. Maybe he'd have better luck at the next town. He'd picked up a cotton backpack for fifty cents at the same thrift store, and he dropped the duct tape into it with his other clothes and the remaining protein bars. The next town was twenty miles down the highway, and when he left the Wal-Mart parking lot, he turned in that direction. By nightfall he'd be twenty miles closer to St. Louis, and her.

Annabelle owned a 1994 Lincoln Continental that she paid the teenage boy who mowed her lawn five dollars a week to drive around the block so that it wouldn't "rust up." Though the behemoth hailed from an era whose time would never come again and had no place in an age where stopping at the gas pump could max out your credit card, Megan had to admit it was the most comfortable vehicle she had ever driven. The trunk accommodated her grandmother's three hard-sided suitcases and Megan's overnight bag with enough room left over for a billiard table, and when Megan saw the backseat she joked that it was roomier than some motel rooms she had stayed in. Annabelle could stretch out her legs in the plush front seat and even nap if she wanted to, which she did for a couple of hours along the way.

During one of these naps, Megan called her mother. To have done otherwise would have been negligent to say the least, criminal to say the most. Her mother screeched about kidnapping and irresponsibility and threatened to send the state patrol after Megan if she did not turn that car around this very minute. Megan just held the phone away from her ear and promised to call her mother when they stopped for the night.

"Leave it to you to do something like this!" Her mother returned, near hysteria now. Her mother could approach hysteria at the drop of a hat. "You always were just like her, but this is the craziest thing you've ever done! You two deserve each other, do you hear me? You deserve each other!"

"Yes, Mother, I know," Megan replied, watching the road.

"The woman has a rod in her hip! How are you expecting her to sit in a car all day?"

"The car is very comfortable," replied Megan. "In fact, it's more comfortable than the couch in my family room." She and Nick had always disagreed about that couch. He liked its big, deep seats. She thought it looked like a pickup truck and sat like one too.

"Oh, no. Tell me you didn't take that car of hers. It hasn't been driven in years! What if you break down on the highway? In this heat? Are you insane?"

"I have AAA."

"She just got out of the hospital! Do you have any idea how many medications she's on? You made sure she *brought* her medications, didn't you?"

Megan shot a quick glance at her sleeping grandmother. She hadn't thought of that. She hadn't thought of any of it. Her hand tightened on the phone. "Mother, I've got this," she said firmly.

"Don't take that tone with me! Let me talk to her. Let me talk to her right now."

Megan said, "I'm losing the signal, Mom. I'll call you later. I love you."

She disconnected and turned off the phone, and when she glanced again at her grandmother, she saw Annabelle had one eye open, watching her. She winked at Megan, turned her head more comfortably on the plush seat back, and went to sleep again.

But still, she worried that her mother might be right. Maybe this *was* the craziest thing she'd ever done. And she didn't mean that in a good way.

Annabelle was awake by the time they crossed the border into Arkansas and wanted to stop and have their picture taken at the welcome sign. Megan would have preferred to stop at the welcome center itself, which was safer, cooler, easier to park and only a mile or so ahead, but she knew better than to argue with her grandmother. This was a tradition. So she pulled the big boat off the road, turned on the hazard flashers, and positioned her grandmother in front of the sign with as much efficiency as possible. Of course Annabelle wanted Megan in the photo too, so with one arm around her grandmother's shoulders and the other one stretched as far as it would go in front of them, she snapped the photo with her cell phone. The resulting picture showed two women squinting against the sun and the gasoline fumes, their hair blown wildly by passing traffic, with the welcome sign completely obscured.

Megan wondered for the first time who had taken that photograph ninety years ago, and why he or she had not arranged his subjects so that the lettering on the sign was visible.

Ten minutes later they pulled into the spacious, air-conditioned Arkansas Welcome Center. While waiting for her grandmother to return from the restroom—it always took her forever—Megan took out her phone and Googled the nearest motel with a sit-down restaurant. She found a Best Western forty miles away, which was perfect. It had a pool, too. They would have a nice meal, a good old-fashioned sleepover, and in the morning head for home, their adventure complete.

Their last adventure.

Megan felt her throat tighten, and she squeezed her eyes tightly shut for a moment, blotting out the bustle and echoes of the busy rest stop, and almost, but not quite, managing to blot out the memory she had of this woman she had so loved all her life lying so still and frail on the hospital bed. When she opened her eyes again her grandmother was coming toward her, moving purposefully with the aid of her silver-tipped cane, a collection of colorful brochures in her hand. Megan was seized by a sudden intense urge to gather the woman up, usher her to the car, and drive her straight home.

Her mother was right. This was crazy.

"We mustn't miss the Little Rock Science Museum," Annabelle said as she reached her. "It says here they have a meteorite that's over thirty-six million years old. Frankly, I wonder how they can be certain how old it is—after all, it came from outer space, what possible frame of reference can they use?—but I've never seen a meteorite up close and I think it would be worth a stop." She glanced at the phone in Megan's hand. "Are you making reservations? Be sure to pick some place with a sit-down restaurant. "

Megan drew a breath to say something about having no intention of going to Little Rock, about turning around and driving straight home now that they'd had their little jaunt, but instead she heard herself saying, "I haven't ever seen a meteorite either."

"Well, don't let yourself get to be ninety-seven before you do." Annabelle tapped her lightly on the arm with the brochures. "Do you know what I saw over there by the brochure stand? One of those fancy cappuccino machines. Why don't you get us a couple? I'll go find a table out of the sun."

When Megan came out of the building with two of the vending-machine cappuccinos, her grandmother was sitting at one of the concrete picnic tables overlooking the grassy dog walk area, several brochures open on the table before her. She wore a pair of reading glasses to study it, but replaced them with her oversized Marilyn Monroe sunglasses when Megan slid onto the pebbly concrete bench across from her.

"Thank you, sweetheart. I remember when you were lucky to find a water fountain at one of these places, and a big treat might be a Coca-Cola chest." She removed the lid from her drink, careful not to disturb the skim of froth that floated on top. "I'll tell you the truth, everyone says Coke lost its flavor when they changed the formula, but that wasn't it. It was the glass bottles. That and the big red ice chests they used to sell them in."

Megan said, "Gram …"

Her grandmother said, "Your mother is a bully. I don't think she means to be but she is. It's probably my fault." She sipped the hot coffee. "I'm a bit of a bully myself."

Megan had to smile at that. "You probably don't mean to be."

"I most certainly do." Her tone was indignant, but her expression was hard to read behind the sunglasses. "How else can I get my way? I hope if I've taught you nothing else, it's that you have to fight for what you want."

Megan sipped her coffee and said nothing.

"She means well, I suppose," Annabelle went on, "but I worry about who she's going to have to push around when I'm gone. Don't let it be you."

Megan looked at her grandmother. "She's worried about you. And she has a right to be."

"She most certainly does not," replied Annabelle with an adamancy that surprised Megan. "I'm ninety-seven years old and if I drop dead before I finish this sentence, I've already lived longer and better than the good Lord ever promised. When she's a hundred years old, she can do whatever she damn well pleases, but until then she needs to worry about the things she can do something about and stay out of her elders' business." Annabelle hesitated for a moment, and added, "God bless her meddling soul."

Megan smothered a laugh. She sipped her coffee and looked at Annabelle tenderly. "You know you're my favorite grandmother, don't you?"

Annabelle inclined her head. "Naturally."

Megan said, "And you also know a woman who just got out of the hospital two days ago should be at home in bed watching game shows and sipping tea, not cruising all over eastern Texas and western Arkansas in this heat."

Annabelle returned her attention to one of the brochures. "Did you know that this part of the country was mostly settled by Confederate soldiers who refused to take the loyalty oath when the North won the Civil War? They were branded outlaws and forced to flee west."

"That explains a lot," murmured Megan.

"My mother was a huge aficionado of the Civil War. She was always taking me to tour the important sites ... Manassas, Bull Run, Gettysburg. She thought it was romantic. I suppose it is, in a way. Just imagine. Perfectly respectable young men, land owners, classically educated, accustomed to all the finer things in life, suddenly turned into outlaws by their own government. Running for their lives with nothing but a gun and a horse. My goodness, it certainly makes you think, doesn't it?"

"Gram," said Megan patiently, "we were talking about you."

"We still are." She looked up and smiled. "The outlaw."

Megan said, "And you're expecting me to be your partner in crime."

Annabelle reached across the table and took her hand. "You always were."

And that was when Megan realized that was not entirely true. They had always started out as partners, with Megan's enthusiasm for the adventure as high as her grandmother's. But when the moment actually came, Megan's courage inevitably failed. She had been terrified of snakes and malaria in Africa, and had changed their reservations three times. She froze on the zip line platform and Annabelle had been forced to push her off. It was supposed to be the two of them who'd gone skydiving, but Megan had backed out at the last minute. She always intended to follow through, she always *wanted* to follow through, and when she started out, all filled with excitement and revved up by her grandmother's enthusiasm, she was the kind of person who *could* follow through. But in the end another part of her always took over.

The part that had become an accountant instead of a pastry chef.

Megan said quietly, "Why do you keep taking me on these adventures?"

And even though she couldn't see her eyes behind the dark glasses, her grandmother was thoughtful long enough that Megan knew she understood why she asked.

"Because," Annabelle replied, "one of these days you're going to *know* why. And when you do, you won't have to ask anymore."

Riddles. As a child Megan had loved them. As an adult, not so much.

She said, a little gruffly, "Don't you die on me."

"I shall try very hard not to."

"I'm serious."

"So am I." Annabelle began folding the brochures. "Now let's get on the road, shall we? We can finish our coffees in the car."

Megan reached to gather up some of the brochures and then paused, looking at her grandmother curiously. "The battle of Bull Run," she said. "That was in Virginia, wasn't it?"

"Of course. Everything worth mentioning happened in Virginia. Just ask any Virginian."

"What I mean is—isn't it a park? A national park?"

Her grandmother tilted her head thoughtfully. "No dear, I believe you're thinking of Manassas National Battlefield Park. Lovely place. Monuments, restored building, beautiful parkland."

"Right, that's it," Megan said. "Do you think—you said your mother liked to tour Civil War sites. Is it possible that the sign the picture was taken in front of was for *that*? Manassas?"

"No," her grandmother replied slowly, "there are no mountains in Manassas. But it was very likely taken on the way to one of those battlegrounds. "

"So all we have to do is to find a likely route between the town you lived in as a child and the most popular Civil War sites."

Her grandmother lifted her dark glasses to look at Megan and there was a delighted sparkle in her faded blue eyes. "And the best way to do that," she said, "is to go back where it all started." She grinned and flung a wiry arm around her granddaughter's shoulder. "Set a course for Virginia, my girl. We're going home."

Which was where, of course, her grandmother had intended to go all along.

Josh had learned early on that nobody but weirdoes offered a ride to a young man walking beside a highway, so he didn't even try hitchhiking. He'd been able to afford a ticket on a bus that was going in the right direction once or twice, but most of the time the most reliable form of transportation was his own two feet. Those feet were getting pretty beaten up, especially since the shoes had started to go, and sometimes the blisters bled through two pairs of socks. He was starting to limp a little. But for the most part he didn't mind walking. It made him feel as though he was doing something.

All his life he'd had a plan. He'd planned to get into Harvard, master computer science, spend ten or fifteen years perfecting artificial intelligence, retire on the income from his companies by the time he was thirty. Travel the world. Get married. Have a couple of kids who looked just like their mother and who would run to him squealing "Daddy! Daddy!" whenever they saw him. They would spend summer vacations at the beach and winter vacations at a snow-covered ski lodge. He would teach them everything he knew. They would adore him. He would never, ever leave them or let them down.

Sometimes plans didn't work out. But that didn't mean he could stop making them. He'd spent the past fourteen months on a new plan: Get to Leda, get his girl out of there, get a job, any job, get an apartment, rebuild his life. It didn't matter where, or how. What mattered was that they would be together, they would be safe, and from there he could make another plan.

But how was he supposed to get to Leda if he didn't know where she was? What if she wasn't in Kansas City anymore? What if …

His mother used to say that "what if" was like a horse without a bridle; it could run forever if you gave it its head. Josh bit down on it, focused on his feet plowing through the dust and stubble at the side of the road, and when he looked up, what he saw made him stumble to a stop. He had to blink several times just to make sure he wasn't imagining it. A couple of cars whizzed by, blowing his hair back from his scalp in their hot exhaust. He squeezed his eyes shut, and looked again. It was still there. A battered tan and white Winnebago was pulled off onto the shoulder a couple of hundred feet ahead, and a gnome-like little man in plaid shorts was bending under the open hood.

Josh started walking toward him. There really wasn't much choice.

Artie looked up with a big smile when Josh was close enough to cast a shadow, just as though he had been expecting him. "She just died on me," Artie explained, wiping the wrench in his hand on a greasy blue towel. "Just puttered to a stop like a tired old cow. When I tried to get her started again, there was barely a click. I've got plenty of gas," he added helpfully, offering Josh the wrench.

Josh ignored the tool, which was of the wrong size and type for a job like this, and dragged his gaze from the sweaty, beaming face of the man he'd had no expectation of ever seeing again to the disabled vehicle in front of him. With a growing sense of helpless inevitability, he moved forward and bent to look under the hood.

He had never seen an engine this old, but there had never been a mechanical device that was foreign to him. He quickly traced down the hose that had been jarred loose by the last pothole Artie had hit, reconnected it and tightened the clamp, then checked the battery. He glanced at Artie. "You got any soda?"

"Sure thing." Artie beamed at him. "Coke, Pepsi, Mountain Dew ... What's your preference?"

Josh said, "Coke." And he turned quickly back to the road-weary mechanisms under the hood because looking at Artie standing here on the side of an Idaho road several hundred miles away from where he had left him made Josh feel as though he had somehow tumbled through the Looking Glass. And maybe he had.

In another moment Artie returned with two cold cans of Coke. He handed one to Josh and popped the other one open for himself. "Hot work," he said, sipping from the can.

Josh opened his can and poured the contents over the battery connectors, watching the coffee-colored liquid eat away at the corrosive buildup there. Artie regarded him in amazement. "Well, will you look at that?"

Josh said, "Try to start it."

Artie hurried into the cab and turned the key. After a couple of minutes of grinding, the engine caught and chugged and settled into a more-or-less normal rhythm. Artie left the engine running and stepped down from the cab, grinning. "Purring like a kitten," he exclaimed, raising his voice to be heard over the sound of the sputtering and clanking motor. "Where did you learn that?"

Josh closed the hood and wiped his oily hands on the towel Artie offered him. He met the other man's eyes evenly. "Prison," he replied.

Artie showed absolutely no surprise. "Is that a fact? Well, lucky for me you did. Come on in, get out of the heat. Have yourself something to drink, now that you gave up your Coke to this thirsty beast." He slapped the side of the van and chuckled at his own joke, squinting in the sun.

Josh said, "I was going to steal your money. All of it."

Artie stopped chuckling.

"I found your bank bag the night you picked me up. I was going to take off with it as soon as you stopped."

Artie looked at him for a moment, nodding thoughtfully, his sun-squinted eyes unreadable. Then he said, "We'd better get on the road before this baby dies again." He slapped the fender affectionately and turned toward the driver's door. He stopped and looked back before climbing inside, though, his expression curious. "Are you coming?"

Josh was too astonished to move. "Wait. Are you kidding me? You're offering me a ride?"

"Kansas City, wasn't it?" He smiled his funny little smile and winked. "On my way. And considering the shape this bucket of bolts is in, it sure wouldn't hurt to have a good mechanic onboard."

Josh didn't hesitate another minute. He scrambled around to the passenger door and pulled himself inside.

"You know something?" Artie said, grinning. "You could have saved yourself a lot of trouble—not to mention shoe leather, from the looks of it—if you hadn't been so quick to leave me behind back there at the campground. Kansas City was on my way back then too, but you seemed in such an all-fired hurry to get going there didn't seem much point in mentioning it."

Josh said, "I didn't really learn that trick with the Coke in prison," he said. "I learned it from some muscle movie I saw on TV." He made sure Artie was looking at him for the next part. "But I was in jail," he said. "Fourteen months. Possession."

Artie waited for another moment, but Josh didn't know what else to say. He had no idea what was going on in the other man's mind, if anything. He was ready for Artie to tell him to get out, and in fact his hand had started to reach for the door handle when Artie put the wagon into gear and turned his attention to the road. The man was as much of an enigma as ever.

Josh sank back into the battered seat and fastened his seat belt. His feet, now that he had taken the weight off of them, throbbed. Then he looked at Artie and thought of something else to say. "I'm sorry," he said. "You know, about the money."

"I know you are, son." Artie checked the oncoming traffic in the side mirror before coaxing the behemoth off the shoulder and back onto the road again. "All's well that ends well, my mother used to say."

Josh almost smiled. "My mother used to say that too."

"She must have been a good woman, your mom."

Josh looked at him sharply. "How would you know? You don't know anything about her."

"I know she raised a pretty good boy," Artie replied mildly.

So many angry, defensive, and confusing retorts bubbled to Josh's lips that he almost choked on them. Thankfully, he was unable to utter any of them, and it was a long time before he could say anything at all. In the end, all he could manage was, "You don't know anything about me either."

"I know enough."

Josh gave a derisive grunt. "Yeah, most people figure knowing a guy's an ex-con is enough."

"Actually, that's interesting, but it's not what I meant. I learn most of what I need to know about a person from what they don't tell me."

Josh looked at him cautiously.

"For example," Artie went on easily, "I know you're the kind of fellow who always tries to do the right thing. You didn't have to tell me that. I just know."

"Yeah, well," Josh muttered, and turned his gaze back to stare out the windshield. "Not everybody always agrees on what the right thing is."

"Doesn't matter. All that matters is that you know what it is."

Josh said in a low, almost inaudible voice, "That sounds like something my mother would say."

"Doesn't surprise me a bit."

Artie was quiet after that, letting the miles roll by in an off-key symphony of bumps and squeaks and whines as the Winnebago clattered down the highway, and it was a long time before Josh felt like talking again. When he did speak, it was merely a gruff, "What are you doing on the road in the middle of the day, anyway? I thought you only liked to drive at night."

"Oh, I gave that up. Turns out you miss too many little miracles, driving at night. Why, I might even have missed you."

Miracle. Josh had never thought of himself as a miracle before, or anything close. But what else would you call something like this? Miracle might not be entirely accurate, but it was close enough. He said, because the moment seemed to call for it, "Well, I don't know much about miracles, but I appreciate the ride."

"Oh, I've stumbled on all kinds of miracles since I started looking for them. Found a perfectly good socket wrench on the side of the road. Got off the highway to get something to eat, and you'll never guess where I ended up. A place called Art's Crossing. Art, just like my name! Best hamburger I ever ate, too. Yesterday, I happened upon an ice cream factory where they were having an open house. Guided tours and free samples at the end. Now, that's what I call a miracle. Met a bunch of nice people, and just about ate my fill of chocolate chip, and everybody I saw was smiling. Of course, you don't meet too many people who aren't smiling when they're eating ice cream, you ever notice that? The point is, I never would have found any of those things driving at night." He glanced at Josh. "You like chocolate chip, Josh?"

"Yeah," Josh said. "Yeah, I like it fine."

"Well, what do you know about that? Just so happens I stashed a box of chocolate chip ice cream bars from the tour in that freezer back there. Why don't you help yourself?"

Help yourself. Josh stared at him. "Dude," he said, "you've really got to stop saying that." And Artie laughed.

Josh found the box of ice cream bars in the tiny freezer compartment on top of a pound of hamburger meat and a box of frozen corn. He took out a bar, his mouth watering, and, on second thought, helped himself to another. When he edged back into the passenger seat, he unwrapped one of the bars and passed it across the console to Artie. Artie smiled his thanks, and Josh unwrapped his own bar. "My mother loved to dance," he said, without looking at him. "Sometimes she would put on a Sinatra CD and just dance around the house. Sometimes I would dance with her. I was just a little kid, but she made me feel ten feet tall."

Artie smiled. "That's a nice memory."

Josh nodded slowly. "Yeah. I've got a few of them."

"I like talking about good memories. It's almost like living them again."

"Yeah, I guess." He sank back in the seat, and took a bite of his ice cream. Before he knew it, he was telling Artie about the ice cream stand in Central Park he remembered as a kid, and how his folks always pretended they were going to say no when he begged to stop, but in the end he always got the cone. And after a time, he discovered Artie was right about something else: it was hard not to smile when you were eating ice cream.

SIX

No great artist ever sees things as they really are. If he did, he would cease to be an artist.

Oscar Wilde

The county courthouse was one of those quaint small-town structures Paul and Derrick had admired about Blue Valley, Virginia, when they first moved there. It was built of peach colored orchard stone, nestled against a background of rolling blue mountains, and boasted a big oak tree in front that shaded stone benches and flower-lined paths. The only thing missing was the perennial couple of old men in straw hats playing checkers. It even had a clock tower with a clock that chimed the hour every forty-five minutes, and had been doing so for so long that no one in town even cared what time it was anymore. It was, in short, the epitome of the kind of good old-fashioned Americana that Hollywood in the 1940s had made everyone believe in. And it was, on this day, a symbol of doom for the small mountain community's two newest residents.

Paul wore Armani, Derrick wore Gucci, and they both wore Hermes ties. Derrick had opted for a subtle tone-on-tone stripe that complemented the pale blue of his shirt, but Paul wore a flashy pink silk tied in an elaborate trinity knot against his deep lavender shirt, declaring as he left the house that if he was to be hauled off to the penitentiary at the end of the day, he would at least do so in style.

They were directed to Courtroom C, a small chamber adjacent to the main courtroom with wood veneer paneling, folding metal chairs, and no windows. The surroundings were hardly an appropriate setting for the gravity of the situation they faced, and a single shared glance confirmed their disappointment. There were only a dozen or so people present, all of them milling about and chatting amiably, and three of them looked familiar.

Bridget smiled and waved at them as she made her way over. She was wearing her pink suit as Paul had requested because, he said, he wanted to look out over the audience as his fate was sealed and see nothing but the kind of beauty that would sustain him during the long dark months ahead. She kissed first Paul, and then Derrick. "My, don't you both look nice!"

Paul pressed her fingers to his lips somberly. "It was good of you to come."

Lindsay, less formal in a white denim jacket over a green print sundress, squeezed Paul's arm. "You know we wouldn't let you go through this alone."

Paul was momentarily drawn out of his gloom as he glanced at Lindsay's sandaled feet. "Pumps, darling! That outfit practically *weeps* for pumps!"

"He's been like this all day," Derrick confided, bending to kiss Lindsay's cheek. "He always resorts to fashion when he's upset, while I ..." he patted his stomach regretfully, "resort to food. I had six muffins this morning. They were small," he added quickly as he saw the reprimand start to form in Bridget's eyes.

"Courage, Camille." Cici came up behind them and placed a hand on each man's shoulder. "Things are usually pretty straightforward in a small town like this, and it will all be over before you know it. Why, if we were back in the city you'd still be waiting for your court date this time next year. Isn't that Harrington up front?"

Paul looked as though he wanted to make some comment on her outfit—khaki pants and a sleeveless white blouse which, if she had not had such ridiculously toned arms would have been a travesty on a woman her age, and not even a scarf or a necklace for flare—but Derrick pulled him away.

Harrington Windale, of Windale, Levinson, Parker and Smythe, sat on one of the folding chairs at the front of the room, using his briefcase as a lap desk while he tapped out something on his iPad. He glanced up when Paul and Derrick reached him.

"Oh, good, you're here," he said. He finished whatever he was typing and closed the screen. "This shouldn't take very long."

Derrick shook his hand fervently. "Thank you so much for coming. Will there be much testimony, do you think? Will you want us to take the stand?"

"I've prepared a statement," Paul assured him, reaching into his coat pocket. "Perhaps you'd like to take a look at it before the case is called."

Harrington looked mildly perplexed. "Really, gentlemen, it's not that complex."

Derrick looked anxiously at the two oak tables at the front of the room. They looked a lot like school room surplus. "Which one is the defense table? Shouldn't we take our places?"

Harrington said, "It's actually just a matter of having the paperwork approved. Didn't my assistant explain that to you?"

"We didn't hear anything after the words 'court appearance,'" Derrick admitted unhappily.

"But I stand ready to take over our defense," Paul assured him, "if you find yourself unprepared. And we have three excellent character witnesses ..." He turned and waved broadly to Cici, Lindsay, and Bridget, who hesitated, then started forward. "Pillars of the community, solid as stone. I can get more if you like. There's Purline, and Harmony ..."

"Maybe not Harmony," Derrick put in apologetically.

"Maybe not," admitted Paul. "But the postman and the UPS driver are practically fixtures around Hummingbird House, and I'm sure they would stand up for us, not to mention ..."

Derrick interrupted gently, "You're babbling."

Paul looked for a moment as though he might take offense, and then sighed, rubbing his hands together anxiously. "I know."

"But if ever a man had a right to babble," Derrick assured him quickly.

"Why don't you both just have a seat," suggested Harrington, "and I'll let you know if I need you."

Paul said, "Well, if you're certain ..." And he started to sit beside the attorney.

"Back there," said Harrington, "in the audience."

Paul started to object, but Derrick touched his arm meaningfully. "We're paying him a fortune," Derrick whispered as he guided Paul away. "Let him do his job."

They met the three ladies in the aisle and had just filled in the short row of metal chairs when a uniformed bailiff came into the room from a side door and announced, "Court is in session."

He was followed by a bald man in a judge's robe, and Paul and Derrick shot to their feet. Since they were the only ones who did so, however, they quickly sat down again.

The judge took a seat behind the largest oak table and gestured to Harrington. Harrington gathered his briefcase and went forward.

"That could be good," Cici whispered to Paul.

"It could be bad," he replied worriedly.

"They look friendly," Bridget whispered.

"Harrington is very well known in legal circles," Derrick replied confidently.

"They certainly are finding a lot to talk about," Lindsay observed.

"That could be good," Paul said, watching.

"It could be bad," Derrick said.

"I should go see if I can help." Paul started to rise, but Cici caught his arm from one side and Derrick from the other, pulling him back into his seat.

Paul pulled his arms away in mild indignation, brushing the creases from his coat. He looked as though he might overrule them both, but at that point Harrington gathered up his papers and his briefcase, said something pleasant to the judge, and came toward them, smiling.

"Well then, as I promised, all taken care of," he told them. "And I've still got plenty of time to get in a golf game. There's a course about an hour from here I've been dying to play."

Cici grinned broadly and punched Paul playfully on the arm. "See, I told you!"

Lindsay exclaimed, "Congratulations!" and Bridget beamed, adding, "But who could be mean to two guys as nice as you?"

Paul stared at Harrington in disbelief, and Derrick looked as though he might drop to the floor and kiss his feet at any moment. "Do you mean," Paul managed on an exhaled breath, "we're not going to jail?"

"Of course not." Harrington clapped him on the shoulder as they left the courtroom.

"And the fine?" Derrick added cautiously.

"No fine. I told you it was just a matter of paperwork. Your license will be issued as soon as you complete twenty hours of community service.

All you have to do is take these forms down to the county clerk's office ..."

But Derrick was already gushing his gratitude, pumping Harrington's hand enthusiastically, and Paul blotted his brow with a folded pink pocket square, bracing one hand against the wall for support. It was Cici who, with a shrug, took the papers the attorney extended and glanced at them.

"Twenty hours," she said. "Is that each, or together?"

"A piece," Harrington replied, managing to extract his hand from Derrick's effusive grip. "Being listed as individual owners, the charges were naturally filed individually."

Derrick looked at Cici. "Twenty hours?"

And Paul straightened slowly, reaching for the papers. "Of what?"

"Community service," Cici replied, with only a slight note of exasperation. "Weren't you listening?"

"It's all fairly self-explanatory," Harrington said. "You just have to have your supervisor sign off on the number of hours you complete, and then follow the instructions for filing the papers. Your liquor license will be issued within two to three weeks after that, but the shut-down order will be lifted within twenty-four hours, so you can open your business again."

"Oh, look," said Lindsay, taking the papers from Cici. "They even give you a list of acceptable places to serve your time."

Paul snatched the papers from her, studying them in growing dismay, and Derrick exclaimed, "Community service! We don't have time for community service! We have a grand opening to plan."

"It won't be much of a grand opening unless you're actually, well, open," Lindsay pointed out.

Derrick explained anxiously, "It's not that we wouldn't *like* to serve the community. We've always been very community-minded people. But the timing couldn't be more inconvenient."

Harrington lifted an eyebrow. "I suggest you find a moment to make it convenient, gentlemen. Because if you don't do so in the next seven days ..." he turned over a page from the stack in Paul's hand and tapped a paragraph, "you're going to jail."

He smiled, nodded to Cici, Lindsay, and Bridget, and said, "Good to see you again, ladies. Now, if you'll excuse me ..." he glanced at his watch, "I have a golf game." He added to Derrick and Paul, "Call my office if you have any questions." And he headed toward the exit at a brisk pace, followed by the stunned blank gazes of his two clients.

"Can we stop payment on his check?" Paul wanted to know as soon as the door closed behind him.

"Oh, come on, guys, it's not that bad," Lindsay said.

"Twenty hours is one week of a part-time job at Starbucks," Cici added.

Paul straightened his cuffs. "Since I passed over my opportunity to be a barista in the seventies," he replied grumpily, "I'm afraid I wouldn't know."

"Maybe you'll get a second chance," Derrick said. "There has to be a community organization in town that serves coffee."

"Oh, look, there are all kinds of interesting things you can do." Bridget took a paper from Paul's stack and read out loud. "Highway Department ..."

Derrick looked horrified. "Stand out in the middle of the road all day holding up a *Slow* sign for construction crews? I don't think so. With my complexion I'd be nothing but a walking sunburn in two hours."

Cici pointed out, "Usually it's beautification."

Derrick looked hopeful until Lindsay clarified, "Picking up trash." And then both Paul and Derrick shuddered.

"Animal shelter," Bridget went on.

"Maybe they're looking for a dog groomer," Paul muttered.

"Recycling Center ..."

They both threw up their hands in protest and Paul said, "I seriously wouldn't have a thing to wear!"

"Senior Center, Parks Department ..."

"That might be fun," Derrick said.

"Picking up trash," Cici said, and his face fell.

Paul said, "Nothing in the fashion industry, I presume."

"Meals with Love, library." Bridget returned the paper to Paul. "That's it."

Paul looked at Derrick. Derrick looked at Paul. "Library," they agreed.

"We'll start first thing in the morning," Derrick said, looking relieved. "Twenty hours of shelving books, how hard can it be?"

"I worked in the school library in high school," Paul added, looking slightly less depressed than he had been a moment ago. "I practically memorized the Dewy Decimal System. And in a small town like this, the library can't be very busy. There's sure to be plenty of free time for us to plan the grand opening."

"And Internet," added Derrick, almost cheerfully. "Don't forget Internet access."

Bridget looked concerned. "I don't think ..."

"Our library back home even had a coffee bar!" Paul reminded him, delighted.

"I don't think ..." Lindsay put in, but Derrick interrupted.

"Ladies, let us buy you lunch," he invited expansively, extending his arms to Bridget and Lindsay.

Paul offered his arm to Cici. "You don't suppose they'll make us wear those awful orange jumpsuits, do you?"

Cici exchanged a resigned look with her two friends, then took Paul's arm, patting it in reassurance. "I don't think so," she said, and smiled. "Now, where shall we eat?"

The Winnebago was faster than walking, but just barely. In fact, the only advantage it had over putting shoe-rubber to the pavement was that the blisters on Josh's feet had a chance to heal. That, of course, and the free food.

Artie had an unreasonable fascination with meandering. He would take an unmarked byroad over a highway any day of the week. He couldn't pass a Dairy Queen or a Waffle House without stopping—about which Josh couldn't really complain because when the bill came, Artie cheerfully paid it, assuring his companion, "You can get it next time," but of course next time never came—and there was not a flea market, Indian museum, snake farm, antique shop, country café, or county fair into which the wheels of the old Winnie didn't seem to turn, like a compass swinging to magnetic north.

Josh volunteered to share the driving in hopes of making better time, but being in the passenger seat only gave Artie a better view of the signs advertising obscure attractions and scenic highways. After a day or two, Josh found himself falling into an almost Zen-like state, something that had served him well in prison. There were things he couldn't control. Fighting them was a waste of energy. He couldn't reach Leda on the telephone. He couldn't push the Winnebago's speedometer over fifty. He couldn't make Artie stay on the highway. All he could do was be patient. He had waited fourteen months. He could do this.

At a yard sale outside of a little town called Victory, he found a pair of Reeboks that fit for two dollars, and three pairs of almost-new socks for fifty cents. He was long past thinking about the time when he would have gone barefoot before wearing someone else's used socks, but every now and then it hit him: here he was, Josh Whitman, who had once lost a jacket at a high school football game that cost more than the average man's dress suit, feeling like the luckiest guy in the world to have found a pair of sneakers at a yard sale that actually fit. And for a moment he was taken out of himself, wondering, as though from a very great distance, whose life he was living. And realizing in the same instant that it didn't matter. The important thing was that he was living. Because he had things to do.

"You remind me of another fella I knew once a while back," Artie observed, watching Josh lace up the shoes. "Walked everywhere he went. When he wore holes in his shoes, he'd line them with newspaper. Said walking was the best way he knew how to get where he was going, because if a man couldn't count on his on two legs, what could he count on in this world?"

They had stopped at a KOA somewhere in Indiana; nice showers, big pool, and a community house that was serving not-horrible barbecue platters for $5.00 each. Josh had paid for his own meal out of his dwindling stash, and now they were back at the campsite, sitting around the campfire while Artie brewed his coffee and melted marshmallows for the long-awaited s'mores. Their next door neighbors had the radio on a little loud, and the family on the other side had a yappy little dog that only barked louder when its owner shouted "*Shut up!*" Life on the road.

Josh glanced at him, tightening the laces. "Let me guess. Johnny Appleseed, right?"

Artie chuckled. "Nope. Never had the pleasure. This fellow was a lawyer. I never had much use for them myself—lawyers, that is—but he made quite a reputation for himself. They called him Honest Abe, but just between you and me he was no more honest than any other lawyer I've ever met, if you know what I mean."

Josh rolled his eyes but said nothing. He was accustomed to Artie's eccentricities by now, and had decided they were the cost of passage. And in some ways, he actually enjoyed them. The man was a nut, but he was entertaining.

Josh flexed his feet inside the new shoes and then, cautiously, put weight on them. Padded inside athletic socks and surrounded by arch and ankle support, his battered feet felt as though they were encompassed by clouds. Unconsciously, he let out a sigh of pure pleasure.

Artie retrieved a bubbling marshmallow from the fire, grinning as he slid it onto a square of chocolate between two graham crackers. "Be sure you put your feet in the right place, and then stand firm," he said. "That's what he used to say."

Josh looked at him across the fire. "Abraham Lincoln?"

"Right." Artie passed him the sandwich of graham crackers and marshmallow, and Josh took it, pulling his camp chair closer to the fire.

Josh said, "So what are you, a history professor or something?"

Artie let forth with his strange cackling laugh, leaning back so that his feet left the ground. "Heavens, no. Just a student of human nature. Just a student."

Josh bit into the cookie and Artie watched his face grow soft, eyes twinkling. "Good, huh?" He threaded another marshmallow onto the skewer and passed it to Josh. "The trick is to keep them coming. Where'd you go to college, Josh?"

"Harvard."

"Ha!" There was a spark of amusement in his tone as he speared another marshmallow for himself. "You can always tell a Harvard man."

Josh watched the edges of the marshmallow he held over the fire grow golden, and he turned it expertly.

"Ah, you've done this before, I see," Artie observed.

Josh shrugged. "I've been to camp. Computer camp, space camp, tennis camp, riding camp, you name it."

"Lucky kid."

"I guess." He took two graham crackers and a square of chocolate from the paper plate on the ground between them, checked for ants, and then slipped it between the chocolate and graham crackers, squeezing gently until the hot marshmallow softened the chocolate.

"So what did you study?"

"At camp?"

"College."

Josh licked a bit of dripping marshmallow from the edge of his sandwich. "Science and engineering. You know, computer stuff."

"Impressive."

"Not really." He hesitated. "Turns out I wasn't as good at it as I thought I'd be."

"Oh yeah?" Artie looked up from spreading his melted marshmallow across a square of chocolate, using his skewer as a knife. "What are you good at then?"

"Nothing." Josh frowned. "Not everybody has to be good at something."

"Sure they do. It's why we're here, you know, to be good at something, and then let it shine. Why, like my old friend Ben Franklin used to say—you know he wrote that book, *Poor Richard's Almanac*—he used to say, What's a sundial in the shade? Of course ..." He pursed his lips, thinking that over. "That might be why they invented clocks."

Josh felt a reluctant grin tug at his lips even as he gave a sharp, dismissive shake of his head. "What are you, some kind of nut or something?"

"Or something," agreed Artie amiably. "So what are you, Josh?"

Josh gazed at the flames. "A mess," he said.

"Well, that much is obvious."

The marshmallow Josh held over the fire was turning black. He jerked it out but not soon enough; a blue flame licked its way up the side and he blew it out. He tried to remove the charred blob of melted sugar and cursed as he burned his fingers.

"What I meant was," Artie went on, ignoring him, "how did a Harvard man end up at a truck stop in Las Vegas without a penny to his name?"

Josh scowled at his scalded fingers, plucking stiff pieces of charred marshmallow from the tips. "Lost it all at Black Jack."

"Is that right?"

The mild way in which he spoke told Josh he was willing to believe the lie, but Josh didn't have the energy to sustain it. "No," he said. "That's not right."

Josh found a napkin and wiped the burned candy off the skewer. Artie waited. He threw the napkin into the fire. "We were on our way to Vegas to get married." He spoke slowly, and addressed the campfire. "My girlfriend and I. We got pulled over, the cops searched the car, I ended up serving time in Nevada. They let you out with what you had in your pockets when you went in, and I didn't have much. What I did have got stolen at the first bar I stopped at to make a call." He shrugged. "That's how."

Artie gave a sudden sharp bark of laughter, his eyes glittering with delight in the firelight. Josh stared at him in disbelief. "You think that's funny?"

Artie raised a hand in self-defense. "No, no, no, of course not! Not a thing funny about it. It's just that I love being right, and I knew I was right about you. The minute I saw you out-foxing those men at the truck stop I said to myself, Now there's a young fellow who's got what it takes. He's going to make it just fine, that's what I said to myself, you just wait and see, said I, because that young man has got what it takes. And how about that? I was right!"

Josh's frown deepened, and he started to push to his feet. "You're certifiable, that's what you are. "

"Sit down, sit down." Artie waved him back, eyes still dancing. "You don't understand. Here, have some of this coffee. Goes with the s'mores like you wouldn't believe."

Josh hesitated, and took the cup of coffee from Artie's outstretched hand mostly because his only other choice was to go back inside the hot RV and stew in his own discontent. It was white ceramic with a couple of chips, and had the faded slogan "See Rock City" emblazoned on the side. It looked like an antique.

He regarded Artie suspiciously. "What do you mean, I don't understand?"

"Why you fascinate me." Artie settled back in his camp chair, cradling his own cup. "There aren't too many young men who could go from tennis camp to Harvard to hard time in prison to landing flat broke on the side of a highway and still manage to get themselves from Las Vegas to Utah using nothing but their own two feet and the strength the good Lord gave them. That takes moxie, son. That takes character. Like I said, I'm a student of human nature, and that is one story I want to hear."

Josh muttered, "Yeah, well I'll send you a copy of my memoir."

Artie let forth with another cackling laugh. "That'll be one for my collection, yes it will. I hope you don't intend to make it a work of fiction, though. I've always found the truth to be much more interesting."

Josh took a sip of the coffee. Artie was right, there was something about the campfire smoke that gave it a flavor like none he'd ever tasted, and it melded with the lingering sweetness of marshmallow and chocolate on the back of his tongue like the long deep notes of the bassoon melted into a symphony orchestra. "Whatever."

Artie laughed again. "*Whatever*? From a Harvard man? They were a lot more articulate back in my day. Why, if Mr. John Harvard—or John

Adams, for that matter—could hear you say that he'd turn over in his grave. Now there was an interesting fellow," he mused. "John Adams, not John Harvard, who I never had the pleasure of knowing ..."

"Oh for God's sake," said Josh impatiently, "will you let it go already with the eyewitness-to-history shtick? And Harvard, too, while you're at it. That was a long time ago."

Artie just smiled. "Maybe for you." And then he said, out of nowhere, "Your dad didn't really kill your mother, now did he?"

Josh looked long and deep into the coffee. "I never knew my real dad," he said. "He died of cancer when I was two. There were always pictures of him and stuff around, like my mom wanted me to remember him, but I always felt a little bad that I couldn't."

Artie said nothing, and the silence made Josh's words sound empty and self-pitying. He cleared his throat, brows knitting briefly with embarrassment and impatience with himself. "Anyway, my stepdad ... I can't remember a time when he wasn't around. He practically raised me. He was my father's best friend, so he kind of naturally was around all the time, and he was the only person I ever called Dad. My mother said it was right after that—right after I started talking—that she knew it was okay to marry him." This time his smile was a bit more genuine, if sad. "He was a good guy. He treated me right. Like I said, he wasn't much of a baseball-in-the-park kind of guy, but that was okay because neither was I. Oh, we had our fights, just like anybody else, but we had some good family times, too. He made sure that whatever I needed, I had before I even thought to ask for it. He told me once it was a promise he'd made to my dad—my real one—when he married my mother, that neither one of us would ever want for anything he could provide. I never thought about that much until now, but that didn't mean just a good school and clothes and tennis lessons and a house in the country. It meant going to soccer games when he didn't even know anything about the game, and Disneyworld when he'd rather take my mother on a cruise. And sometimes it meant saying no." He was silent for a moment. "Of course, you don't appreciate things like that when you're a kid. You think they're your due, and I guess it's part of a dad's job to make you think that. At least while you're little.

"I was in my third year at Harvard and things weren't going all that well. My folks wanted me to come home for Christmas, but I knew it was going to be a hassle, a lot of talk about straightening up and taking responsibility for my life, and I just didn't want to hear it, you know. It wasn't like I didn't already know what a screw up I was. I made out like I was going to stay on campus and study, but I went to Aspen with a bunch of the guys instead."

He gazed down at his coffee cup again, absently tracing the curve of the handle with his finger. "Seems my folks thought it would be a good idea to drive down and surprise me for Christmas. It was snowing, some drunk came out of nowhere, and by the time they tracked me down my mom was in a coma and they said she would never wake up again."

Artie nodded. "Your dad was driving?"

For a moment Josh appeared not to hear him, so absorbed was he in the design his finger was making on the handle of the cup. Then he gathered his thoughts with a visible effort, and he said, "Yeah. But it wasn't his fault. I guess I always knew that. It just didn't matter."

He seemed to recognize for the first time that the cup held coffee, and he took a sip. "I didn't believe the doctors, of course. I thought if I hoped hard enough and prayed hard enough … if I sat with her long enough, and talked to her long enough, and kept believing she'd come back to me … but she just lay there with her eyes open and her head all bandaged up, not even looking like herself. Like all the soul was gone out of her. I talked to her, I held her hand, I kept expecting her to blink and turn her head and smile at me, but she didn't know I was there. And all the time I just kept getting madder and madder at my dad because he wouldn't even *try* … he just sat in the waiting room staring at the wall looking all shrunken and haunted, just staring. He wouldn't even come in the room. I guess … well, later I guess I heard that he'd already been there, doing exactly what I was doing, not leaving her side, for over a week while they were trying to find me. He knew. He already knew what lay at the end of the road."

Josh let a silence fall, and after a time, Artie spoke into it. "There's a native tribe along the Amazon whose word for parent is *hiabwi*. It means 'those who go before.' Those who go before always see the end of the road first. That's their job."

Josh said softly, "Yeah." He was silent for a moment. Then he went on, "The doctors kept telling me we had to make a decision. They said there was no hope. They said she was gone already, that whatever was inside of her that made her my mom had died before they even got her to surgery. But people come back from comas all the time. Five, ten, twenty-five years later, they wake up and they're fine. I just wanted to see her one more time, you know? To say some things ... to tell her stuff. But my dad said it was time to let her go. He said it was what she wanted. He said he had papers. I said I would get a judge to stop him. He said I was dishonoring her memory. I said he was a murderer. The last thing I said to him was when I had him pinned up against the wall screaming in his face that he had murdered my mother. I walked out of that hospital, and I never even said good-bye. To either of them."

"Ah," said Artie, nodding thoughtfully. "And that's really how you ended up all alone on the side of the highway without a penny to your name."

Josh blew out a long breath. He felt weary to the bone, aching in his spirit, but somehow lighter, too. Relieved. "Yeah," he said. "More or less."

"You know," Artie said after a moment, "I heard somebody say one time that refusing to forgive is like drinking poison and expecting the other person to die. Makes a lot of sense to me."

Josh looked at him across the fire, the strange little man with his crooked face made even stranger by the colors and shadows that played across it. He said softly, "The only trouble is that I'm not sure who should be forgiving who."

He stood up, tossing the dregs of his coffee toward the fire. "I'm going to get some sleep."

"The quality of mercy is not strained," Artie said.

Josh said, "Don't tell me—you were friends with Will Shakespeare too."

Artie chuckled. "Nah, the man was a lunatic. Owed money to everybody in town, too, who wants a friend like that? But he did have a good idea or two, despite himself. The quality of mercy. I like that one."

Josh, shaking his head, couldn't stop a small smile. "Good night, Artie."

The librarian, a small, quick woman with short pale hair and red-framed glasses that were easily half the size of her face, was named Amelia Brendt, and she seemed a bit overwhelmed by the two dapper gentlemen who presented themselves before her bright and early the following morning, ready for duty. They had checked and double-checked on the dress code, and were assured that street wear would be perfectly appropriate for their first day of community service at the public library. Orange jumpsuits were not, apparently, standard issue, so they opted for sports coats, khakis, and loafers or, in Paul's case, driving moccasins worn without socks because he refused to completely abandon his sense of personal style for the sake of the provinces. Now that the stress of the trial was over, however, he was able to be much more relaxed about his attire and decided against neckwear.

Amelia Brendt peered up at them over the top of her glasses from behind the check out desk, looking puzzled. "Really, gentlemen," she said, "you didn't have to bring me your resumes."

"We thought it might be helpful," Paul explained, "for you to know our backgrounds so that you could place us more efficiently." What he had really wanted her to know, of course, was that they were respectable citizens and business owners, not common criminals, lest there be any misunderstanding at all in that respect. To make certain, he had included at the top of both resumes a detailed report on the infraction that had resulted in their becoming victims of the justice system which had, in turn, led to their appearance now before her, in search of a way to be of service.

"We take our civic duty very seriously," Derrick added. "As you'll see there …" he indicated the papers in her hand, "I was an art history major, so perhaps I might be most useful at the research desk. That way when any calls come in regarding art, I'll be available to field them."

"Um, we actually don't have a research desk, per se," she replied, glancing around the fourteen-hundred-square-foot facility in bewilderment, "and I really can't recall the last time anyone asked a question about art." At his looked of horrified dismay, she assured him quickly, "We have several art teachers in the community. Usually people with a question would simply ask one of them."

Derrick looked both cautiously relieved and disappointed. "Oh. Well, I suppose that's all right then." He added helpfully, "Our friend Lindsay is an art teacher. Perhaps you know her. Lindsay Wright."

She drew breath for a reply but at that moment a woman came up with a stack of books and she excused herself to attend to them. Paul took out his BlackBerry and discreetly checked his messages while she was gone. "Still nothing from Lester Carson," he murmured, frowning. "I've been calling him for two days. I know he got the invitation, I talked to his secretary."

"I thought she said he was in Beijing."

"She did, but he was due back Monday. I told her to enjoy the basket of blueberries that the invitation was packed in and I sent him a bottle of '97 Montrachet yesterday."

"I knew sending perishables was a bad idea," Derrick worried. "We should have just sent everyone wine."

"That would have spoiled the theme, wouldn't it? The point is, I can't call him again, he'll think I'm stalking him. But how can we not have the travel editor from the *Times*? If he doesn't come, what's the point?"

The librarian returned and Paul quickly pocketed his phone, smiling at her. Before she could resume their conversation, he spoke up. "I'm sure you noticed that my background is in journalism. Perhaps you've read my column?"

She smiled politely but clearly had no idea what he was talking about. He tried not to be offended—

after all, what could one expect in the country?—and redoubled his efforts to make her feel comfortable. "Many's the fine hour I've spent in the library, naturally. The original Carnegie Library—that's in New York—"

"I'm familiar with it," she assured him with a lift of her eyebrow.

"Yes, of course," he said quickly, moving on. "It was practically my second home when I was at Columbia." He felt compelled to explain, "Columbia is a—"

"University, yes, I know," she said, and sighed. "Gentlemen, to be perfectly honest, generally our community service workers are teenagers who've been caught shoplifting or driving without a license. This isn't a program that was designed for—shall we say?—the utilization of specialized skills. I don't think …"

At that moment, a door marked "Auditorium" opened on a cacophony of tiny voices and closed again. A rather harried-looking woman in a messy bun and a print dress that appeared to be stained with greasy handprints hurried over. "Excuse me, Miss Brendt, I don't mean to interrupt, but have you heard anything at all from our volunteers? We have twenty-seven children today and with only SueAnn and myself I just don't see how we can manage show-and-tell *and* refreshments. We're barely keeping order as it is. Is there anyone you can call?"

She started to reply, then smiled slowly. "No need," she said, and turned to Paul and Derrick. "Your volunteers are here."

At first it seemed manageable. The Children's Librarian, whose name was Cynthia, explained as she hurried them toward the Auditorium, "We're in the middle of our Summer Reading Program. Today the children were asked to bring something that reminds them of a character from their favorite story, which means things are a bit more hectic than usual."

"I really don't know much about children," Paul warned her. "I don't even have any nieces or nephews."

"I'm excellent at arts and crafts, though," Derrick put in.

"Oh. Well, that's good to know. But you really won't be interacting with the children today. If you could just serve the punch and cookies, it would be a huge help."

Paul smiled. "I have been serving punch and cookies since I was twelve," he assured her. "It will be my pleasure."

"And of course," she added, swinging open the door, "help wrangle the animals."

At first they thought she was referring to the children, and given the chaos into which they stepped, it was an easy mistake. A posse of noisy boys and girls was gathered in something vaguely resembling a circle around a young woman with a picture book. Her name tag read Miss Sarah, and she looked barely older than her charges. Though her voice was all but drowned out by the bouncing children who shot their hands up in the air and called, "Miss Sarah! Miss Sarah!" "Miss Sarah, Jeffery is sitting on me!" and "Miss Sarah, is it my turn yet?" she gamely soldiered on, a frozen smile on her face as she held up the book to show the pictures. Every time she turned the picture book toward her audience, of course, more children leapt to their feet to see, and they hardly ever resumed sitting again. But the real zoo was not gathered around the beleaguered storyteller; it was lined up against the opposite wall, and it was, in fact, a real zoo. A liver-spotted beagle barked from its wire cage, a kitten yowled, a frog flung itself repeatedly against a clear plastic box, and a rooster crowed. There were other odd-looking objects against the wall as well—a glittered feather boa, a ladder made out of tin foil, a kite shaped like a shark.

"I'm starting to think my early childhood education was sub-par," Paul murmured, staring at the collection.

"*The Owl and the Pussycat,*" Derrick said with a note of triumph in his voice.

"What?"

"The kitten. They were supposed to bring something that reminds them of a character from a story. The kitten is from *The Owl and the Pussycat.* Am I right, Cynthia?"

Cynthia glanced over her shoulder at him, distracted. "Yes, I suppose so. Now, we've set up this long table for the refreshments. You'll find the tablecloth and paper plates in that cabinet over there, and the cookies are in the overhead cabinet. I'll bring the punch from the break room. Just fill the paper cups and line them up … oh, the paper cups are—"

"Really, my dear, we can manage," Paul assured her. "You just run get the punch, we'll take care of everything else."

She did not look convinced. "We'll serve refreshments right after show-and-tell," she said. "That should give you plenty of time, but we do have almost thirty children today, so …"

Derrick found the plastic tablecloth and shook it out with a snap. "Never fear, fair lady, we are on the job."

Paul's phone buzzed as she hurried away, still looking uneasy, and he glanced at the ID. His expression changed dramatically, and he quickly answered, "This is Paul. Thank you so much for returning my call."

Derrick moved close and before he could ask, Paul mouthed "Bobby Flay!" Derrick gripped his arm and held his breath.

"Yes, that's right, the fifteenth," Paul said. "Naturally, we'll be responsible for all accommodations and all amenities … yes, of course. Farm-to-table, absolutely … I completely understand, no problem at all. Totally artisanal, yes, that's absolutely our trademark ... We're expecting quite a few well-known names from the entertainment and political arenas, and the party will last the weekend. It really will be quite special. Yes, that would be wonderful … I certainly do … Thank you, I look forward to it."

He disconnected and turned to Derrick, who breathed, "You did not just get Bobby Flay to cater our grand opening."

Paul held up a cautionary finger but his eyes were brilliant with excitement. "Almost. It's very nearly a sure thing. That was his assistant. She's going to call me back."

"You," declared Derrick, "are a genius! How did you do it? Who did you call? You are a master networker! You should give lessons."

Paul agreed modestly, "I really am, aren't I? But it wasn't really that difficult. I was the first non-food critic to write about him when he first opened his restaurant, and he called to thank me personally. Then I met him again at Madeleine's party—you remember, you spent the entire next week pouting because you were on that buying trip and missed the party."

"I did not pout," Derrick said.

"Anyway, we chatted for a while, and he said the next time I wanted to come to the restaurant to call him personally and he'd make sure I had a table ..."

Derrick pressed his hand against his chest. "You never told me that!"

Paul tapped his forehead. "Genius, remember? I was saving the favor."

"Okay," Derrick said, his mind racing, "this totally ups the stakes. You do not bring in Bobby Flay for anything less than the best." He whipped out his phone and started scrolling through his contact list.

"The invitations have already gone out," Paul reminded him. "Sixteen pints of handpicked artisanal blueberries packed in locally crafted artisanal baskets cunningly wrapped in butcher block paper with the date and time printed in gold and a handwritten invitation tucked inside. We were up all night. It's done."

"I'm talking about the entertainment," Derrick replied, not looking up. "These people will expect something more than our clever wit and charming good looks."

"I told you, the chamber orchestra—"

"I had something a bit more current in mind." He drew in a breath and looked up, alight with a new idea. "You know who we should get?"

"Celine Dion."

"I wish. No, that girl—oh, what's her name?—who won *American Idol* a few seasons back. Cute, blonde …"

"They're all cute and blonde."

"I read somewhere she's even from this part of the country. She's huge on the charts. Everyone loves her."

"Carrie Underwood?"

He looked up from his Internet search, eyes bright with delight. "No, but that's a fabulous idea! Who could be more artisanal? Do you know her agent?"

"I don't know everyone," Paul was forced to admit, a little uncomfortably. "Besides, I'm not sure Carrie Underwood is quite the right fit."

He started tapping keys again. "Who's that other one? Actress, singer …"

"Miley Cyrus?"

Again his face lit up. "I love it! Perfect! Do you know anyone who can call her dad?"

Paul returned a dry look. "I'm not even sure I know anyone who knows who her dad is. Besides, do you think Miley Cyrus is quite right for our brand?"

"Patty McClain!" exclaimed Derrick, ignoring him. "That's who I'm thinking of. You know her, she's on the radio every minute. And yes ..." He tapped more keys. "I'm right! She's from Charlottesville—that's barely a minute from here!" He lifted his eyebrows as he read the screen. "Seven million records. Definitely. Definitely, that's who we have to have." He started swiping the screen. "Surely we know someone who knows someone who knows her agent."

Cynthia came through the door just then lugging two gallon jugs of a liquid the color of antifreeze, casting a puzzled glance toward the table which had not been set and the cookies which were still in the cabinet. Derrick tucked away his phone and hurried to help her, while Paul began to unpack paper plates and cups with all possible efficiency. While they poured twenty-seven cups of the chartreuse-colored liquid and artfully arranged two chocolate-chip cookies and a folded napkin on each paper plate, show-and-tell began.

The beagle, inspired by *My Little Puppy* and not, as Derrick had insisted, Snoopy from *Charlie Brown,* was brought out first and stood barking and lunging to the end of his leash while the little boy who was inspired by him shouted, "Sit! Sit!" and the other children shrieked with excitement and laughter. Miss Cynthia lost no time in thanking little Todd for his contribution and escorted the beagle back to its cage. As Paul explained to Derrick that Snoopy was, in fact, a comic strip character and not a character in a book and therefore ineligible for this event, a little girl stepped to the front of the room with the frog in the plastic box.

"Now isn't that nice?" Paul said approvingly. "No gender stereotypes. Good for her." He applauded enthusiastically with the rest of the group.

"*The Frog Went a'Courtin'* ," said Derrick.

"That's a poem, not a book."

"This is my pet, Toady," said the little girl to a clatter of "oohs," "ahhs," and quite a few "eewws" from the girls. Paul and Derrick chuckled. When prompted by Miss Sarah, the child added, "He's from my favorite story, *The Frog Went a'Courtin'*".

Paul missed Derrick's smirk because just then his phone rang. He turned his back to the room to answer but Derrick got close to his face, whispering, "Is it—"

Paul nodded and said into the phone, "Paul Slater." Then "Yes, of course I'll hold." He pressed the phone to his chest and told Derrick, "Holding for Bobby."

"Oh my God, you're holding for Bobby Flay." Derrick began to fan himself and Paul turned away again, covering one ear against a sudden burst of excitement from the show-and-tell circle.

There was a click and Paul straightened his shoulders and smiled broadly, just as though the person on the other end of the line could see him. It was only the secretary. "I'm so sorry, it will be just a few more minutes. Do you mind holding?"

Her last word was all but drowned out by a squeal and Paul covered his ear again.

"Is everything all right?"

"Yes, yes, just fine. Not a problem. I can hold."

"Thank you so much."

"Children, children, please take your seats! Make a circle, make a circle!"

Paul glanced over his shoulder and saw a level of chaos he could have previously only imagined. Children were streaming everywhere, overturning chairs, crawling under tables and scrambling over them, screaming and laughing at the top of their lungs. Derrick was trying to herd a couple of them back toward the story circle, shooing them like geese, while Miss Cynthia stood in the center of the room and clapped her hands sharply, looking completely at a loss for what else she might do to restore order.

The little girl who had had the frog charged toward him, crying, "Toady! Toady!" and Paul realized what all the excitement was about approximately half a second before the frog bounded through the air from a nearby table and landed in the punch bowl. Green punch erupted across the table, spraying Paul's face and jacket and shoes. Squeals of excitement and laughter broke out as more children rushed the table and Derrick rather desperately tried to ward them off. The little girl dived for the frog in the punch bowl and Paul ducked as the slimy creature, now even greener than before, squirted through her fingers and into the air.

It was at that moment that a voice said in his ear, "Paul, I'm so sorry to keep you waiting."

Paul, straightening, heard Derrick cry, "Be careful!"

And the little girl screamed, "Toady!" just as Paul stepped back and felt a sickening, squishy crunch under his foot.

Everything got very still. Paul closed his eyes slowly, unwilling to look, afraid to move.

One of the children said, "Ew, gross."

Paul swallowed hard, opened his eyes, and turned slowly to face the stunned faces of his accusers. "Um, Bobby," he said, "I'll have to call you back."

At Ladybug Farm

"Well, you know Paul," Bridget said with a sigh, setting a basket of fresh-baked blueberry muffins on the table. "He was horrified. Distraught. Beside himself. He offered to buy the little girl another frog, but where do you go to buy a frog?"

They liked to have breakfast on the side porch in the summer, and the white wicker table was set with a bright blue and yellow tablecloth and Bridget's Wedgewood-patterned china. Lindsay came up the steps with a handful of giant blue hydrangea blossoms, and Cici followed Bridget out of the kitchen with the coffee pot. Cici groaned out loud as she poured the coffee.

"Of all the things to happen," she said.

"And of all the people for it to happen *to*," Lindsay added. She took a vase down from a weathered wooden cabinet mounted to the wall and went to fill it from the utility sink around the corner.

"So he tried to give the little girl's parents twenty dollars but they just thought he was weird," Bridget went on. "And the librarian asked them—nicely, he said—not to come back."

"Well," Cici said, "you do have to sympathize with her point of view. Seriously, I can't imagine two people less suited to handle a roomful of six-year-olds and their farm animals."

"It's just that they take everything so seriously." Bridget went back into the kitchen and returned in a moment with a bowl of fruit in one hand and the butter dish in the other. "Now they're worried they won't even be able to get a library card."

At this, Cici had to compress her lips against a bubble of laughter. "I'm sorry," she said at Bridget's look, "I just got a mental picture of that frog jumping into the lime Kool-Aid."

Even Bridget's lips dimpled with that. "I'm sure it wasn't funny at the time."

Lindsay set the vase of hydrangea blossoms in the center of the table and sat down, reaching for a muffin. "Well, I suppose it could have been worse."

Bridget sat down and stirred cream into her coffee. "It was. They didn't get Bobby Flay for their grand opening after all. It turns out he's going to be in Italy the whole month of August." She sighed. "I don't know who's more disappointed, them or me. You know they hired me to cater the breakfast the next morning and the very thought that a real chef might be tasting my cooking ..."

"You *are* a real chef!" Lindsay protested.

Cici added, "You have your own restaurant, don't you?"

Bridget grinned wryly and shook her head. "Thanks, guys, but I don't think I'm ready to take on an Iron Chef yet, and ..." she held up a hand in protest, "before you even suggest it, there's not enough money in the world to persuade me to cook dinner for that grand opening, even if they did ask me, which they know better than to even try. You know I love them, but can you imagine working for them on an event like this?"

Her two friends shuddered appropriately, and Cici said, "Derrick told me they invited Katie Couric."

"They knew each other from college, didn't they?"

"That was a long time ago."

"And Neil Patrick Harris."

Lindsay's eyes lit up, and she paused with a neatly sliced and buttered muffin partway to her mouth. "Oh, I'd love to meet him. I've loved him since *Doogie Howser.*"

"I think he hates it when people say that," Cici said.

"Wait," Lindsay said, "we are invited to this thing, aren't we? I mean, the celebrity part, not the breakfast, no offense, Bridget."

"We'd better be," Bridget said, "after all those blueberry baskets we helped them wrap. Of course," she added, "they were sweet enough to order Ladybug Farm gift baskets for all the rooms—the deluxe edition—which is bound to be fabulous for business. So even if I don't get to meet Bobby Flay or Doogie Howser, I can't complain."

"We're invited," Cici assured them. "To cocktails *and* dinner." She bit into her muffin and added, "Fabulous muffins, Bridge. We should take the boys some this afternoon."

"It's going to take more than muffins to cheer them up, I'm afraid," she answered.

Lindsay said, "Who are they going to get to cater the dinner now?"

"I have no idea. I'm sure Paul has some more contacts up his sleeve, but it's awfully short notice."

"Not to mention," Lindsay added, "a bit of a logistical challenge for anybody willing to take it on. Remember all the trouble we had getting vendors out here for that wedding we did? We had to get chairs from the funeral home! And we wouldn't even have thought of that if it hadn't been for Paul." She took another bite of her muffin and said, "That's why I've decided to have my wedding catered on site." She winked at Bridget. "And on my budget, it's a good thing she's a friend."

"Speaking of which," Bridget said, "how are we coming on picking a date?"

Lindsay shrugged. "No rush. Dominic will be back this weekend. We'll talk about it then."

Cici scooped some fruit onto her plate. "Anyway, the boys have got bigger problems than finding a caterer. What are they going to do about their community service now that they've been kicked out of the library?"

Bridget put down her fork, her expression unhappy. "It's not good news."

The other two looked at her curiously.

"The only place that could take them on such short notice," she said, "was the animal shelter. They start today."

SEVEN

Experience is simply the name we give our mistakes.

Oscar Wilde

Megan had met Nick twenty-two years ago at a wedding. She was the bridesmaid in the ugly cocoa brown organza dress with a yellow sunflower pinned to the sash, and he was the caterer who was making such a ruckus in the kitchen that the guests were starting to give each other alarmed looks. She was the one the mother of the bride grabbed by the arm and ordered, in a desperate whisper, to "For God's sake, find out what's going on!" before the bride, who was currently posing for photos and calling for her mother, got wind of the disturbance. Megan had been on the receiving end of the stressed out bride's disappointment more than once over the past several weeks, and she lost no time in complying.

She could hear the shouting and the crashing long before she reached the kitchen of the reception hall, and she burst through the door just in time to be splattered by a froth of cream and pastry that had been thrown by a fat man in a chocolate-stained white apron at a curly haired blond man who had ducked just as Megan came through the door. Berry sauce dripped from her sleeve and heavy cream frothed the sunflower sash like snow. The man with the curly blond hair straightened slowly, looking at her with a mixture of suspended rage and stunned horror in his churning green eyes. Everything in the kitchen was suddenly quiet. The uniformed servers, the assistants, even the bartenders daring hardly to breathe. He said very quietly, "Are you all right?"

Instead of answering, she replied calmly, "Is there anything I can do to help?"

He walked over to the fat man, who, to his credit, was now looking much more frightened than angry, and jerked the apron right off his neck. He said quite clearly, "Get the hell out of my kitchen."

While the erstwhile dessert-thrower scrambled away, rubbing the rope burn the straps of the apron had left on his neck, the other man turned back to Megan, running an agitated hand through his curls as he snatched up a napkin. "I'm so sorry about the dress. We'll pay for it, of course. You're sure you're not hurt?"

She took the napkin from him and began to brush ineffectually at the mess on her dress. "Don't worry about the dress. This is actually an improvement." She dipped a finger into the berry sauce, tasted it, and grimaced at the sour taste. "On second thought …"

He grinned at that. "I see you are a woman of discriminating taste. You wouldn't by chance be a pastry chef, would you?"

She wiped the berry sauce off her fingers and replied, "I'm not a pastry chef, but I hardly ever throw my desserts at people. And I'm pretty sure I can do better than this."

That was when he, with laughter dancing in those fabulous green eyes of his, took her arm and said, "You're hired."

Later he would tell her he had known he was going to marry her the moment she had said, in that oh-so-calm voice of hers, "Is there anything I can do to help?" And later she would tell him she had fallen in love with him because he had thought, even for an instant, that she was pastry chef.

And much, much later, eleven years later to be exact, he would look into her eyes and say sadly, "You've changed, Megan. You're not the girl I married anymore."

And she would say in a small tired voice, "I never was."

She was not a pastry chef, nor would she ever be, but she rescued her friend's wedding dinner with a tiramisu made from store-bought ladyfingers and chocolate ganache, and had lost her heart to a passionate green-eyed Italian who didn't even blink an eye as he served it to the bride's table and told them it was a treasured family recipe featuring an imported chocolate liqueur produced only in a small hill town in Tuscany. Since the bride and groom were honeymooning in Tuscany—a fact Megan might have let slip as she was chopping and melting ordinary baker's chocolate for the ganache—they declared Nick a genius and tipped him half again the cost of the entire dinner.

Megan and Nick had laughed about that for years. They never went to an Italian restaurant without ordering the tiramisu. And it always made them smile.

"Aren't you going to eat that?" Annabelle asked, eyeing the untouched dessert in front of Megan.

Megan blinked and came back to the present. "Oh," she said. "No." She pushed the dish of tiramisu across the table to her grandmother. "I really don't know why I ordered it. I'm stuffed."

"I can't imagine how." Annabelle picked up her spoon and scooped up some whipped cream. "You barely touched your lasagna."

"It wasn't very good."

"Neither is this." She wrinkled her nose and put down the spoon. "How did you know?"

Megan managed a small smile. "Canned whipped cream," she said.

"Ah well, you can't expect five star dining every night when you're on the road."

"Especially when you choose to dine at a place called Pizza and More."

"Beggars can't be choosers, my dear."

Megan looked around for their waitress to request the check. "Well, it wasn't *that* bad."

Her cell phone rang. She checked the caller ID and rejected the call. "It's Mom," she explained. "I'll call her later."

They were just outside of Nashville, which wasn't the shortest possible route, but her Grandmother insisted on seeing the Grand Old Opry and Megan had to admit she was looking forward to touring Music City herself. They were already three days behind the schedule Megan had plotted in her head—a schedule that she should have know would turn out to be useless—partly because her grandmother kept finding things she wanted to see, and those things were always off their route, but also because everything with her grandmother took longer than planned. "I'm ninety-seven," Annabelle kept reminding her. "Nothing about me is as fast as it used to be." And the truth was, Megan didn't mind taking it slow. They drove four or five hours a day with long pit stops for lunch or sightseeing or just so that Annabelle could get out and stretch her legs. They checked in to their motel in late afternoon, had a leisurely dinner, and Annabelle would be tucked into her bed with the remote control by seven. Sometimes Megan would walk around the motel grounds or sit by the pool until dark, but most of the time she enjoyed sitting with her grandmother, watching the Food Channel or reading until they both grew sleepy. They were in their own little world, and as long as they were on the road, nothing outside the two of them could intrude. Megan could forget what she had left behind, and what awaited her when she returned home. She still did not know why they were traveling or what, exactly, they were looking for. In a way, it didn't really matter. But still, every now and then, curiosity poked its head up and she remembered that this great meandering adventure did, in fact have a point—more or less.

"Gram," she said as she glanced over the check the waitress set before them, "I've been meaning to ask. Who took the picture?"

Her grandmother sipped her coffee. "What picture, dear?"

"The picture that started this cross-country trek." Megan counted out some bills. "That picture."

Her grandmother reached for her purse, and Megan assured her, as she always did, "My treat."

And her grandmother replied, as she always did, "At least let me leave the tip."

"Thank you," Megan replied with a smile, because it would be pointless arguing with her.

Annabelle pulled out two dollar bills and left them on the table. Megan surreptitiously tucked another three under her plate. "You and your mother were both in the picture," she explained. "So who was behind the camera?"

Annabelle appeared to consider that as she lifted her coffee mug again. It was one of those generic white ceramic mugs with not even the embellishment of a logo on the front, which meant the restaurant could not afford to squander money. Megan tended to notice things like that.

"Why," said Annabelle after a moment, "my father, I suppose."

Megan's brows came together. "Wait a minute. You said he died before you were born. In the war, right?"

Annabelle's perfectly powdered and made-up face creased into a mysterious smile. "Well, now, that's the gentle lie they told back then, isn't it? The fact is, I don't think the fellow even went to war, much less died there. All I know for certain is he never bothered to marry my mother."

Megan sank back against the sticky vinyl booth, astonished. "Well, I'll be … How do you know that? Why did you keep it such a secret?"

"Oh my, I didn't keep it a secret. It was kept from *me*. Until Mother died, and I found this." She opened a zippered compartment in her purse and pulled out another small, stiff photograph in shades of faded sepia. She passed it to Megan.

The photograph was of a young man in a white shirt kneeling with an arm around a blond-haired little girl. His face was turned toward hers and there was a tenderness in his expression that even the faded, imperfect snapshot could not disguise. The little girl, who Megan recognized as the child Annabelle, had an arm draped around his neck and was grinning broadly into the camera.

"Turn it over," Annabelle suggested softly.

Megan did so, and read the faded brown handwriting out loud. "Jackson and Annabelle." She looked back to her grandmother, puzzled.

"My father's name was Jackson, at least according to my mother. She didn't talk about him much but I do remember she always smiled when she said his name. She was in love with him all of her life, I think. She never remarried … or I should say, married." Annabelle smiled. "He looks pretty good for a man who died ten years earlier, doesn't he?"

"Wow," Megan murmured, looking at the photo again. "A scandalous secret in the family. What do you know about that?"

"Look closely at the picture," Annabelle said. "I'm wearing the same dress I was in the other one. I think the two pictures were taken on the same day."

"Why … it could almost be the same place," Megan said, squinting to make out the details. "Maybe taken from a different angle? I don't see the sign, but those mountains in the background definitely look familiar. "

"And look what we're sitting on," prompted Annabelle.

Megan brought the photograph closer, then farther away, trying to make it out. "A bench?"

"Steps," said Annabelle. "Stone steps. In my dream I'm going up a set of stone steps."

Megan's eyes widened. "Oh my goodness. I just got a chill. What else happens in your dream?"

"I'm looking for something," Annabelle said, "something my daddy gave me. A birthday present, I think. I don't know what it is, but it's terribly important that I find it. The details fade as soon as I wake, but it all seems very vivid at the time. I've had the dream all my life."

"Oh my goodness," Megan said on a breath, "after all these years … Do you think there really was a birthday present? Or could it be, you know, metaphorical?"

Annabelle shrugged. "Goodness, child, your guess is as good as mine. I suppose I'd have to go into therapy to find the real answer, and at my age it seems rather academic. What I do remember is a fight between the two of them, my mother being very upset, and I remember we left very early in the morning, before it was light, and in a great rush. I cried because I didn't get a chance to say good-bye." Her expression grew melancholy for a moment. "The happiest summer of my life ended in one of the saddest moments of my childhood memory."

"Which is why," said Megan softly, "you've been dreaming about it ever since."

"My mother never spoke about him again," Annabelle went on, "at least not to me. My theory is that my mother took me to visit with him that summer in hopes, somehow, that he would come back to us. When he made it clear that wasn't going to happen, she took me away in the middle of the night without saying good-bye, breaking both our hearts. But, that's just a theory. I do know though that we would receive money from time to time, and it had to be from him. Sometimes it was considerable—enough for a piano, or a new ice box—other times there would be an extra present under the tree, or a roast on Sunday when I knew we could barely afford chicken. And I think this photograph ..." she gestured toward it, "may have been the last—perhaps the only—time I saw him."

Megan started to return the photograph to her grandmother, but Annabelle waved her away. "You keep it, sweetheart. You're in charge of the family history now."

Megan tucked the photograph carefully into her wallet, shaking her head a little in wonder. "As mysteries go, I've got to admit, you've definitely outdone yourself. But you know, there is a much easier way to find out who your father was than to go all the way back to Virginia. Why don't you just send for your birth certificate?"

Annabelle chuckled a little. "That's not as simple for someone my age as it is for you. I tried finding my birth certificate when I applied for social security, but it had been lost in a fire or flood or some such nonsense decades before. Besides, it's not the *who* I'm interested in, don't you see? At this stage of the game, what difference could that possibly make? It's the *why*. I want to know the story, my dear. There's always, always a story. And in the end, it's hardly ever what you expect."

"All in all," observed Paul, sinking onto the plush, down-upholstered tapestry sofa with a glass of scotch, "I have had better days."

"You know what they say," agreed Derrick. "Sometimes you're the donkey, and sometimes you're the tail."

The look Paul gave him spoke volumes about what he was trying hard *not* to say.

Purline stood in the center of the room, hands on hips, scowling at both of them. "And if you think for one minute that I'm going to be cleaning up after all them animals—"

It was at that moment that they heard the door to the back garden open, followed by the scrabbling of little paws on expensively refinished wood floors. Paul lurched to his feet in alarm as a herd of small-to-midsized dogs flooded into the room, followed by Harmony with a kitten under each arm.

"Harmony!" Paul exclaimed. "I thought we agreed the dogs are to stay in the garden!"

"Well, I tried to explain that to them," replied Harmony reasonably, "but they seemed to be having a bit of trouble with the concept of boundaries." A scruffy looking Pekinese mix that Derrick had promptly named Cozette caught the hem of Harmony's flowing gown between its teeth and began to tug. "It's not as though the garden is fenced, you know," she added, calmly disengaging her garment from the jaws of the playful Pekinese. "That would make it all so much easier."

Paul sidestepped an impromptu game of chase between a fuzzy poodle-mix called Roxie Hart and something vaguely resembling a cocker spaniel that Derrick, whose theme had quickly become obvious, called Eliza Dolittle. Paul glared at Derrick. "We are not," he said, loudly enough to make certain he was heard over the sudden outburst of yapping from Eliza, "building a fence."

"Well, you needn't look at me as though it was all my fault." Derrick bent to scoop up an ugly little bulldog mix called Gaston, who was sniffing suspiciously at the fringe of the three-hundred-year-old Oriental carpet that anchored the room. "You're the one who said we couldn't possibly leave all those animals to be executed."

Holding the squirming little dog at arm's length, he crossed the room and thrust it toward Harmony. This action caused the two kittens, Grizabella and Mr. Mestopheles, to squirm from her arms and shoot across the room, sending a crystal vase and an imported French lamp tottering dangerously in the process. Purline saved the vase, scooping an excited Roxie Hart out of her path with her foot, and Paul steadied the lamp, holding his glass of scotch high as a daschund—now known as Sweeney Todd—scooted through his feet in hot pursuit of Grizabella.

"Just our luck," he agreed dismally, "that our volunteer work should fall on Expiration Day."

Purline stared at him, once again sweeping a curious Roxie out of the way with the toe of her sneaker. "Expiration Day? What's that?"

"It's the day when all the animals that have been in the shelter for over a week are, well …"

Derrick helped him out by slashing a finger across his own throat and supplying, "Expired."

"Good Lord above," exclaimed Purline, eyes widening. "They didn't expect you to …?"

"No, no, no," Derrick assured her.

Paul added, "But, knowing what was scheduled, we would have been complicit."

"You know what they say," added Derrick. "All that is necessary for evil to thrive is for good men to do nothing."

Purline looked slightly skeptical. "Well, that's all fine and good," she said, tugging her shoelace out of Roxie's mouth, "but what are you going to do with all these dogs and cats?"

Derrick looked at her hopefully. "Purline, you have children. Wouldn't they like—"

"No," she interrupted firmly. "I'm not taking home any of these puppies, like I didn't have enough to do already, with a husband and two kids, not to mention this place." She shook her foot to dislodge the poodle, ignoring Derrick's crestfallen look. "It's your mess, you fix it."

Harmony cradled Gaston against her bosom. The little dog was almost swallowed up, and squirmed in protest. "You know," she said thoughtfully, "it's become quite trendy for B&Bs to offer a rent-a-cat program for travelers who are forced to leave their pets at home and just want something to cuddle up with at night."

"Seriously?" said Paul, looking as though he expected a pie in the face at any moment. "Rent a cat?"

"No, wait," Derrick said excitedly. "I read about a similar program back home. Someone was renting out dogs to joggers who wanted a running companion but who didn't want all the trouble of keeping a dog."

Paul turned his disbelieving looked on Derrick. "And they charge *money* for this?"

"That's the stupidest thing I ever heard of," declared Purline. "What are you going to do with all these critters when you're not renting them out to some fool who wants to run with a dog or sleep with a cat? Put them in storage?"

Once again, Derrick looked deflated. "She has a point," he told Paul, plucking Grizabella off his pants leg. "We probably should have thought this through."

"We're going to have to find homes for them," Paul said, with a note of finality that would not have sounded out of place at Waterloo.

"How?" said Derrick. "We don't know anybody here. And we have a grand opening to organize."

"And when fleas start hopping on all them fancy movie stars y'all invited you're going to wish you'd never laid eyes on any of these dogs," declared Purline with a nod of her chin that was a mere harbinger of the *I told you so* that was to come. "Meantime, I guess I'll start cleaning out that shed out back and you can keep them there tonight. I'll probably get bit by every copperhead in the county doing it, too." She paused and fixed each of them with a meaningful look, but no one volunteered to help.

She bent down and finally picked up the poodle that had been nibbling at her shoes, tucked it under her arm, and muttered as she left the room, "What kind of name is Roxie Hart for a dog anyway? I reckon we'll just see about that."

Paul's expression was a mirror of the alarm on Derrick's, and they said at once, "Exterminator."

"First thing in the morning," added Paul, brushing at his sleeve and then his shoulder uneasily.

"And don't forget to leave a check for the limousine company," Harmony said, tickling a heavily panting Gaston under the chin. "It has to be done no later than tomorrow if you want to reserve twenty cars for the fifteenth. I held your wine order with a credit card but they'll invoice you later."

Paul and Derrick exchanged a quick look. Derrick cleared his throat. "Um, Harmony, on the subject of credit cards …"

"Oh!" she exclaimed, "I almost forgot in all the excitement. I have a caterer for you. I called Emeril—"

"Lagosse?" gasped Derrick, and even Paul's eyes widened. "You got Emeril Lagosse to cater our party?"

She gave them an odd, almost dismissive look. "Of course not. He's filming a special, and he couldn't get here in time anyway. But he recommended that young fellow at Daffodil in New York …"

"Wait a minute," said Paul, cautiously impressed. "I read about him. First Michelin star, fastest rising young chef in the fusion scene …"

"And, unfortunately, booked," said Harmony. "But he recommended someone who'll be much better for our purposes, and best of all he's available. He wants you to call and discuss the menu. I left his number on your desk."

Paul smiled politely, trying to mask his disappointment. "That was nice of you, Harmony. Thank you."

"Not at all," she replied cheerily. "If you need me for anything else, I'll be supervising this little fellow in the garden. Something tells me it's time for another tinkle, isn't it, pretty Gaston, isn't it, baby? Time to tinkle-winkle?"

She left the room, cooing and rubbing noses with the singularly unimpressed Gaston, and Derrick went to the sideboard to pour himself a drink. When he was certain she was out of ear shot, he returned to Paul and whispered, "Do you suppose we'll ever get paid?"

"We'd better," Paul whispered back, "if we're expected to book twenty limousines from National Airport."

"God only knows who she hired to cater."

"Well, it wasn't Emeril, that much we know."

Derrick sighed. "I'll check it out in the morning."

"Speaking of bad news," Paul added in a low, but slightly more normal tone, "Heidi is out. She's filming too."

"Well, that's one," said Derrick glumly. Then he brightened. "But there is good news."

Paul sipped his scotch. "I'm breathless."

"Jenny Franklin—you know, she used to come into the gallery all the time, never bought anything, but always talked like an expert—anyway, she's friends with Donovan Handel whose hairdresser knows Courtney Mitchell who does Addison Paron's nails who works for Patty McClain's agent!" He tossed back a satisfied gulp of his bourbon. "And *I*," he pronounced, "have her personal e-mail address."

Paul spent a moment trying to unravel the connections, then gave up. "Congratulations," he said. "There's more good news, you know."

Derrick looked at him curiously.

"We've already completed our first ten hours of community service."

Derrick nodded in pleasant agreement, and then his contentment began to fade. "The bad news is," he said, lifting his glass, "we still have ten to go."

Derrick's silver Volkswagen Touareg hybrid bumped and lurched over the rutted dirt driveway, its cargo section filled with foil-wrapped plates that smelled suspiciously like an elementary school lunchroom. Honeysuckle and wild roses, long since out of bloom, grabbed at the windows with sticky fingers from either side, and both men instinctively shrank back, peering ahead in consternation. Past a rusted-out silo and a tumbled-down split rail fence shot through with tall fescue, a weathered gray shack came into view, its front porch sagging like an old woman's chest. Derrick pulled up in front of the steps and turned off the engine.

The windows were dark, and the wild grass that served as a yard was tall enough to be used as a hedge. Derrick said uneasily, "Well."

And Paul agreed, "Well."

He consulted the slip of paper on the console upon which he had written directions. "This has to be it."

"I suppose."

For another moment, neither of them moved. Then Paul got out of the car, opened the hatchback, and selected one of the plates. Derrick followed, carrying the box that contained a bottle of sweet tea, six ounces of coffee, a jar of peanut butter, and a loaf of white bread. He couldn't help glancing surreptitiously at his watch. Nine hours, thirty-six minutes to go.

They made their way cautiously up the creaky steps and knocked on the door. They waited. Paul knocked again. There was not so much as a stirring inside.

Derrick slid an anxious glance in Paul's direction. "You don't suppose he's …"

Paul scowled, but he looked distinctly uncomfortable. "Of course not."

Derrick consulted his notes again. "Well, it says here he's eighty-five."

Paul knocked harder.

"I'm not sure what the procedure is," Derrick went on, worried, "in the case of the … you know, unexpected demise of a customer. I knew I should have taken that CPR course at the Community Center last year."

Paul's shoulders were stiff and he shifted his weight slightly from one foot to the other, a sure sign of suppressed agitation. "In the first place," he said, "they are not customers, they're clients. In the second place, in the case of the demise of one of these clients, I don't think CPR would—"

The door opened suddenly and a crepe-faced, bow-shouldered man with a cigarette hanging from his bottom lip glared at them. "Who the hell are you?" he demanded.

Derrick pushed himself forward, smiling broadly. "Hello there, Mr. Briggs," he said warmly. "I'm Derrick Anderson and this is Paul Slater, with Meals with Love. We have your—"

The door slammed in his face.

Paul lifted his eyebrows, glancing at Derrick. He knocked again.

The door jerked open. "Get the hell off my stoop with that crap," said Adam Briggs, cigarette bobbling, "and come back here when you've got something a man can eat."

"But," said Paul quickly, wedging his foot in the door just as it was about to slam shut again, "this is a nutritionally balanced, low-sodium, low-fat, carefully prepared three-course meal designed especially for you."

The other man stared at him as though he had spoken Latin. He leaned forward slightly, sniffed the air, and drew back in disgust. "Smells like crap," he declared. "You got any peanut butter?"

Derrick fumbled to edge the box through the door. "Actually, yes. But I'm sure—"

The man on the other side of the door grabbed the box, kicked Paul's shin with surprising acumen, and slammed the door on them both the moment Paul jumped back, yelping and rubbing his bruised shin.

"Are you all right?" demanded Derrick, alarmed.

"All in the line of duty, my good man," replied Paul with a pained expression. He stretched out his leg and flexed his foot inside his Ferragamos, checking the crease of his trousers. "I'll live." He looked at the foil package in his hand. "But seriously. How bad could it be?"

Derrick looked worried. "Do you suppose we get credit for hours even if they don't take the food?"

Their next stop was at a far more appealing little cottage at the edge of town belonging to one Abigail

Freeman. Though small and in need of painting, its owner obviously still possessed some pride of property, as evidenced by the fragrant wildflower garden that bordered the well-weeded front path, and the pots of blooming geraniums that lined the steps to the front porch. The door was opened by a plump woman on a scooter chair, her silver hair immaculately coiffed, her print dress neatly ironed. She beamed up at them, her smile gradually fading as she saw what they offered.

"Hi," began Derrick cheerfully. "My name is Derrick, and this is my friend Paul. We're from—"

"Meals with Love, I know," said the woman with a resigned sigh. She backed the scooter away from the door. "I suppose you might as well come in."

Paul and Derrick exchanged an uncertain look, then followed her through the small, cluttered house to the kitchen, where a yellow enamel table was scattered with magazines and unopened mail, and the sink was filled with dishes. The house smelled of pine cleaner and neglect.

"I don't suppose they remembered my lemon pie," said Abigail. "They never do. The one thing I always ask for, I don't know why they can't remember."

"Well," said Derrick, summoning enthusiasm, "I'm sure this will be delicious, even without the pie."

"I'm sorry the place is such a mess," she said. "It's not as easy for me to get around to things as it once was. But if you'd sit a spell, I'll bet I could find a teapot and a couple of cups."

She looked so cautiously hopeful that it was hard for Paul to say, "Well, we do have quite a few more meals to deliver ..." And when her expression turned to the kind of forgiving resignation that spoke of how very many times she had heard that excuse before, he added quickly, "But we'd love to visit with you for a few minutes while you eat your lunch."

Her face lit up with excitement. "I'll start the tea. I might even have a box of gingersnaps around here somewhere that hasn't gone too stale."

Derrick began clearing the table. "Now, Miss Abigail, don't you worry about that. We're here to serve you."

She beamed at him. "Well aren't you sweet? It does get lonesome all by a body's self, and it's nice to have company. I just wish the food was a tad more on the tasty side."

Paul placed the plate on the table in the spot Derrick had cleared. "I'm sure you'll enjoy what we brought today. Let's see what we have here. Why, look ..." He peeled back the foil. "We've got creamed carrots, creamed, um, spinach, some nice ..." He examined the entree closely. "Nice, um, chicken ..."

"Turkey," corrected Derrick, sotto voce.

"Right, turkey in gravy ... shall I cut it for you?"

"And some really, really lovely bread and peanut butter," added Derrick enthusiastically, smiling as broadly as possible. "Please, Miss Abigail, just give it a try. Just pull your chair up here, right next to the table, I'll find some silverware ..."

The older woman looked at the offering with barely disguised dismay, then lifted innocent, faded blue eyes to them. "But I couldn't possibly eat all this by myself," she said. "Please, bring three plates. I insist on sharing."

Paul looked at Derrick. Derrick smiled weakly. "Maybe," he said in a tone very similar to the one Sydney Carlton might have used when facing his executioner, "just a taste."

"It was unspeakable," Paul told Harmony that evening over Purline's baked hen and oven-roasted potatoes served with sliced yellow tomatoes in a balsamic vinaigrette. "The spinach was …" he suppressed a shudder, "canned."

They dined on the enclosed porch where once dozens had enjoyed Sunday brunch accompanied by Paul's creative cocktails, trying to ignore the dismal sight of all those tables and chairs stacked in the corners and the way their voices echoed around the empty room. The windows were open to an evening twilight and a light breeze caused the candle flame to dance inside its hurricane globe. The peaceful vista of the winding stone paths and distant mountains was broken only by the sound of a half dozen yapping dogs, who had apparently finished their own dinners and were looking for something to do. Everyone at the table pretended to ignore them.

"Please," said Derrick with a small groan. "I'm trying to eat."

"And it was creamed in …" He swallowed hard. "Evaporated milk."

Derrick put down his fork, forced to clear the memory with a sip of wine.

"Well," said Harmony practically, helping herself to another slice of chicken, "that's what they have at the food bank."

Paul said, "Food bank?"

"Of course. That's where the food for these kinds of programs comes from."

"My guess would have been prison," said Derrick.

Paul sighed. "The worst part was, I don't think our supervisor was very happy with us at all. We were three hours late getting back, but what were we to do? The conditions that some of these poor things lived in were appalling. Naturally we had to tidy up a bit before we served the food—and I use that term loosely."

"They were so lonely," added Derrick. "The only hope we had of getting them to eat that awful fare was if we stayed to chat with them."

At that moment one of the kittens launched herself onto the window screen and clung there, tail twitching, like a lizard on a wall. Derrick quickly jumped up and pried her off, checking the screen for damage before releasing the kitten to the floor, where it scampered away as though a bear were in hot pursuit.

"You know," observed Harmony wisely, "you really can't keep those dogs locked up like that much longer. Even if they do have the run of the place during the day, they are starting to complain about the accommodations."

Derrick gave her a dry look as he resumed his seat. "So I noticed."

"Next on our agenda," Paul assured her. He transferred a slice of tomato that was easily the size of a melon onto his plate. "Unfortunately they only gave us credit for three hours work today—which was how long our route should have taken, according to the driver who had it before us." He sliced the tomato and made an appreciative sound as he tasted it. "Entirely possible, I suppose," he added, "if all one did was drop off the food and didn't even wait for the clients to toss it in the trash bin."

"It's so sad to think about people having to live like that when we have so much," Derrick said, delicately buttering a corner of one of Purline's homemade biscuits. "I'm just not sure I can face it again tomorrow."

Paul paused in the act of cutting another bite of tomato and looked up at Derrick, the light of an idea slowly beginning to dawn in his eyes.

"That's right," he said, "we do."

The next morning they bounced up the rutted dirt drive again, and the aromas that came from the wicker basket between them made even their mouths water. There was a lasagna made with tomatoes fresh from the garden, chicken salad with apples and walnuts, a fresh vegetable medley, and cornbread still warm from the oven. The only thing marring the heavenly aromas that filled the car came from the backseat, where the bulldog mix Derrick had dubbed Gaston paced excitedly back and forth, panting his foul-smelling breath from one window to the next.

"I'm sure this is against some health code," Paul complained. "Why did you have to bring him anyway?"

"Harmony says when you save a life you're responsible for it," Derrick replied, jaw set stubbornly. "And she's right. The dogs deserve to get out once in a while, even if it is only to go for a ride."

Paul pulled the car up in front of the ramshackle house, set the brake, and picked up the basket. But when Derrick went around to open the back door, he put his hand up firmly. "The dog," he told him, "stays in the car. We're breaking enough rules as it is."

Trying to disguise their trepidation with determinedly squared shoulders, they marched up the steps and knocked loudly on the door. Paul stepped back quickly, protecting his shins, when it was finally opened.

Mr. Briggs glared at them. "You again." He actually spat on the floor, barely missing one of Derrick's oxblood loafers. "What do you want?"

Derrick took the basket from Paul and thrust it through the door. "We felt bad that you didn't get anything to eat yesterday," he said.

"So we brought something we hope you like better," Paul said.

"You can keep the basket," added Derrick, and started to back away.

The old man opened the basket suspiciously and peered inside. He broke off a piece of cornbread and stuffed it in his mouth. "Hey," he said, yellow flecks of cornbread dripping from his lips, "this ain't bad." He peeled back the lid on the chicken salad container and scooped out a bite on two fingers. He tasted it. "Not bad at all."

Paul smiled, relieved, and Derrick said, "We're glad you like it. Bon appetit."

They started to turn and go down the steps, but Mr. Briggs stopped them with a sharp, "Hey!"

They turned back cautiously.

"What's that you got there?"

After a moment they realized that he was peering at the ugly little bulldog who was bouncing in the backseat of the car, fogging up the window with his breath and clawing at the glass. His expression was wistful. "I used to have me a dog like that. Best friend I ever did have."

Paul looked at Derrick, an idea clearly dawning in his eyes. Derrick turned to the man in the doorway. "Mr. Briggs," he said, "would you like to meet Gaston?"

On Ladybug Farm

"So you know Paul," Bridget said, "he never saw a need he couldn't meet, an occasion he couldn't rise to …"

"A scene he couldn't overplay," supplied Cici. "And Derrick, God bless him, is even worse."

Bridget grinned. "Right," Bridget said. She set a platter of peanut butter cookies on the wicker table as she settled into her rocking chair on the front porch. "After the success with Mr. Briggs, they went back over the entire route with plates from their own kitchen—and may I say, I'm talking about real china—filled with leftovers from dinner and baskets of fresh vegetables from their garden. Everyone was so appreciative that they did it again the next day, and the next."

"The perfect solution," said Lindsay, nodding approval. "They're overwhelmed with all that produce, and that poor cook of theirs has already filled two freezers and a pantry."

"Not entirely perfect," Cici pointed out, "unless they're going to start their own lunch program. I mean, they can't keep it up forever."

Bridget chuckled. "I think that girl they've got working for them let them know the long and short of that on the second day. By the end of the week she was cooking lunch for forty-two people! Still, I think they would have found a way to keep it up if their supervisor hadn't caught on. It seems there was a sixty-eight percent increase in applications for the program virtually overnight, and she got suspicious. It didn't take much snooping to find out they were taking the lunches from the Meals with Love kitchen, tossing them in the dumpster, and substituting their own."

Lindsay groaned. "Oh, don't tell me she's pressing charges. If they have to go back to court ..."

Bridget laughed. "No chance. The people in the program would have her lynched. No, she wrote off the rest of their community service hours in exchange for the promise that they wouldn't come back."

Lindsay stretched over Cici to help herself to a couple of cookies. "Now that's what I call a happy ending. And ...," she toasted Bridget with a cookie, "we got a few benefits too."

Bridget shrugged it off. The cookies were left over from the six dozen she had baked, along with a lemon pie and an angel food cake, to accompany the lunch plates. "It was the least I could do."

"I do feel sorry for the people on their route though," Cici said. "Now they have to go back to that awful dreck they were eating before."

Bridget raised a cautionary finger. "Not entirely. Paul and Derrick are donating their excess produce to the food bank, and as every cook knows, a good meal starts with fresh ingredients. Not to mention the fact that as soon as the restaurant opens again,

Paul and Derrick will be delivering the leftovers from brunch to everyone on their route on Sunday afternoons—served on fine china with cloth napkins, of course." She added, "It's no trouble for me to bake an extra cake or pie for the weekend, and we might get some of the other ladies in town to contribute."

"Well now, that really *is* a happy ending," Cici said, raising her wine glass. "To our friends—the nicest guys I know!"

The other two clinked glasses and drank, and then Bridget said, swallowing hastily, "And you didn't even hear the best part. You know all those animals?"

Cici looked at her suspiciously. "Yes."

"They're all gone! They found homes for each and every one of them. Purline took the little poodle, which," Bridget conceded reluctantly, "proves she's got a good heart, I suppose. And the rest of them went to the people on their route who were starving for someone to love and look after—and to look after them. All except one, of course."

She reached down and scooped up the kitten formerly known as Mr. Mestopheles, who had been twining through her ankles. She smiled as she snuggled him against her face. "I think," she said, "I'll call him Ratatouille."

EIGHT

There are only two tragedies in life: one is not getting what one wants, and the other is getting it.

Oscar Wilde

Josh was almost out of minutes. Every time he looked at the counter on his cell phone, what he thought was, *Almost out of time, almost out of time ...* And then the panic would rise in him in waves, choking off his breath and clouding his vision with a red haze. He had called information for the number of every name he could remember, but who had a landline anymore? Finally he remembered Leda's cousin Lenny had been working at the Twelfth Street Pizza Hut before he left, and he took a wild shot and called there. Of course Lenny had been fired months ago, but the assistant manager who answered the phone happened to know him and happened, also, to think the firing was less than righteous, and when Josh told him he was an old friend, he gave up Lenny's cell number without hesitation.

Josh was down to twelve minutes on his phone when Lenny answered. "Lenny, this is Josh. Josh Whitman, you remember me."

A hesitation while Lenny's brain, whose synapses had never been particularly fast to fire even when he wasn't high, made the connection. Then he said, "Josh, my man! Last I heard you was in the pen."

"Yes, that's right. I'm out now."

Josh breathed out a long slow breath and let his heartbeat return to normal. They had stopped at a Laundromat just outside of Hayesville, Kansas, because the last two campgrounds they'd pulled into had not had laundry facilities and Artie insisted he was running out of clean shorts. It killed Josh to be so close—a day and a half of driving at most, but what could he do? Even when he got to Kansas City, he had no idea how to find Leda, so he'd tried to use the time, and a good cell phone signal, productively. Finally it had paid off.

He drew in a shallow breath of humid, bleach-scented air and walked quickly to the glass front of the building, away from the sound of the radio playing in the background and the rhythmic click and clack of the driers. Artie was sitting in one of scuffed plastic chairs, smiling and nodding to himself as he read a magazine, and a tired-looking woman in denim shorts was folding laundry on the table in the middle of the room. Josh could see them both reflected in the window against the night background of a rain-washed parking lot and a neon sign across the street promising quick title loans. "Listen, Lenny, I'm trying to find—"

"You're out, that right? Hey, man, that's great! You in town, man? You looking for some first-class stuff?"

"No, I don't … what I mean is, I'm looking for Leda. I tried calling her but her phone doesn't work."

"Hey, man, she can't afford no phone. Her old man done left her with all them kids to feed and she can't barely even feed herself, man. I do my part, you know what I'm sayin', but a man's gotta take care of himself too, man. What you want with her, anyhow?"

Josh's hand tightened on the phone until he was very much in danger of cracking the case. Lenny had never been a very reliable source of information, and if he really didn't know why Josh was looking for Leda, he could hardly be counted on to know much else. But Josh had to try. "Listen," he said, "is she still in that little house down on Beaumont?"

"Oh, hell, no, man, she got kicked out of there back in April, you know what I'm saying? No rent-y, no sleep-y." He cackled at his own bad joke.

Josh struggled to keep his voice calm. He thought that if he could reach through the phone he would have had Lenny by his scrawny neck by now. "You happen to know where she went?"

"I guess I do, man. Ain't I been crashing on her floor for the past month myself?"

Every muscle in Josh's body sagged with relief. *Thank you, Jesus,* he thought, and then, in almost the same instant, *Let it be true.* Knowing Lenny, his memories of the past month could have actually taken place a year or more ago. Josh hoped he sounded calm and casual as he said, "That's cool. I was thinking about dropping around to see her. You too, if you're there. You got the address?"

"Yeah, she's over at the Bluebird Apartments on Howard Street, man. Number 212. It's a dump, but it's a roof, you know what I'm saying. Listen, you come see me and I'll fix you up with some first-class stuff, man. You in town?"

"Thanks, Lenny." There was more he wanted to say, more he wanted to know, but he was down to five minutes. He could ask the questions, but he was afraid of the answers. He had to see Leda. That was all that mattered. "Thanks a lot. Listen, Lenny ... tell Leda I called, okay? If you see her, tell her I'm on my way. Can you do that?"

"Yeah, sure man, I'll tell her. Course, I don't know when I'll see her again. Don't know what happened to her after the landlord kicked her out. All them kids, too."

"What?" A wash of cold drained through Josh and his voice was hoarse. "Are you saying she's not at the Bluebird any more?"

"Hell, man, how should I know? I ain't seen her in weeks."

No, no, no no .... His fist tightened on the phone until his knuckled went white. "Damn it, Lenny, you just told me you'd been sleeping on her floor for a month!"

"Well, I guess that was a while back. I don't know where she went after that. But I tell you what, when you get here, you be sure to look me up, man. I'll fix you up with some first-class stuff."

Josh was breathing hard when he jabbed the disconnect button and thrust the phone back into his pocket. *So close, so close …*

"Damn it," he whispered through lips that felt numb and dry. *"Damn it."*

He wanted to put his fist through the plate glass window. He wanted to tear every machine in the place out of the wall. He wanted to scream his rage at the top of his lungs, and keep on screaming. He wanted to cry.

Instead he did what he always did, what had gotten him through those last dark months of prison, what had kept him walking when his feet were bleeding, what had kept him alive even after he'd thought the reason for living was gone. What had made his heart smile even when it was broken.

He reached into his pocket for the photo, but it wasn't there. He checked the other pocket, and then he remembered. It was in his other jeans. He had changed because Artie had insisted on washing …

He whirled around and saw Artie, no longer in the plastic chair, pulling wet laundry from one of the washing machines and transferring it to a dryer. He charged forward, shouting, "What did you do? God damn it, what did you *do*?"

He shoved the startled little man away from the machine and reached inside, flinging damp articles of clothing on the floor until he found the jeans he was looking for. The woman at the folding table stared at him, looking alarmed, but he barely noticed. He untangled the wet jeans with frantic, clumsy motions and wedged his fingers inside the front pocket, the pocket where he always kept it, and what his fingers caught was a wad of damp, shredded paper. His lips formed the word "No" but he wasn't sure he actually said it. He pulled the shredded scraps out because he had to. He stared at the mess in his hand, all bleached and soggy and balled together. There was nothing left to save.

Nothing.

Artie came up next to him, looking puzzled. "Did you leave something in the pocket, son?"

Something white hot and sharp-pointed rushed through him and erupted from his throat with an inarticulate roar. Somehow Artie was against the wall and Josh had fistfuls of his shirt twisted in his fingers and he was screaming, "Do you know what you've done, you stupid son of a bitch? You had no right! Do you hear me, *you had no right*!" And suddenly it wasn't Artie's small, misshapen face in front of him, but his dad's. It wasn't Artie's mild, startled hazel eyes he was looking into but his stepfather's swollen, bloodshot brown ones, streaked with grief and helplessness. The sound he heard in his ears was no longer his own ragged breathing but the sound of broken sobs echoing down the cold white corridor of an empty past.

Josh stepped away abruptly, releasing Artie's shirt. He was dimly aware that the woman at the table had taken out her phone and was punching three digits, keeping a wary eye on him as she did so. A quavery kind of tension still sang through his veins, a mixture of terror, grief, and rage, and he brought the back of his hand to his mouth uncertainly, blotting the spittle that had caught at the corner of his lips.

Artie said, "What's wrong, Josh?" And there was nothing more than gentle concern in his tone, or his voice. "You okay?"

Josh's throat was in a clutch and he couldn't have answered if he'd wanted to. He pushed through the door of the Laundromat and out into the hot wet night just as the girl was putting away her phone. He heard Artie call his name but he just squeezed his eyes shut, shoved his hands deep into his empty pockets, and kept on walking.

The Grand Old Opry turned out to be everything Annabelle had hoped it would be, and Megan, who had not expected anything at all, enjoyed herself mostly because her grandmother did. Afterwards they took a bus tour of the music district that included lunch at Jimmy Buffet's restaurant, and, despite the fact that Annabelle was laughing and clapping along with the live music just like everyone else, she left her cheeseburger mostly untouched and Megan could tell she was exhausted by the time they returned to the hotel room.

Annabelle was in the shower when Megan's mother called. She had taken to turning off her phone during the day and simply checking in with her mother in the evenings. It was much simpler that way. Nonetheless, she knew without checking there would be three or four messages from her mother if she took the trouble to look. "Hi, Mom," she said as she sank down onto the corner of her bed and kicked off her shoes. "I was just going to call you back. We've been touring Nashville all day and there wasn't—"

"Nick called me," her mother said in a voice that was tight and clipped. "He said you weren't answering your phone. He tried calling your grandmother's house but of course there was no answer. He was afraid something was wrong. So he called me."

Megan closed her eyes and exhaled slowly through her nose. She could feel her throat start to tighten and there was a heavy, thudding knot in her chest where her heart used to be.

"Imagine my surprise when I realized he had no idea you had taken off on your little madcap road trip," her mother went on coolly. "And imagine how foolish I felt when he told me you hadn't been living together for almost two months. When were you going to tell me, Meg? Ever?"

Megan said, with her eyes still closed. "I'm sorry, Mother. I thought …"

"What *did* you think, Megan?" Her mother's voice was approaching shrill. "Or did you think at all? Could you tell me that for just once? Then maybe I'll be able to sleep tonight!"

"I thought," Megan managed, with her eyes still closed, "we could work things out."

As her mother's voice grew more strident, Megan's voice grew smaller, quieter. In fact, her whole presence seemed to shrink, curling into itself like one of those human-sized balloon dolls that was slowly losing its air, until she knew that in another sentence, maybe two, there would be nothing of her left except the withered remnants of what she should have said.

So when her mother replied sharply, "Well, it didn't sound to me as though that was going to happen any time soon!" Megan opened her eyes. And she saw her grandmother standing at the open door of the bathroom, wrapped in her fluffy pink robe with the legs of her silk pajamas just visible below the hem, watching her with interest.

Megan drew a breath. "What did Nick call about, Mom?"

"He said his lawyer had some papers for you to sign. You can just imagine what papers those might be! The minute he mentioned lawyer, that's when I knew something was wrong. Something my own daughter hadn't even bothered to tell me about when we were standing in the same room together, when we talk on the phone every day, when ..."

Megan said, "Thanks, Mom. I'll call him back." Her eyes were on her grandmother, who nodded approvingly. "Everything is fine here. Gram sends her love. I'll check in with you tomorrow. Good night."

She disconnected and hesitated for a moment before checking her call log. There were three missed calls from Nick. He hadn't left a message on any of them.

So then, she thought, and the pit of pain that opened up inside her was bottomless and cold and empty. *It's over.* But what had she expected?

Annabelle sat on the edge of her own bed, wedged off her slippers, and swung her feet up slowly onto the bed, using her hands to guide the leg that was stiffest. She propped up the pillows behind her back and reached for the remote control, flipping through the channels until she found a home renovation show they both liked. Megan slipped on her shoes.

"I think I'll go down to the bar for a little while," she said.

"Bring me a gin and tonic, will you, sweetie?"

Megan forced a wooden smile as she bent to fasten her sandals. "Sure thing."

"The problem with your mother is that she's afraid," said Annabelle conversationally, and that was when Megan realized her grandmother had not turned up the volume on the television. "Afraid things will sneak up on her, get out of control, behave unpredictably. That's why she's such a pain about everything, really. She's just trying to keep life manageable."

Megan straightened up slowly, one sandal yet unbuckled. Her grandmother's eyes were on the television, her finger on the remote control.

"It was my fault, of course. I taught her—I taught all my children, really—that the world was an uncertain place and that they must always be wary of what lurks around the next corner. I didn't mean to. I thought I was protecting them. But it turns out, you can only teach what you know. And what I knew was the uncertainty and insecurity of a fatherless child."

Megan smiled tightly, and even that effort felt as though it might crack her face. "Mother has never seemed to me to be particularly insecure."

"Of course not. You never let the enemy see your weakness."

That surprised Megan. "The enemy?" There was a note of amusement in her voice. "Are you saying my own mother sees me as an enemy?" Although, as she thought about it, the idea did not seem completely unreasonable.

"She sees life as the enemy. By the time I realized that it was too late to undo the damage, which is probably why I tried so hard to make sure you were better equipped than either she or I ever were to deal with whatever life threw your way." Annabelle smiled a little, dryly. "That was my intention, dear. I'm sorry if it didn't work out that way."

"Oh, Gram." Megan let her shoulders sag. "The things that are wrong with my life now have nothing to do with you. Or with Mom, as much as I'd like to blame her. I managed to screw this up all by myself."

She could feel her grandmother's eyes on her, but Megan could not turn to look at her. She took a breath, and she said softly, "Nick wants a divorce."

"I take it you don't."

Megan shook her head. Until that moment she hadn't even asked herself what she wanted. Now at least she knew, but she wasn't entirely sure that was a good thing.

Annabelle said practically, "Do you think there is anything you can do to change his mind?"

Again, Megan shook her head, her throat too tight to speak.

"Do you mind if I ask why?"

Megan drew in a shallow breath through her nose. She said in a small voice, "Nick thinks I had an affair."

There was no reply for a moment. Then Annabelle said, "Did you?"

Megan was silent for a long moment, and then she started to cry.

Josh made it as far as a Waffle House two blocks away before the pain and adrenaline gave way to shame. He took an empty booth and ordered chili fries and coffee. The waitress refilled his coffee cup twice while he let the fries grow cold. He tried to eat, but every time he picked up his fork he felt as though he might choke. How the hell had he managed to screw everything up so badly? Again?

He was not at all surprised when Artie slid into the bench opposite him. He barely even looked up. "How'd you find me?" he said.

Artie returned in that jovial way of his, "It wasn't that hard. You couldn't get far with your feet in the shape they're in, and this was the first place that served coffee. I'll have a cup, black, if you don't mind," he added to the waitress who'd stopped by, "and a grilled cheese sandwich would hit the spot on a wet night like this. How about you, Josh? You want a sandwich?"

Josh muttered, "Nah, I'm good."

He lifted one of the soggy fries with his fingers and let it fall again while he waited for the waitress to return with the coffee, not meeting Artie's eyes. She set a mug of coffee before Artie and topped off Josh's cup. When she was gone, Josh sat back, cradling his mug in his hands, and looked at Artie.

"Seems like I'm always saying I'm sorry to you," he said. "And you're always finding me so I can say it."

Artie gave a little shrug, smiling. "You know what they say—good things will chase you down if you let them. Seeing as how it was you that found me the last time, there just might be some truth to that."

Josh frowned, too low and dispirited and tired of it all to even try to figure out what that meant. "What are you doing here, Artie?"

"Just getting out of the rain, is all," replied the other man, sipping his coffee as he settled back against the booth. "My, that's good coffee. What about you? What are you doing?"

It was a long time before Josh could summon up the energy to reply. "Giving up," he said at last, heavily. "I'm just sitting here ... giving up."

Artie seemed unsurprised. "Harder than you thought, huh?"

Josh picked up another french fry, twirled it in some cheese, and let it drop back to the plate. "Yeah," he said. "Just like everything else in my life."

They sat for a while, surrounded by the fragrance of fried food and hot coffee, the clatter of the kitchen and the hum of voices, and then Artie said, "You know how many pioneers in the old west died of thirst in the desert?"

Josh sighed. "No."

Artie started to say something, thought about it, and admitted, "Well, neither do I. But I do know how many documented reports there were of people who died of thirst within fifty feet of water. Two hundred fifty-nine. Can you imagine? They came all the way across the country on foot, on horseback, in covered wagons. They left most of what they loved behind. They buried children, husbands, wives, and parents on the journey. And they gave up when they only had fifty feet to go."

"Let me tell you something, Artie," Josh said without looking up, "and you can take this to the bank. Even if that story is true, not one of those two hundred fifty-nine people gave up because they thought it was too much trouble to try to make it to the watering hole, or because they didn't think it was worth it, or because they thought they'd just sit there and think about it for a while before going on. They gave up because they'd already given everything they had and they couldn't go another step. They gave up because they had no choice. Because that was the only thing left to do."

The waitress came with Artie's grilled cheese, and he dug into it with gusto, giving Josh alert, interested glances between bites. Finally he said, "So what is it, exactly, that you're giving up on, if you don't mind my asking?" And when Josh gave no reply, he suggested, "Yourself?"

Josh made a small sound that might, under other circumstances, have been a smothered laugh. He shook his head, slowly, once. "I gave up on that a long time ago."

"Is that a fact?"

"Yeah." Josh let out a breath. "That's a fact."

He glanced at Artie, seemed to debate with himself for a moment, and then sank back against the booth. "What the hell. I guess I owe you the truth, at least. For your human nature study."

Artie's expression went soft with delight. "Why, I would be obliged. Truly."

Josh picked up his coffee, started to take a sip, and put the cup down again. He met Artie's gaze. Artie gave him a brief, encouraging nod and took a bite of his sandwich.

Josh said, "Things went downhill after my mom died. I emptied out my savings account and lived on that for a couple of years. A lot of it went to drugs. That's how I met Eva. She was a sweet girl, no more messed up than I was, but fragile, you know? She needed taking care of. The funny thing is, I got straight because of her. Because I was afraid if I didn't, something would happen to her and I wouldn't be able to stop it. You know how some people, even messed-up people, are just good for each other? It was like that with us. With me, she wasn't messed up. She even managed to stay clean for a while, a long while, and it almost felt like we could have a normal life. We were living with her sister in Kansas City, a nice woman with a husband and kids and everything, and I got a job—no big shakes, just managing the computer department of one of those big electronics stores, but it was real money coming in. Enough for us to move out, get married, the whole enchilada. The only problem was, she couldn't stay away from her old friends. She had a baggie full of cocaine in her purse when the cops pulled us over that night. She said it wasn't hers, she was just holding it for a friend, and the thing is, that was probably the truth, but it didn't matter. I couldn't let her go to jail, so I put the baggie under my seat and told the cops it was mine."

Artie nodded thoughtfully as he took a bite of his sandwich, looking interested but nothing more. "That was pretty noble."

"It wasn't noble." He took a gulp of his coffee. It tasted bitter in the back of his throat. "It was what I had to do." He put down the cup. "I made sure she got back to her sister and had a place to live while I was doing my time. There wasn't much I could do for her while I was locked up, but her sister Leda was a good person and I knew she'd do the best she could until I could get there."

"So that's who you're trying so hard to get to in Kansas City." Artie smile. "Your girl, Eva."

Josh was silent for a long moment before he shook his head. "She died two months before I got out. Overdose." His lips compressed bitterly. "I went to jail for her. And she couldn't stay straight two more lousy months." He gave a small sharp shake of his head, as though to fling off the thought. "She always said she couldn't do it without me. I guess she was right."

Artie put down his sandwich. His small hazel eyes were rich with understanding. "Ah," he said, "no wonder you're so angry. Betrayed by everyone you've ever loved."

Josh didn't even bother to answer that. "She sent me a picture. It was the last thing I had from her. I made sure I always kept with me, no matter what else I lost. It was like having her with me. It was all I had."

Artie nodded slowly. "You kept the picture of Eva in your jeans."

Josh looked up at him, his expression bleak. "The picture wasn't of Eva," he said. "It was of our little girl. My daughter."

Megan blew her nose, balled up the soggy tissue, and pressed the heels of her hands against her wet, swollen eyes. "At first it was the two of us against the world, you know," she said. "It was like …" She found a small smile as she glanced at her grandmother. "Like a great adventure, a grand quest, a quest to make our dream come true. I guess all newlyweds feel that way. But after four years, five years, six, the dream wasn't quite as shiny as it once had been, and even with both of us working day and night we were barely keeping our heads above water. We had to have some money coming in, so I started taking freelance bookkeeping jobs for some of the restaurants around town and eventually ended up managing *Coquette*. For the first time ever things started looking up for us. The business took off, we were able to buy a house, even talked about having children … although how that was going to happen I don't know since we never saw each other. Nick was working fifteen hours a day and so was I, and the thing is, it never felt as though we were working for the same thing."

Her voice was growing tired, heavy with the defeat she had been carrying around for too long. "I should have figured it out a lot sooner, I know. And maybe I did. Martin Craig, my boss, was Nick's biggest competitor, and I was spending every minute of every day with him. Nick's work was my biggest competitor, and he was spending every minute of every day, and most nights, with it. We both told ourselves we were doing it for each other, but I think we knew we were doing it to *spite* each other. Sometimes it scares me, to think how easily love can be turned on its side like that. Almost before you know it."

She looked down at her hands, somewhat surprised to realize that she had shredded the damp tissue into confetti in her palm. She balled up the pieces again. She took a breath. "I didn't have an affair with Martin Craig. But I wanted to. And when we kept working later and later at night in my office, I knew what the danger was. When he kissed me, I might not have kissed him back, but I didn't pull away. And when I looked up and saw Nick standing there, it seemed—I don't know, fair. Inevitable. Like the final rhyme in a poem. Sad, sweet, predictable."

The tears started again, and she pushed them back with her fingers. "He had come to surprise me for our anniversary. He had flowers. I'll never forget the look on his face."

Annabelle silently offered her the tissue box, and Megan pulled one out but did not use it. She simply looked at it for a moment as though having forgotten what it was for. "I could have told him there was nothing going on. I should have told him. He was waiting for me to tell him. He wanted me to tell him. But I couldn't."

"Why not, dear?" asked Annabelle softly. "Why in heaven's name not?"

Megan just shook her head. "I couldn't forget the look on his face," she whispered. "And I couldn't forgive myself for putting it there. No matter what I said or did, it wouldn't make that look go away. Some things are just ... broken. And nothing can ever make them the way they were again."

Annabelle leaned back against the pillows and opened her arms to her granddaughter. Megan crawled into her arms, her head resting on her grandmother's shoulder. They were quiet for a long time, just holding each other. Then Annabelle said, "You're right. Things between you will never be the same again. Sometimes broken things can't be fixed, and trying always leaves a scar. But sometimes the scar is what binds them together, and you'll never know until you try. You've punished yourself long enough. You have to tell your husband the truth, sweet girl. You have to tell him how you feel."

"It's too late. So much hurt, so much distance ... it wouldn't matter now."

"Do you want your marriage?"

Megan whispered, "Yes."

"Then fight for it," commanded Annabelle simply.

"I can't." Megan closed her eyes and then squeezed them tightly for a brief moment to hold back the hot blur of tears. "I'm not the kind of person who can do that. I know you always wanted me to be, I wish I could be, but … I'm not that kind of person. I just … can't."

Annabelle drew in a slow soft breath, fighting back all the things she wanted to say, wished she could say, knowing they would make no difference. It was the final curse of age and wisdom: knowing too much, and being able to do absolutely nothing about it. So in the end she squeezed her granddaughter's shoulders, kissed her hair, and held her, just as she had done when she was a child, until she fell asleep.

Josh said, "Her name is Amy. She is ..." His face, as he struggled to find the words, was so transformed that words were not even necessary. The smile that was in his heart found its way to his eyes. "It's like you can't even describe, you know? How can two such screwed-up people make something so perfect? The first time I saw her I wasn't even expecting it, what she did to me. It was like everything in the whole world changed right then and there was only one thing that mattered and that was making sure that nothing bad ever happened to her, not ever."

He glanced down at his coffee, took a sip. "She was six months old when I left. She used to laugh when she saw me, you know, like she was so happy inside just to see me walk in the room she couldn't keep it in. That's kind of the way I felt when I saw her too. Now she's almost two. She's walking." He said it with wonder. "Walking."

He took a deep breath. "The thing was, Eva had a record, but I'd never been picked up before. I thought I could get off maybe with time served. Turns out I was wrong. Anyway, a baby needs her mother and Eva had been straight for so long ... I thought she could do it. I thought for Amy's sake she could do it. Turns out I was wrong about that too."

By now the smile was completely gone from his eyes, leaving them bleak and stripped. "When Leda called to tell me about, you know, about Eva, she promised she would take care of Amy. It was only two more months. It'd been over a year and I thought Amy would be okay with her for another two months. I thought I could trust her. But in the end ..." His lips tightened, and so did his hand on the coffee cup, and so did his voice. "In the end she was just like everybody else. She boogied. With my kid. And I don't have a clue in hell as to where to start looking for her."

Artie swiped the paper napkin across his mouth, looking thoughtful. He was thoughtful for so long that Josh looked up from the depths of his coffee, waiting for Artie to say something. What Artie said was, "I was just thinking about your dad. He's a grandfather and doesn't even know it. Why didn't you call him when you were arrested, Josh? That's what families are for, to help a fellow out when he's in trouble."

Josh's jaw knotted, and he curled his fingers tightly around the handle of his coffee cup. "I was stupid," he said. "I didn't want him to know ... I thought I could handle it. Now it's too late. He doesn't want to hear from me. Not after everything … I can't go back to him. Not until I can make him proud of me again."

Josh sucked in a breath, and took a gulp of coffee. "Anyway, it doesn't matter now. All this time I thought I could make up for everything if I just got this one thing right. If I could keep this one promise to this one little person who was depending on me to make sure nothing bad ever happened to her. But I blew it. Hell, I don't even know what I was thinking, anyway. What do I know about raising a kid even if I could find her? Look at me, an ex-con, no job, no money … She's better off with Leda, wherever she is."

Another gulp of coffee, and he put the cup down. "So anyway, Artie, thanks for the ride. It's been nice knowing you." He reached into his back pocket and pulled out his last ten-dollar bill.

"That's it, huh?" The shadow of disappointment in Artie's eyes surprised Josh, and irritated him. "You're just going to give up?"

"Didn't you hear me, man?" Josh's tone was sharp; he couldn't help it. "She's gone. I don't know where to look. It's over. And don't give me any of that crap about dying fifty feet from the watering hole. If I knew where the water was, I'd go there. But I don't. It's over."

Artie sipped his coffee thoughtfully. "You know," he said, "you don't spend six years hanging out with the most famous tracker in the world without learning a thing or two. And the first thing Kit Carson taught me was that if you want to find out where somebody went, you start with where they were."

He drained the last of his coffee, slapped a twenty on the table and stood. When Josh just sat there, looking stunned and upstaged, Artie said, "Our deal was for Kansas City. Are you coming or not?"

Josh said, "I told you, she's not there. There's no point."

Artie said, "Fifty feet, my friend. Fifty feet." He moved to the door.

Josh sat there for another long moment, jaw tightening, heart racing. Then he drained his coffee in a single swallow and, for reasons he would never afterward be able to explain, he followed.

NINE

The pure and simple truth is rarely pure and never simple.

Oscar Wilde

The glow of Derrick's smug smile could have powered a small nation as he followed Paul into the kitchen, arms flung open wide as though to embrace the very air itself. "Not only did Dr. Fredericks pronounce me to be in astonishing physical condition for a man my age—astonishing, that was his exact word choice—but he said there was absolutely no sign, none whatsoever, of cardiac disease."

"Yes, I know," replied Paul, returning a quick smile as he checked his messages. "Congratulations. That's wonderful news."

"Says he of little faith." He opened the refrigerator and checked the contents. "Not only that, but he said he had never seen such a remarkable recovery in all of his years of practice. Remarkable, that was his word."

"Yes, I know. I was there, remember?"

Derrick removed a platter containing the remainder of the baked ham from the previous evening's dinner, along with a package of cheese and a loaf of fresh bread from the farmer's market. "He said my blood pressure was lower than his. Lower than yours!"

"That wouldn't surprise me a bit," Paul muttered, swiping a finger across the screen of his phone and scanning the next page.

"Purline was right," declared Derrick. He set the lunch ingredients on the stainless steel center island and went to the cupboard for plates. "It's all about fresh local food, not about how it's prepared. Where is she anyway? I want to talk to her about short ribs for dinner."

"She's right here," Purline called through the open window, "sitting on the porch snapping beans for that soup kitchen of yours. And stay out of that ham, that's for tonight's casserole. You're having cold tomato soup and egg salad sandwiches for lunch. It's in the fridge."

Purline was a bit of a fanatic about fresh air, and kept the tall windows that opened onto the porch open on all but the most stifling days. Since the back part of the house was on a separate air-conditioning unit from the guest quarters, this had not presented much of a problem so far, and Paul and Derrick were actually beginning to enjoy the fresh breezes and garden scents that blew through their living area almost constantly.

Paul went over to the window, saw Purline sitting on the porch deftly snapping green beans into a pot while reading a magazine, and said, "Thank you, Purline. But it's not a soup kitchen."

Derrick quickly put the ham back in the refrigerator and removed the soup and the egg salad, echoing, "Thank you, Purline, found it." Though he wrinkled his nose and mouthed to Paul, *Egg salad*! which was not his favorite.

Purline called, "I heard that!"

Derrick whipped his head around toward the window, staring, and Paul grinned before turning back to his phone. Everyone knew how Derrick felt about egg salad.

Recovering himself with a small shake of his head, Derrick went to the cupboard. "And you know who else was right?" he demanded. "Harmony. She told me my heart was completely healed weeks before Dr. Fredericks did. She told me I'd get a good report, remember? And she was right!"

Suddenly Paul tossed his phone onto the counter, sank down onto one of the red stools and let his head fall back in a brief gesture of despair and surrender. "Well, if she was, that was the only thing she was right about," he said bitterly. "I can't believe this."

Derrick set two woven placemats, two bowls, and two luncheon plates on the counter, looking at him curiously.

"That so-called chef she hired?" demanded Paul. "The one that's supposed to be the hottest up-and-coming young thing in the city? The one that Emeril Lagosse's friend supposedly recommended? He owns a food truck!"

Derrick fumbled for a stool and sat down heavily, slack-jawed. "But—you were going to check him out!"

"What do you think I just did?"

"I mean sooner! I mean before we hired him!"

"We've both been a little busy, in case you haven't noticed. And after Harmony said he'd been written up in the *Post* ..."

Derrick looked at him in mounting dread. "She did mean the *Washington Post*, right?"

Paul just looked helpless and defeated.

Derrick sagged back. "But—but the menu! The butternut squash risotto served with local goat cheese! The Asian pears poached in wine sauce! The grilled Chesapeake Bay scallops served over Swiss Chard and sweet corn fritters with an apple wood-smoked bacon and caramelized onion cream! The smoked trout on sweet potato cakes with a purple basil sauce and apple-carrot slaw fresh from the garden! The—"

Paul raised a hand in self-defense, groaning. "I know, I know. He probably downloaded the entire menu from the Internet. Why, oh why, didn't we take the time to go into the city and taste his food? Why did we trust our entire future to a crazy person?"

"But ... but ..." Derrick stammered, still struggling with disbelief. "Emeril ... Nancy Reagan ..."

"Oh, please! Harmony Haven knows Emeril Lagosse about as well as this, this *fraud* she hired knows crème brulee! And let's not even talk about Nancy Reagan!" Paul sat up straighter, his frustration mounting. "I haven't gotten one single RSVP from any of those celebrities she promised. Mick Jagger—"

"Keith Richards," Derrick corrected absently.

"Either one. Ryan Seacrest, Ann Curry, Heather Locklear ... Purline was right. The only stars she's ever seen were in her head."

Purline called through the window, "Maybe next time you'll listen to what a country girl has to say."

Derrick returned wearily, "Thank you, Purline."

Paul tightened his jaw. "We've got to find someone else."

"We can't! Harmony already sent him a check—and a contract! Besides, who are we going to find at this late date?"

"Well, that's just marvelous! And it is also ..." Paul pushed determinedly to his feet, "the last straw. "I've been nice. I've been polite. I've pretended to be amused by her endless stories and enchanted by her ridiculous pseudo-spiritual nonsense, I've ignored her hideous taste in clothing and don't even get me started on those absurd feather earrings! But this is beyond what even a *southern"*— he put emphasis on the word for Paul's benefit—"gentleman should be expected to tolerate. I am having it out with her once and for all."

Derrick placed a steadying hand on his arm. "We'll both have it out with her," he assured him, "as soon as you calm down. I suppose you've figured out how to fire someone you never hired?"

Paul drew a sharp breath, thought about it, then sat down hard, defeated. "Not yet," he admitted. "But I will."

"Poor old soul," said Derrick. "She meant well, I suppose. She still has to go," he assured Paul quickly, "and she had absolutely no right at all to sweep in here and take over when she didn't have the first idea what she was doing, but you have to feel sorry for her. In a way."

Paul looked very far from feeling sorry for anyone other than himself. "The worst part is I traded on the names *she* gave me to get Yeses from half the people on my list," Paul said. "Now they'll all think I'm the worst kind of name-dropper and a liar as well. My reputation is ruined."

Derrick said, "No, the worst part is that everyone who does show up is going to be eating from a food truck."

"I suppose the good news is that since Lester Carson tactfully declined to respond to our invitation yet again, at least we won't be reading about the debacle in the *Times*."

"That's true," agreed Derrick bleakly. "Only in *Southern Living, Travel and Lodging, Great B&Bs of the United States* and the travel sections of the *Atlanta Journal Constitution,* the *Washington Post,* the *Richmond Times-Dispatch* ..."

Paul held up a hand for mercy, stifling another groan. And while they were still trying to absorb the horror that lay ahead, Purline offered, "See, if you'd called Smokey's Barbecue like I told you, you wouldn't be in this fix."

Paul closed his eyes in a gesture of long-suffering forbearance. "Purline, don't you have anything at all to do besides sit on the porch and listen to private conversations?"

Derrick winced at the perfectly predictable repercussions from that, but Purline did not reply. Just as both men were starting to relax, however, the screen door slammed shut and Purline marched into the kitchen and plopped the bowl of green beans down on the counter. "It just so happens," she informed them, "I've got a gracious plenty to do, thank you very much." She jerked open the utility drawer and took out a box of kitchen matches. "And just for that, I'm not even going to tell you my good news."

Paul and Derrick looked at the matches in alarm. "What are you going to do with those matches?"

"I'm going to burn up all that trash I pulled out of the shed like you told me to," she replied impatiently, "so y'all can bring in your fancy fountains and tents and whatnot for all them fancy party folk that probably won't even show up anyhow." Glaring at them, she demanded, "Well? Do you want to hear it or not?"

Paul said meekly, "Hear what, Purline?"

"My good news." And without giving either of them a chance to reply, she drew up her shoulders, smiled broadly, and announced, "It just so happens that my cousin Trish is coming into town to see her mama on the fourteenth of August and she's staying all week. She said she'd be happy to sing a number or two at your shindig, and seeing as how it was me asking, won't even charge you a cent." Her smile grew into a grin. "How about that?"

Somehow the two men managed to almost summon up a full smile between them. "It just gets better and better," Derrick said.

"Remember that when it comes time to write my Christmas bonus check," replied Purline. "And I need somebody to keep an eye on that fire with a garden hose while I get started on supper. Are y'all going to eat your lunch, or just look at it?"

Derrick sighed. "I'm afraid I've lost my appetite, Purline. I'll come with you."

"I'll clear the table," said Paul. "I'm just not up to doing anything more useful than that."

Purline made a rather obvious effort not to roll her eyes as she tossed him the box of matches. "I'll take care of the kitchen," she said. "Y'all start the fire. Gasoline is in the garden house, next to the lawnmower," she added, as though they didn't know that—which they didn't. The only person who had been near the lawnmower since they had taken over the place was the boy they had hired to mow the lawn once a week.

"We could always ask Bridget," Derrick suggested, uncoiling the garden hose.

"I'd sooner die," Paul said. "After all she's done for us?"

"I suppose it is a bit much," Derrick agreed unhappily.

"Besides," Paul added when he returned from the garden house with a red plastic gallon can marked "gasoline," "she already turned me down."

Derrick dragged the garden hose over to the pile of rotting wood, empty crates, cardboard boxes and unidentifiable detritus that Purline had piled up outside the shed they had used as a temporary kennel for the dogs before they were happily re-homed. "That reminds me," Derrick said. "I stopped by and took Mr. Briggs some of Purline's cake yesterday. His granddaughter was there. She comes over just about every day now to play with the dog."

For a moment, the preoccupation melted from Paul's face. "Now, that's nice," he said. "He was just lonely, that was all. Now he's got a dog and a family to keep him company."

Derrick frowned a little. "He renamed the dog Butch. Why do people do that?"

Paul declined to answer, nudging the pile of trash with his foot. "What is all this stuff? Why did we never notice it before?"

"Spiders," Derrick reminded him, and Paul, remembering, stepped back.

"Well, we're going to have to think of something," Paul said, unscrewing the top of the gas can. "It's too late to cancel. Stand back." He started splashing gasoline over the trash pile.

"Y'all be careful and don't set the shed on fire!" Purline called from the back porch, watching them worriedly.

"That would be one solution," Paul muttered. "Grand opening canceled due to fire."

"Don't even think it. Hold on a minute." Derrick carefully extracted a piece of lumber from the pile and began to poke through the rubble, turning over pieces of plywood and pushing aside an old lampshade. "There might be something interesting in here."

"Well, if there ever was it's in pieces now."

"I suppose so." Derrick poked again at the pile, revealing a section of colorfully painted fence boards.

Paul struck a match.

"Wait!" Derrick shouted, and launched himself at his startled friend, snatching the match from his hand and flinging it to the ground, stomping on it until it was out.

Paul cried, "Are you crazy?"

And from the porch Purline gave a little scream and called, "What? What happened? Who's hurt? I should've known better than to trust you with fire!" She started running toward them.

Derrick, ignoring them both, dived into the rubble pile. He emerged, his trousers smudged, smelling of gasoline, stumbling through the debris and holding the painted fence section carefully in both hands just as Purline arrived. "Purline!" he demanded excitedly. "Where did you find this? You can't possibly have meant to throw this away!"

She looked at him in disbelief, breathing hard. "You mean I ran all the way across the yard over some piece of board that that Harmony woman scribbled on? I thought you was about to set yourself on fire!"

Derrick said, controlling his emotion with an obvious effort, "Harmony didn't paint this. Just tell me, where did you find it?"

She scowled. "In the shed along with all that other scrap lumber. I've got work to do."

Derrick murmured, "From the outrageous to the absolutely sublime."

Paul, reading Derrick's expression, came to look over his shoulder. Though faded and stained with mud and a collection of other unidentifiable substances, the painting could be recognized as a rendering of child with a round face and curly hair. The strokes were broad, the interpretation simple, but it did have a certain unsophisticated charm to it. In the background, with absolutely no effort made at perspective at all, was what might have been the front porch of the Hummingbird House.

Paul said, "I hate to agree with Purline, but it does look like something Harmony would paint."

"But it's not," Derrick said, in his element now. "This painting is at least eighty years old. "You can tell by the paint—pigment boiled in linseed oil. See how the red has held up? The artist was using barn paint. A lot of them did back in the twenties and thirties. They couldn't afford the expensive vermilions, and cadmium was still new—relatively, anyway—and a lot of artists didn't trust it." He held the board at arm's length, studying it. "I like this. It reminds me of something from the Hogpen Montana school."

Paul regarded the painting with new appreciation. "In *our* shed?"

Purline looked skeptical. "Do you mean to tell me you have to go to school to learn to draw like that? My third grader could do better."

Derrick chuckled. "Hogpen Montana was a famous folk artist during the Depression. A lot of people copied his style, and some of them became famous too. That's why they call it a school."

Purline gave a sniff of disdain. "Hogpen is about where it belongs, if you ask me. And don't you even think about bringing that filthy thing in the house. Wash it off with the hose first."

Derrick just grinned at her. "Purline, you are a wonder. If this does turn out to be any good, that Christmas bonus of yours might be bigger than you thought."

Now she looked interested. "Well, I can't say I mind the sound of that." She turned to go back to the house, and then looked back. "Speaking of that woman, when you get ready to give her the heave-ho, be sure to tell her to pick up her toys before she goes. She left her painting things sitting out on the patio like she was expecting her mama to come clean up after her, and then tore out of here without so much of a by-your-leave." She gave a disgusted shake of her head. "Some folks have got no consideration at all."

Paul was nudging the lumber pile with his foot, murmuring, "I wonder what else is in here." But then he looked at Purline. "On the patio, you say?"

Derrick met his gaze of sudden consternation, and asked Purline, "The one underneath the kitchen window?"

Purline said, "That's where she paints every day. But she usually takes her things inside when she's finished."

Derrick's expression grew troubled as he turned back to Paul. "You don't suppose she heard us talking about her, do you?"

A dark flush of embarrassment crept up Paul's face and his gaze was filled with dismay as he looked toward the circular stone patio that sat directly beneath the open kitchen window. It was surrounded by an herb border, with graceful paths opening up onto the wildflower garden. In the center of the patio was an abandoned easel and a watercolor pad dotted with splotches that might have been meant to represent flowers. But no Harmony.

"I think," said Paul miserably, "that would be a very good guess."

Annabelle seemed tired to Megan. But then again, Megan was tired too, having driven almost straight through from Tennessee to the Virginia border. She had thought her grandmother would like to stop and meander through the Great Smokey Mountains National Park or wander off the beaten path to take in some of the historical sites along the way, but Annabelle seemed to have lost interest in side trips. As they grew closer to their destination—though where, exactly, that was, neither one of them was sure—Annabelle became more focused and more eager. By contrast, Megan could feel the dread rising in her chest with every mile that spun under the wheels of the big old Town Car. The closer they grew to Virginia, the closer they grew to the end of the journey. And Nick. And everything she must face there.

Oddly—or at least it seemed so to Megan—her grandmother had not mentioned the troubled marriage again. In a way, Megan was disappointed. It was almost as though she had expected her grandmother, who had always had the answer for everything, to tell her what to do to make it right, to fix everything with a word or a wave of her hand, just as she had always done. But Megan was clearly too old to rely on magic words, and some things simply could not be fixed.

They stopped at the Virginia welcome station and the rise of Annabelle's excitement was palpable as she exclaimed over depictions of historic sites she remembered from childhood, flipped through books and brochures, tasted parched peanuts fresh from the shell and even picked up a package of smoked ham, grinning as she hugged it to her chest.

"I hope you get the chance to leave home someday, sweetheart," she said, "just so you can know what it's like to come back again."

Megan watched her indulgently, smiling. "Why did you wait so long, Gram? You could have come back here any time. You've flown out to see me a dozen times over the years and Virginia is just a minute away. We could have gotten in the car and taken the tour any time you wanted."

Annabelle just shook her head, looking wistful. "It wouldn't have been as sweet back then. There's only one last trip home."

Megan drew a breath to say something, but there was nothing she could have said that wouldn't have sounded silly and inconsequential. Her grandmother saved her the trouble. "We're going to find a room with a kitchenette tonight," she declared, holding up the package of ham, "and in the morning I'll make us eggs and Virginia ham for breakfast."

"And canned biscuits?"

Annabelle's eyes twinkled at Megan's perfectly deadpan expression. Canned biscuits had been a staple with Megan's mother, morning, noon, and night, which was one of the first things that had led to Megan's interest in learning to bake.

Annabelle slipped her arm through Megan's with a wink. "Come on," she said. "The least we can do is send your mother a postcard and let her know we made it this far."

Megan could not suppress a chuckle. "I'd love to see the look on her face when she gets it."

They spent a pleasant five or ten minutes browsing though the postcards, from the generic "Welcome to Virginia" maps of natural resources to the scenic photos of Virginia Beach to the stately "birthplace of freedom" selections from Williamsburg and Monticello and Carter Plantation. Annabelle chuckled over the humorous cards showing babies in mob caps signing the Declaration of Independence and landing in Jamestown, and Megan became absorbed in a rack of historic black and white photo cards from the late eighteen hundreds and early nineteen hundreds. There were pictures of miners and farmhouses, cattle shows and county fairs, tin Lizzies and show horses. Megan, intrigued, realized that the postcard series had been created from old newspaper photos from around the state. She started to look through the rack, occasionally taking one out and turning it over to read the headline. Out of the corner of her eye, she saw her grandmother move toward the check out desk with the package of ham and a couple of postcards, and Megan started to follow. Then she stopped, her heart in her throat.

"Oh ... my goodness," she whispered.

She took the postcard out of the rack and tried to hold it steady, hardly believing her eyes. It was a black and white photo of two bearded men in top hats standing in front of a sign that said, "Wayfarer Inn," holding up a piece of paper between them. Behind them was a long low log building, and behind that in the distance was a range of mountains, one of which looked from that angle remarkably like a Tyrannosaurus Rex.

She turned the card over and read, "Shenandoah Railroad comes to Blue Valley."

"Gram," she said. But her voice was barely above a squeak so she cleared her throat and hurried over to the checkout desk, and her grandmother. "Gram, look!"

Her grandmother, who was engaged in a pleasant conversation with the clerk, turned to her. "Good heavens child, what in the world?"

Annabelle took the postcard that Megan waved and Megan, breath suspended, watched her grandmother's face change as she looked at it.

"Well I'll be," she whispered. "I'll just be."

"That's it, isn't it?" Megan demanded excitedly. "That's the place, and I think you and your mother were standing in front of that very same sign! Look at the building, look at the stone steps. That's it, it has to be!"

She turned to the clerk. "Excuse me, do you have a map? And ..." She turned and took the postcard from her grandmother. "Do you happen to know where this place is? And if it's still standing or open for tours or anything?"

The pleasant young woman took the card and glanced at it. "I'm sure I can find out for you. It will take just a minute."

Megan was practically dancing with excitement as the young woman went over to a computer station. "Gram, can you believe it? Seriously, can you *believe* it? We found it! What are the odds, but we did!"

Her grandmother looked stunned, a little shaken, and suddenly frail. "My goodness," she said unsteadily, fanning herself with the postcards. "What are the odds indeed?" She touched Megan's arm lightly. "I think I'll just go sit down for a minute, dear. You find out what you can."

"Gram, are you all right?"

"Yes, yes, I'm fine. It's all just a bit much, you know. I need a cup of coffee." And she drifted off toward the plastic tables by the window, leaving the smoked ham and the postcards on the counter.

Megan waited impatiently until the smiling clerk returned, a sheaf of paper in her hand. "You're in luck," she reported. "The place is not on our registry of historic places, but I was able to pull up a website and it is still open to the public. Here's the map and the information from the website. You'll just follow 81 practically the whole way. It's a little over an hour outside of Staunton."

"Thank you," Megan said, clutching the papers. She felt as though her grin would crack her face. "You have no idea what this means. Thank you so much. Gram, did you hear that?"

She turned just in time to see her grandmother, clutching a cup of vending machine coffee, crumple to the floor.

"Her things were packed, her car was gone, absolutely no trace," Paul told the ladies as he helped unload Ladybug Farm gift baskets from the back of Bridget's SUV. "I feel wretched. Just wretched."

"Of course, we ran her credit card immediately," Derrick added, his voice coming from a forest of cellophane and ribbon as he carefully made his way up the steps, his arms filled with oversized deluxe baskets. "It cleared with no problem."

"Well, that's something, anyway," said Cici. She held open the door and backed out of the way as the two men, heavily laden, made their way through.

"Unfortunately," Derrick went on, "the whole thing was completely unnecessary. We made some calls to friends back home, and it turns out this fellow with the food truck is legitimate. He serves fine dining cuisine out of a food truck, can you believe it? He was not only featured in the *Post* but in *Food and Wine* and won the *City Life* Sustainable Living award two years in a row for his use of local, artisanal ingredients … in other words, perfect for our grand opening."

"Wait a minute," said Lindsay, "I've heard about him. They say the line for his truck is two hours long. People on Capitol Hill send their interns down to wait in line at 10:00 in the morning."

"Thank you, my darling, as if I could possibly feel any more foolish," Paul said. "Three months in the country and I've completely lost my touch. Not to mention my contacts, my networks, and soon my credibility."

Derrick's expression was pained as he added, "And to add insult to injury, I finally heard back from Patty McClain's agent. It seems she just finished a tour and is taking some time off in Hawaii or somewhere. She's not taking any new engagements."

"Fortunately," Paul declared with grand exaggerated irony, "we have Purline's cousin to step in."

Bridget shared a meaningful look with Cici as she followed Paul through the door, her iPad in hand. Lindsay, bringing up the rear with a handful of hand-painted gift tags, each one an original work of miniature art, said, "Where's the painting?"

The entrance to the B&B, which had once been a dark and cluttered foyer that masqueraded as a reception area, had been transformed under the new owners' direction into a stylish, open gallery entrance, brightened by the addition of skylights, uncurtained windows and photographic gray walls. The oak floors gleamed and bright copper kettles held extravagant bunches of wildflowers and grasses from the garden. The reception desk, a tall mahogany marble-topped piece with scrolled griffons down the front and a brass kick-bar at the bottom, was original to the house, but now highlighted by a gilt-framed mirror behind it and recessed lighting overhead, it was a showstopper. On the walls, each one individually lit, was a small but eclectic collection of art that ran the gamut from primitive to modern extremist, with Lindsay's realistic wildlife and landscape paintings—which had been called "sweet" and "charming"—bridging the gap. The newest edition was not hard to spot at all. While Paul and Derrick lined up the gift baskets along the wall for distribution to the proper rooms later, Lindsay absently handed Derrick the stack of hand-painted tags and went to stand before the fence-board painting, examining it critically.

"Lindsay, these are stunning," Derrick said, looking through the gift tags. Each one was a different scene from one of the Hummingbird House gardens, which he intended to frame in 24-carat gold, personalize, and attach to a gift basket with silk ribbon.

"My invoice is enclosed," she murmured, folding her arms and pursing her lips thoughtfully as she scrutinized the painting more closely.

"And Bridget, these are lovely," Paul said, indicating the baskets. Then he sighed heavily. "Although I have to be honest, it's starting to look as though we might not have any choice at all except to cancel. We trusted everything to Harmony—the florist, the decorator, the caterer, the wine vendor, the musicians ... And she left without leaving the contact list. We have no idea if she really made arrangements with all those people, and, if she did, what those arrangements were; what she ordered or when she ordered it ..."

Cici stared at them. "I can't believe you trusted all that to a stranger. Didn't you keep records?"

"Well, we were a little busy," Derrick defended, "what with the meals, and the animals, and frantically working the phones to try to get the press out here. And you have to understand, she never really asked us about anything, she just did it. And," he admitted, "we let her."

"But it's not as though we turned over the checkbook to her," Paul said. And then he added bitterly, "Although I suppose we might as well have. How could we be so naïve?"

Bridget looked at them both almost apologetically, and then she said, "Actually, your checkbook was probably the one thing you didn't have to worry about." She brought up a document on her iPad and handed it to him.

"Your invoice?" Paul took it curiously.

"Worse," said Derrick, reading over his shoulder. He added softly, "Oh, dear heaven."

Paul turned curious, reluctant eyes to the document, read a few lines, and groaned. "No," he said, reading further. "No, no ..."

"I know we shouldn't have interfered," Cici said apologetically. "But you have to admit the whole thing was a little odd."

"I kept asking myself who would name their baby Harmony Haven," Bridget added. "So I looked it up."

Paul glanced at Derrick. "Something that might have occurred to us to do."

"It turns out her parents would," Bridget went on.

"Meredith Haven and Lynwood Haven," put in Cici.

"Of the HavenHome Hotel empire," Bridget finished.

"Harmony Haven is the heiress to one of the biggest hotel corporations in the world," said Derrick, his expression stunned. "And we were worried about her credit card."

"She told us she worked for Nissan," Paul said, almost accusingly.

"She did." Bridget gestured him to read on. "She struck out on her own right after college. During the time she was with Nissan they showed a forty percent growth. She was written up in *Forbes*."

This time Paul did not even bother to stifle the groan. "Please, I can't read on." He thrust the iPad back toward Bridget. "Someone bring me a kitchen knife and let me do the honorable thing."

"Before you do ..." Derrick, swiping forward one page, turned the tablet toward Paul. The screen was filled with a picture of Harmony, dining with Paris Hilton.

Paul sank back against the wall, eyes closed, waiting to be put out of his misery.

Derrick shook his head in disbelief, staring at the photo. "No wonder she was able to put everything together so quickly. She *is* the hospitality industry. Those vendors must have dropped their teeth when she called."

"But that's good news, isn't it?" Bridget said. "At least you know she did what she said she did."

"And canceled everything the minute she left," Paul said morosely. "Why wouldn't she? We were awful."

"Actually, "Derrick corrected politely, "you were awful. I just agreed with you."

Paul glared at him. "You called her a 'poor old soul.'"

Derrick winced. "I did."

Paul turned back to Bridget. "We could try to call and re-hire everything but we don't know who to call. And good luck trying to replace them two days before the event. It's a disaster. An utter disaster."

Lindsay, completely oblivious to the drama that was taking place behind her, stepped back from the painting and pronounced, "I like it. It's a shame about the signature, though."

Derrick came forward, glad for the distraction. "It might not matter," he told her. "There's an inscription on back, written in the same lead pencil as the signature, and even though the writing has faded on the signature, the inscription is perfectly readable." He smiled. "The good news is, of course, that pencil leaves an impression in soft wood, so I'm confident I'll be able to recover the rest of the signature in time."

"How much do you think it's worth?"

"It depends on the artist, of course," Derrick said, "but I would guess a couple of thousand, at least."

Cici's eyes widened at that. "For something you found in the *trash*?" She came over to give the painting a more thorough examination, taking out her glasses. At length she took off the glasses and turned her skeptical gaze on Derrick. "No offense, Derrick, but if you can get two thousand dollars for that, you need to win salesman of the year. Your paintings are *so* much better," she added to Lindsay.

Purline appeared abruptly through the arched doorway to the back hall, wearing denim shorts and a tight "Kiss Me" tee shirt, clutching a dishtowel in her hand. Her ponytail was swinging and her eyes were wide with alarm. "I thought you all told me you fixed your troubles with the law!" she accused in a stage whisper.

Paul pushed himself away from the wall, and Derrick turned to look at her.

"Why?" Paul said cautiously.

"We did," Derrick insisted. "What's happened?"

"Well, you'd better get that fancy lawyer of yours on the phone, then," Purline said, "because there are two government men in the kitchen, with badges and guns. And they're looking for you."

The McDonald's where Artie decided to have lunch—the man was wild about McDonald's hamburgers—turned out to be only a couple of blocks from the Bluebird Apartments on the outskirts of Kansas City. That might have been a coincidence, but Josh didn't think so.

He didn't have much hope in Artie's plan—start with where she was—but he didn't have a better one. Besides, the little guy had brought him this far; the least Josh could do was try. So he left Artie in the McDonald's parking lot with a paper sack full of hamburgers, chortling over some 1960's sitcom on the Winnie's grainy 13-inch television screen, and he started off down the kind of street where beer bottles and condoms littered the cracked sidewalks and guys hanging out around their battered Chevys gave him dark suspicious looks.

The Bluebird was no better than he had expected; a single squat cement block building with a dumpster out front and the last names of residents written on adhesive tape in front of a row of mailbox slots on the outside wall. Leda's name was nowhere to be found, but that did not surprise him. He went down the row until he found the name and apartment number of the Super, then knocked on that door.

An Asian man in a soiled tee shirt answered, and when Josh told him he was looking for Leda, he replied, "Yeah, when you find her tell her she owes me three hundred dollars." And slammed the door in his face.

Start with where she was. So he did: 212 was locked up tight and dead silent: 213 and 214 didn't answer his knock; 216 looked at him with narrowed eyes through the slit between door and frame that was permitted by the chain, and muttered, "Never heard of her," before he'd even finished speaking; 218 was a woman with carrot-colored spiked hair wearing a tank top and bike shorts. He could hear the baseball game on loudly in the background, and saw over her shoulder a man stretched out on the sofa beside a stack of empty beer cans. When Josh told her who he was looking for, she said, "Nah, can't help you." And she started to close the door.

Josh, by this time, hadn't expected anything more, but for some reason he tried anyway. He said, "Well, if you do hear from her, tell her Josh was here, can you do that?"

The woman hesitated, then said abruptly, "Hold on." She closed the door.

Josh stood there in the dank, smelly hallway with its stained industrial carpet and its smudged walls, uncertain whether to stay or go, until he started to feel like an idiot. "Crap," he muttered, and just as he was about to turn away, the door opened a crack again and the woman appeared with an envelope in her hand.

"I thought you was her ex," she said, and thrust the envelope at him through the opening. "Sorry about that. She left this, in case you was to come around. She said to tell you sorry about your car, but they had to sell it for parts when Eva—well, I guess you know about that. That's all that's left."

Josh opened the envelope and flipped through the bills inside. A hundred eighty-two dollars. He felt a mixture of despair and urgency rise up inside him, threatening to choke off his voice. So close. *So close …*

"Where is she?" he managed. "I need to know where she went."

The woman nodded curtly toward the envelope in his hand. "She wrote the address on the back," she said. "Said she couldn't wait for you any longer."

Josh read the block printing on the back of the envelope, and felt hope turn, once again, to despair. "Virginia?"

The woman said, "That's where her mama is." And she closed the door before he could say anything else.

He stood there staring at the handwriting on the back of the envelope for a long time, feeling hopeful and hopeless and sick and exhausted all at the same time. No phone number, not even her mother's name. Just an address in some little berg he'd never heard of in Virginia. *Virginia.* It might as well have been Mars.

Unless …

With sudden determination, he thrust the envelope into his pocket and left the building. He started walking fast, and then broke into a jog. A young man didn't run in this neighborhood without getting some piercing looks, but he didn't care. He waited impatiently for traffic to clear across the street from McDonald's, then dodged between a lumbering delivery truck and a windowless step van—no doubt a rolling meth lab—to race across the street to the parking lot. He was ready to shout, "Artie!" when he came up short, breathing hard, and looked around.

The Winnebago was gone.

There was a guy and a girl eating french fries in a faded red Camaro, an empty pickup truck, and a jeep. A black woman came out of the restaurant, noisily scolding two fussy kids. Josh went inside. He checked the men's room. He walked quickly around the parking lot. Two cars were in the drive-through line. Neither of them was a Winnebago.

Artie had left him behind.

The disappointment that rose in his throat tasted bitter; it ached in his sinuses and burned behind his eyes. What had he expected? After all, their deal had been for Kansas City. But, damn, he was going to miss the crazy little dude. Not just the wheels, not just the sound of another voice on those long empty highways, not just the outrageous stories and funny snippets of altered history … but him. And he hadn't even gotten a chance to say good-bye.

"Damn it," he whispered, and he actually had to blink a couple of times to clear his vision. What was he supposed to do now?

That was when he looked up, and saw the bus station.

Lester Carson dropped his briefcase on the floor, shrugged out of his jacket, and was about to go to the bar to pour himself a drink when he stopped, staring at the giant fruit arrangement on his black marble foyer table. He started to ignore it and walk on, but found himself unable to. He turned back, picked up an oversized, glistening red globe by the stem, and called, "Mrs. Goddard!"

She came bustling around the corner, drying her hands on a paper towel. "I'm sorry, Mr. Carson, I didn't expect you back so soon. I was just having a bite of lunch."

"With this?" he held up the mysterious fruit, looking puzzled. "What is it, some kind of pomegranate?"

She smiled. "Amazing, isn't it? Actually, it's a cherry, and it's delicious. The basket is from Paul Slater—all organic fruit from his garden in Virginia."

Lester regarded the fruit skeptically. "Mrs. Goddard, I have traveled all over the world, and would you like to know what I've discovered to be the only difference between organic fruit and that which is commercially grown?" He dropped the cherry delicately back into the basket. "Worms."

She looked amused. "How fortunate that he sent the basket to me, then, and not to you—as a thank you for the effort I've put into trying to persuade you to respond to the invitation to his grand opening."

He groaned out loud. "All right, then it's official. I'm a cad. For God's sake, will you just write something up? I'll sign it. I'll send flowers. I might even ..." he cast another rather pained look at the fruit basket on his way to the bar, "eat the fruit."

She picked up the fruit basket. "You'll have to fight me for it."

Lester's phone rang. He took it from his pocket, checked the ID, and answered quickly, his heart pounding.

"Good news," said the man on the other end without preamble. "I've arranged a meeting."

The private detective was a former Army intelligence officer, and a man of few words. Over the months of dealing with him, Lester had learned to emulate his example, although a hundred words, a thousand, were bubbling up inside him, closing his throat, choking his chest. *Who? Why? Where? When? How?* And perhaps most importantly, *Are you sure?* Please, please God be sure ...

But the other thing Lester had learned in his brief sojourn into this aspect of covert operations was that men like this one did not respond well to questions, and they were always sure. He turned away so that Mrs. Goddard could not see the war of emotions on his face, and he said into the phone simply, "Where?"

"Virginia."

"I can be there in three hours." If he had to move heaven and earth.

"No good. Tomorrow, four o'clock. We pick the place, neutral, public. There's a Holiday Inn about an hour away ..."

Lester thrust his hand through his hair, frowning, trying to focus. "An hour from what? Where are you?"

"A little place in the middle of nowhere off 81, between Charlottesville and Staunton. It's called Blue Valley."

And suddenly, miraculously, it all fell into place. Lester Carson turned to look at the fruit basket Mrs. Goddard was re-wrapping in its protective cellophane covering and he thought, as though from a great and objective distance, *There is a God. What do you know about that?*

He said, "I think I know a place we can meet. I'll call you back."

"Make it quick. And Mr. Carson—if you're serious about this, bring your lawyer."

Lester Carson pressed the disconnect button and turned to his secretary. "Mrs. Goddard," he said, very calmly, "will you please get Paul Slater on the phone? It turns out I'm available for his event after all."

"Mr. Slater, Mr. Anderson." The man with the bald head and the grim expression held out a badge for them to examine. His counterpart, a younger man with a pair of sunglasses tucked into the pocket of his suit coat, moved with quiet purpose around the room, looking out the windows, peering through doorways. "I'm Agent Keller and this is Agent Morrison. We're with the United States Secret Service."

Purline, Bridget, Cici, and Lindsay crowded in close behind Paul and Derrick, all of them knotted so tightly together that when the other man, the one who had been introduced as Agent Morrison, tried to edge past them to get to the doorway through which they had just entered, the entire group shifted, as one entity, to the right.

Paul swallowed hard, staring at the badge the agent presented. Derrick clutched Lindsay's arm. It was Cici who spoke, carefully. "Secret Service? As in White House?"

The agent spared her a brief glance. "That's right. We've already cleared the guest list, and we're here to do a security sweep of the premises. It's routine in the case of a possible visit by the former First Lady."

Lindsay smothered a yelp as Derrick's fingers dug into her arm. He said, "Do you mean … she *is* coming? Here? She's coming here? To our party?"

"That's not for me to confirm or deny," replied Agent Keller, flat-faced. "As I said, this is standard procedure. Now if you'll excuse me, we should be out of here in a matter of minutes."

"Yes, yes, please, of course, be my guest." Paul waved him through the door and the others, after a moment of shocked immobility, scattered apart. "Whatever you need, anything at all, just make yourself at home."

He ushered the agent toward the front of the stairs and hurried to follow, pausing only to look back over his shoulder and mouth, *Oh. My. God.*

Less than half an hour later they all stood on the front porch and watched the black SUV disappear down the drive. Even Purline looked impressed. "The real White House," she said with a shake of her head as she turned to go back inside. "Wait till I tell my kids about this."

And Derrick agreed, still looking somewhat stunned, "Unbelievable."

Bridget cautioned, "It's not a sure thing. Just because they cleared this place doesn't mean she's coming. She's pretty old, you know. "

"No, but it means she *considered* it," Lindsay said. "That's impressive enough, in my book."

Derrick repeated, "Unbelievable."

Paul said, "You know what this means, don't you?"

They all looked at him.

"We *really* can't call it off now," he supplied bleakly. "I don't have Nancy Reagan's phone number."

As though on cue, his cell phone rang. He glanced at the ID and, with a pained expression that suggested it could only be more bad news, excused himself to answer it.

Cici grinned, shaking her head. "You really don't get it, do you?"

Derrick's expression was a little offended. "I'm sorry, Cici, but I don't see anything funny about this at all. Paul is right. We can't call it off now. We have one of the most revered first ladies in modern history coming to our grand opening and we don't have a caterer, a florist, a wine list ..."

"And there is no one in the world better equipped to pull this off than you and Paul," Bridget said.

Cici gave an emphatic nod. "Your dream house falls into a sink hole and you end up owning the only B&B in the county—and then proceed to turn it into a restaurant that people drive an hour and a half to come to. You lose your liquor license and end up starting a charity. You find a two-thousand-dollar painting in your trash pile. You take in a stray and she turns out to be an heiress. You lose the heiress and gain a First Lady. So what if none of those fancy Hollywood types bothered to RSVP? If she hadn't invited them, you wouldn't have started working your own network, and now you've got the entire east coast A-list on its way here. "

"And they are going to have a fabulous time," Lindsay said. "Do you know why?"

"Because you've never given a bad party in your life, for heaven's sake," said Bridget.

"Your only problem," Lindsay added, "is that you make everything so complicated. You try too hard. Keep it simple. That's why you moved here, isn't it? For a simpler life? Just relax, things will work out. They always do."

"Because," said Cici, "some people have the magic touch. You guys are two of them."

Derrick looked less than convinced. "Well, at least we have a caterer."

"And wildflowers are very trendy," Lindsay added.

Bridget kept a straight face, but her eyes twinkled as she offered, "And don't forget Purline's cousin is ready to sing. "

Derrick was about to respond to that when Paul came back onto the porch, an odd and thoughtful look on his face, as though he couldn't decide whether to be delighted or horrified. "That was Lester Carson," he said. "It turns out he can make it to the grand opening after all." He met Derrick's gaze with a look of cautious disbelief in his own. "We're going to be written up in the *New York Times*."

Derrick caught his breath, hand pressed to his chest, and seemed for a moment not to know what to say. Cici did.

"See, what did I tell you?" She grinned. "Magic."

TEN

The true mystery of the world is in the visible, not the invisible.

Oscar Wilde

Megan sat in a blue vinyl chair in the Intensive Care waiting room, hugging her arms and rocking back and forth gently, almost imperceptibly, nursing her pain like she would a fussy child. She had been there all night, drinking coffee, pacing back and forth, praying. A doctor had talked to her about cardiac failure and leaking blood vessels that were too fragile to repair. The nurses had brought her a blanket and sympathetic progress reports—still unconscious, stable but critical, doing as well as could be expected—and had allowed Megan to go in and stand beside the bed for five minutes every four hours. They told her Annabelle Stephens was dying.

But they didn't know Gram.

She had called her mother. And then she had spent the longest time staring at Nick's number on her contact list, needing him, wanting more than anything in the world to call him, aching for the sound of his voice, the strength of his arms around her, his chest beneath her cheek while her tears soaked into his shirt. And unable to make herself push the buttons.

Megan looked up hopefully as the nurse approached, and the other woman was smiling. "She's awake," she said gently, and Megan leapt to her feet. The nurse stopped her with a light hand upon her arm. "I don't want to give you false hope. Very often terminal patients will recover consciousness and lucidity near the end. Go and sit with her, and take all the time you need to say good-bye. It could be an hour, or another day, or only a few minutes."

Megan gave the other woman a tolerant look, and pulled her arm away. "Thank you," she said. "But with all due respect, I've heard that before. And you don't know my grandmother."

Annabelle was propped up against the pillows, an oxygen cannula taped in place beneath her nostrils, a clear IV dripping into her arm. Monitors beeped and glittered. Megan smiled as she approached the bed. "This was funny the first time, Gram," she said.

But the effort to return Megan's smile seemed too much for her grandmother, and Megan's chest tightened with alarm. Annabelle fluttered her fingers, and Megan came to sit beside her, folding her grandmother's hand inside her own. It was cold.

"Looks like Moses and I have something in common," said Annabelle. Her voice was weak, but steady. "Neither one of us is going to make it to the Promised Land."

Megan tightened her hand around Annabelle's fingers. "Stop talking like that. You're going to get up and walk out of this hospital, you know you are."

Annabelle's face softened with compassion, and she lifted her free hand as though to touch Megan's face, but could not quite make it. "Ah, sweet girl," she said. "You always knew this was going to be a one-way trip, now didn't you?"

Megan's chest flooded with tears and her eyes went hot, but she pressed her lips tightly together, refusing to give voice to the pain. *No, no, no ....*

The door swooshed open and Megan turned, dashing away tears. Her mother, disheveled, un-made up, wearing wrinkled cotton slacks and a misbuttoned sweater, rushed toward the bed. "Thank God!" she whispered. "I thought I would be too late!"

Annabelle smiled then as her daughter sank down beside her, clutching her other hand. "No, Marion, honey. You're right on time, just as you always are." She let her head sink back against the pillows and the lines in her face relaxed into contentment. "This is nice," she said. "My two girls together, here at home. Where we belong."

Marion bent her head over her mother's hand. "Mother," she said thickly, "I never got a chance to tell you … that was why I was so upset when you left town … all these years I never got a chance to thank you for what you've done for my little girl." She looked at Megan, her eyes wet and ravaged, and filled with a silent plea for understanding. "For giving her what I couldn't. The time, the patience, the confidence … You helped her become the woman I always wanted to be."

Megan stared at her mother, her breath caught somewhere in the back of her throat, but she couldn't speak. She didn't even know what to think.

Annabelle said, "I only wish I could have given it to you, sweetheart."

"You tried," said Marion. She brought her hand, still linked with Annabelle's to her face to wipe away the drenching tears. "I never had the courage to take what you were offering. But I've always loved you for trying. Please believe that."

Annabelle's eyes, once tired and faded, suddenly grew brilliant, as though lit from within, and the faintest flush of color came to her face as she turned to Megan. "Oh, my goodness!" she exclaimed softly. "I remember now! I remember the birthday present my father gave me!"

Only seconds ago she had been a frail and fading vessel for the life that sustained her, but now she was animated, her voice strong and her muscles full of life. Megan laughed through her tears as hope and relief soared through her. "I told them not to count you out, Gram! I told them!"

Her grandmother looked at her intensely, her expression filled with joy. "It was the best present a little girl could ever have, and do you know why?

Because it meant he loved me. I want you to have it, and every time you look at it remember how very much you were loved. Promise me you'll find it, sweet girl. Don't let our great adventure die in this room."

Megan squeezed her grandmother's fingers happily. "Of course I'll find it, Gram. We'll find it together."

Annabelle smiled and squeezed her fingers back. She looked then at Marion and said, "Now. Let's talk about the funeral."

At the distress that crossed her daughter's eyes, she raised a hand of protest. "I know, I know, you already made other arrangements. But it'll do you good to improvise. I want to be buried in the family cemetery at that little church outside of Falls Creek, Virginia. I know it's still there, I looked it up on the Internet. The pastor's name is Jacob Williamson, and I'll just bet if you get to work on your charm he'll do everything he can to accommodate you. I want the place filled with pink roses, and you should call one of those worthless nieces of mine and have them ship you my white silk Diane Von Furstenberg dress, the one with the beading on the sleeves. And the Jimmy Choo heels. I know no one will see them but I've been waiting twenty-five years for an occasion special enough to wear them and it just doesn't get any more special than this."

She looked at her stunned daughter sharply. "Shouldn't you be writing this down? I know it's a lot of work, but I wouldn't trust anyone but you to get it right."

After another stunned and motionless moment, Marion scrambled through her purse until she came up with a pen and paper. She began writing furiously. Megan shared a grin with her grandmother.

"Now," said Annabelle, "I want all the nephews and sons-in-law to be pallbearers. They'll have to fly in from all over the country, but since I haven't seen most of them in thirty-five years, it seems only fitting. And see if you can schedule the funeral for the middle of the week, will you? They'll all have to take off work and that will really piss them off. Now, for the processional I want the choir singing, 'At Last.'"

Marion stopped writing and her eyebrows flew up, but Annabelle demanded, "What? If it's good enough to inaugurate a president, it's good enough for me. Besides ..." her expression softened, "that was the last song your father and I danced to. Good times. Then," she went on, "after everyone has given me all their rave reviews, and they're carrying out the casket, I want you to play *Fifty Ways to Leave Your Lover*. The original Simon and Garfunkle cut will do fine." To Marion's horrified look she responded brusquely, "Oh, loosen up, sweetie. It'll do you good."

Megan burst into laughter. "Gram, you are a card!" She dropped a kiss onto her forehead. "Do you know how much I love you?"

Her grandmother patted her cheek. "I hope it's a lot, sweet girl, because your job is the hardest one. I want you to leave this hospital room right now, before your mother can talk you into staying and helping her with all the things she's got to do, and I want you to drive to that place we've been looking for, and have your picture taken on the front steps sitting just where I was sitting all those years ago. Then I want you to have both pictures blown up really big, and set them on either side of the casket, so that the whole world—or at least the ones that give a damn—can share our last adventure, and it will give them something to talk about for years to come. What do you think about that idea?"

Megan smiled. "I think it's one of the best ones you ever had. And as soon as you get out of this place that's exactly what we're going to do. You can be the one to take the picture."

Annabelle smiled. "Oh, sweetheart," she said with a sigh, "I wish I could."

And then she closed her eyes, and she died.

Derrick and Paul had spent the past two days calling event planners, booking agents, florists, limousine companies, wine vendors, and decorators up and down the east coast. None of them had ever heard of the Hummingbird House grand opening, and when they were asked, on a note of hope that grew fainter with each call, about availability, they either laughed or hung up. Now they faced each other blearily over coffee seven hours before the first guests were due to arrive, all but ready to admit defeat.

"Whoever she used, they're not in the phone book," Derrick said, "or on the Internet."

"Of course not. She's HavenHome Hotels. She has her own people."

Derrick rubbed a hand over his stubbly cheek, groaning out loud. "How could we not have noticed even one name?"

Paul frowned. "I'm used to delegating. So are you. The only reason we knew about the caterer was because you signed the check."

"And thank God I did. She must have used her personal credit card or her own good name to secure the others." Derrick took a sip of his coffee, staring at the kitchen clock with its maddening, unrelenting, steadily ticking second hand. "At least we'll have food, although God only knows who we'll have food for if she canceled the limousine service."

Paul, on the other hand, was gazing out the window, where a steady gray rain was fogging up the screens and digging mud puddles in the garden. His expression was surprisingly reflective. "Do you know what I've been thinking?" he said. "We did this exact same thing with the girls when we first moved here. It was easier to let them take care of things, so we did. Before long we were counting on them to take care of things. And when they put their collective feet down about it, we just went looking for someone else to depend on. We should have listened to them in the first place. All of this is Karma. We deserve it."

Derrick considered this unhappily. "You're right, of course. What does it take for us to learn our lesson?"

Paul sighed and turned away from the window. "I, for one, feel sufficiently schooled. Maybe the girls are right about something else, too. Maybe we have been trying too hard. Simple. Artisanal."

Derrick looked skeptical. "It's too wet to pick wildflowers," he said. "And you're not seriously suggesting we let Purline's cousin sing?"

The sound of a large truck rounding the drive distracted Paul from what he was about to say. He glanced at his watch. "That must be the caterer. He said he'd be here by nine." He stood and forced a smile. "Game faces," he advised. "We're on."

Derrick said, "Can't I just sit here and cry?"

But after another moment and a last, bracing gulp of coffee, he followed Paul out onto the front porch. And he stopped.

"Good lord," he said, peering through the rain at the steel-sided tractor-trailer that was now screeching a back-up beep as it maneuvered its way around to the entrance, "did he bring his whole kitchen?"

"That can't be the caterer," Paul said, alarmed. "How many people does he think he's going to feed?"

Behind the huge truck came another, smaller van, followed by several cars. Two men jumped out of the cab of the big truck and went around to open the trailer. Paul called, "Um, can I help you?"

Derrick grabbed two umbrellas from the stand by the door and handed one to Paul. The men swung open the back doors of the trailer and jumped inside. "Hello!" Derrick called. They started down the steps.

People began to swarm from the van and the other cars. More vans pulled up. A giant basket of lilacs and a small dogwood tree bobbed down the driveway, carried by two women in black suits with black umbrellas. From the big truck there came a huge clatter as steel poles were tossed on the ground. A young man dashed through the rain with a huge plastic-wrapped roll of what appeared to be brown paper under his arm. "Morning!" he called as he ran up the steps.

Paul, turning in almost a full circle from the truck to the steps, replied, "Excuse me, may I ask ...?"

A man in jeans and a rain slicker jogged up to Derrick, his hair dripping. "Hi," he said, "where's the kitchen?"

Derrick, slack jawed, pointed, and then the air was pierced by a decibel-shattering mechanical screech. Everyone winced, stopped, and turned. "Listen up!" called a megaphone-amplified, mercifully familiar voice. "No one, and I mean no one, enters the house until the floors are covered! Tents go east and north. Stay out of the flowers beds! Dogwoods in the foyer, lilacs in the dining room. Fountains, follow me. Move it, people, move it! "

She marched through the rain in a long black cape, fuchsia striped galoshes, and an oversized red rain bonnet, looking huge, ridiculous, and magnificent. She lowered the megaphone as she approached and called, "Hello, boys."

"Harmony!" they exclaimed on a single breath, and rushed toward her, splashing through the mud, umbrellas bumping.

"Are we ever glad to see you!" Derrick cried, beaming as he reached her. "We thought—"

"Harmony, I am so dreadfully sorry," Paul said, grasping her hand. "Can you ever forgive me?"

"Thank you, thank you so much for coming back." Derrick grasped her other arm and led her toward the house. "We've been just miserable over what happened. I know we don't deserve your forgiveness, but if you would just give us a second chance ..."

She looked from one to the other of them with big, confused eyes. "What on earth," she demanded, "are you talking about?"

They stopped, falling back a step, looking at each other, looking at her. Rain spattered and popped on their umbrellas and seeped into their shoes. Finally Paul said, "What I said the other day ..."

"Didn't mean a word of it, of course," Derrick put in quickly.

"It was rude and thoughtless and I'm most abjectly sorry ..."

"But if you could ever see your way to forgive us ..."

Harmony handed Paul the megaphone and tucked one hand through his arm, and the other through Derrick's. "Fellows," she said, "you are really very sweet, but sometimes you can be a little weird. Whatever it is you've got on your minds, could it wait? We have a grand opening in a little over six hours!"

They started up the steps, and Paul and Derrick shared a look of abject bewilderment and utter relief over her head.

At the top of the steps, Paul dropped her arm, gathered his courage, and stepped in front of her. "Harmony," he said formally, "it occurs to me we've never properly thanked you for all the effort you put into this event. I would like to take the opportunity to do so now. Thank you," he said, "with all my heart."

Derrick took her hand, bowed and kissed her fingers. "Thank you," he echoed.

Harmony dimpled. "Well, are you just the cutest things? It was my pleasure, gentlemen, because the spirits tell me this is just the beginning of a long and prosperous partnership."

And before either of them could register alarm at that, she smiled that smile that could melt stone and met Paul's gaze. "By the way," she added, "how do you like my earrings?"

She gave a little toss of her head, revealing two of the ugliest speckled partridge feathers Paul had ever seen dangling from her ears. He returned her smile. He couldn't help it. "I think," he told her in absolute sincerity, "they are perfect."

Megan felt a sweet quiet calm riding in the empty seat of the big old car beside her that puzzled her most of the way across the state. It wasn't until she passed through Charlottesville and was back out on the open highway that she knew what it was. She finally understood why her grandmother had kept taking her on adventure after adventure, even though Megan had continually shied away at the last minute when it came time to face the challenge. She had been afraid, but she had done it anyway. And that was what courage was all about.

She missed her grandmother. She missed her wit, her spirit, her stories, her zany ideas. But she wasn't alone. And after the funeral she was going to go home, she was going to find her husband, and she was going to fight for her marriage. She was going to fight for herself. She knew how to do that now.

It started raining when, according to her calculations, she was little less than an hour from her destination. She let the windshield wipers hypnotize her for a while, and it never once occurred to her, even when the rain grew hard enough to diminish her visibility, that she was driving without her headlights on. When she turned onto the county highway, there was more traffic than she had expected and she fumbled for the GPS she had pulled up on her phone, not wanting to miss her turn. She did not realize she was drifting into the opposite lane until she looked up and saw the headlights slashing through the rain in front of her. By then it was too late.

Josh had stayed on the bus when everyone got off at the rest stop in Charlottesville, and he slept through the change of drivers. He wasn't really sleeping, though; it was more like he was thinking, drifting through possibilities and events and options with a peaceful clarity he really had not had time to know before. When it took everything you had just to stay alive, it was hard to think straight. But maybe all that time with Artie, feeling safe, eating good, not worrying about somebody stabbing him in his sleep or how he was going to get from one place to the next, had done something to his brain. He could think more clearly now.

He knew what he had to do.

He opened his eyes and took out his phone. He pushed the "on" button but nothing happened. He tried again. And then he understood, and there was nothing he could do but smile. The battery was dead. Of course it was. He had a charger, but it was back in the Winnebago with Artie. Of course it was.

He glanced around, looking for a friendly looking person who might let him make a call. A lot of people had gotten off in Charlottesville, and about half the seats were empty. It had started to rain while he slept, and the interior was dimmed by the gray skies and rain-streaked windows. The big wipers swished back and forth, pushing rivers of rain toward the side of the front windshield. And, watching them, Josh got a good long look at the face of the driver in the rearview mirror. The bald head, the oversized, crooked nose, the funny little mouth. He was even wearing red plaid golf pants.

"Artie?" Josh said softly, disbelieving. Then, excitedly, "Hey, Artie!" He pushed himself up and made his way to the front of the bus.

"Artie, what are you doing here?" He grabbed the driver's shoulder happily. "You're a sight for sore eyes, man!"

The driver, who was not Artie at all but a square-faced man with a perfectly normal nose and an annoyed look on his face, took his eyes off the road for only a moment to glance at Josh, but that was all it took. He didn't see the car without the headlights coming toward him until it was too late. Reflexively, he jerked the wheel in the opposite direction, and everything spun out of control.

Peering through the rain-fogged windshield, cursing the taillights that flashed and glowed on the country road ahead of him, Lester Carson steered the rental car with one hand and held the phone with the other. "It's called The Hummingbird House B&B," he told his attorney. "It's off County Road 43. There's supposed to be a sign. The meeting is set for four o'clock so I sure as hell hope you're on the road."

It was at that moment that he realized the taillights in front of him were actually brake lights, and before he could react, the car in front of him started to skid across the road directly in his path, flinging up sheets of water in its wake. He dropped the phone and slammed on the brakes, gripping the wheel in a desperate effort to hold his own vehicle steady. But it was too late.

At the Hummingbird House, candles were lit in every corner. Lush baskets of lilacs and delicate potted dogwoods brought the pastel colors and sweet scents of the outdoors in without seeming overwhelming or pretentious. The air was filled with the tantalizing aromas of hot hors d'oeuvres, and from a beautifully decked fern bower near the restaurant the cellist that Harmony had brought in from Philadelphia played modern classics. Every one of the colored doors was open to welcome their guests, each one marked with a stunning floral topiary interwoven with miniature white lights. Two liveried valets stood on the front porch with umbrellas. A veritable army of uniformed servers lined the foyer. The champagne was poured into sparkling flutes. Gift bags were lined up on silver trays. Cocktail napkins embossed with the Hummingbird House logo were artfully placed in strategic places. Paul wore Armani, Derrick wore Versace, and Harmony wore a beaded floor-length red gown with a gold chiffon jacket and a tiara in her oversized, over-styled, over-sprayed hair. At four o'clock precisely they took their places on either side of the front door, their broad and welcoming smiles belying their nervousness, and prepared to greet their guests.

At four thirty they were still standing there, their smiles more frantic than welcoming.

At four forty-five the champagne was starting to go flat, the hor d'oeuvres had been returned to the kitchen, and Harmony was on the phone with the limousine company. Derrick gripped Paul's arm, who was banging his head deliberately against the wall and repeating, "I knew it, I knew it …"

There was a sudden commotion behind them and they both turned quickly, hope springing into their eyes. But it was only Cici, followed closely by Bridget and Lindsay, all of them dripping rain water on the highly polished floors as they shed their rain coats. "Guys, we're so sorry we're late, but you wouldn't believe the accident on the highway! Traffic is backed up for miles. The only way we made it was by turning around and coming in the back way. We parked on the side of the house, like you told us." Cici stopped and looked around. "You said four, didn't you? Where is everybody?"

Derrick caught the eye of one of the servers, who quickly went to collect the rain coats while another one mopped up water from the floor with a white towel. Paul said, "Accident? Did you say accident?"

"Didn't you hear the sirens?" Bridget looked around for a mirror to check her hair. "Every fire truck in the county must be out there."

Lindsay said, "The worst part is that it was change of shift at the plant, so the road was already a tangle of traffic. It's going to take hours to clear."

Paul and Derrick looked at each other in dismayed comprehension just as Harmony returned, cell phone in hand, and announced grimly, "And that, fellows, is what happened to our limousines. They are being turned back at the county line by the state patrol."

Paul drew in a breath, and let it out empty. Derrick said what he could not.

"That," he said, looking around regretfully, "I guess, is that."

Lindsay placed a sympathetic hand on his arm. "Maybe it won't take them as long as I thought to clear the traffic. I mean, seriously, if they can just get the overturned bus off the road ..."

Paul looked at her in growing dismay. "Bus? Were people hurt?"

"Not according to the radio," Cici said. "At least not badly. From what we could see when we came up the back driveway, it was mostly just a bunch of wet and cold and miserable people standing around waiting for the tow trucks and emergency vehicles to get through."

Bridget looked around with genuine distress in her eyes. "All this food can't go to waste! Surely you can put it back in the refrigerator, tell the chef to hold off on the entrée ..."

"Sautéed scallops," said Derrick sadly, "cannot go back in the refrigerator."

One of the servers came up to Cici with a tray of hors d'oeuvres. "Pate?" he said.

Cici looked torn, but Lindsay reached in front of her and helped herself. "What?" she defended when the other two women looked at her in mild reprimand. "It's going to go to waste."

Paul looked confused. "Wait a minute. What do you mean, you could see it from the back driveway?"

"Well, the bus overturned practically in front of your entrance sign. You know how when you come in the back way there's a little rise ...?"

Derrick said, "You mean all those hurt people are standing out in the rain at the bottom of our driveway?"

"Oh for heaven's sake!" exclaimed Bridget softly, understanding.

Cici looked around for her coat. "I am an idiot," she said.

Paul looked at Derrick. Derrick looked at Harmony. Before either of them could say a word, she raised her arm in the air as though to lead a charge and shouted, "Fernando! Havier! Bring the vans around!"

Lester Carson, nursing a bruised chest from the airbag but no other noticeable injury, made his way through the tangle of vehicles and the dripping rain. In all his worldly travels, he had never seen anything like it—not just the giant parking lot of dented, haphazardly spun cars, pickups, and vans—but the people. The way they went from car to car, making sure everyone was all right, sharing blankets and first aid kits and even take-out cups of coffee and bottled water. He was certainly no hero, but he helped calm down a frantic mother and get her two little boys out of the backseat, and he left his umbrella with an elderly couple who refused to stay in their car but insisted on making sure no one needed their help. He helped a shaken but otherwise completely uninjured young woman whose Lincoln Town Car had skidded off the road climb onto safe ground again; she probably wouldn't realize it until later but that big old dinosaur of a car had probably saved her life. The front fender had actually been clipped by a bus.

The bus was lying on its side across the road, one shoulder resting against the embankment so that the front of the vehicle was tilted at a forty-five-degree angle away from the pavement. The first thing Lester thought was how much worse it would have been had the vehicle landed flat on either one side or the other, throwing all the passengers across the aisle. The second thing he noticed was that both emergency doors were clear and open. Some guardian angel had definitely been paying attention to his job today.

The bus driver, easily identifiable in his uniform, was helping people to the ground in the front. At the back door a young man with scrapes on his arms and a bloodied head had stationed himself inside the door and was easing people down to the ground four feet below. Lester rushed forward to help as a boy of about ten years old was lowered over the side by his arms. He was clearly trying very hard not to cry. Lester grabbed the boy's waist. "I've got you, son."

The mother followed quickly, tumbling into Lester's steadying grip in her haste to reach her child. She was crying, but they were mostly tears of relief. Next was a teenage girl with a punk haircut and a bruised lip, a middle-aged woman with an injured hand, and a dazed-looking man who kept saying, "Holy crap, holy crap." Amazingly, no one seemed to be seriously hurt.

Finally the young man called from inside, "That's everybody!" and he jumped to the ground.

For an endless moment they stared at each other. The chaos, the weeping, the sirens, the chatter, the spattering rain, and the flashing lights all receded around them, shrinking, it seemed, into a single moment of slow and pounding heartbeats, of silent suspended breaths.

Then Josh said uncertainly, "Dad?"

Lester Carson took one staggering step forward and threw himself into his son's embrace, hugging him hard enough to lift his feet off the ground, crushing him and feeling those wiry familiar arms hug him back just as hard. He could not tell whether the hoarse ragged sounds of joy and relief were coming from his throat, or from his son's.

Finally he had to break the embrace, had to look at him again, had to make sure it was real. He cupped Josh's wet and muddied face in his hands, smoothing back the blood-matted hair. He demanded, "Are you all right?"

Josh replied, searching his face, "I don't know. Are you real? Are you really here?"

Lester hugged him again, fiercely. "I'm here," he whispered. "I'm here."

This time it was Josh who stepped back, regarding the older man with the hunger of a beggar at a feast, but his eyes were clouded with shame and uncertainty. "Dad, I'm so sorry. Not just for what happened before but …I've got some stuff to tell you. There's a lot you don't know."

Lester gripped his son's arms, shaking his head, unable to stop looking at him. "Maybe not as much as you think. I never stopped looking for you, Josh. Not ever. By the time you showed up in the Nevada prison system, you'd already been released, and the girl, Eva …" His expression softened. "She was dead. I'm so sorry, son."

Josh's jaw tightened, and he met his father's eyes bravely through the rain. "I couldn't let her go to prison, Dad. I tried to do the right thing. I thought I could take care of her, take care of everything, but it turns out …" he dropped his eyes briefly, "I couldn't." He drew a breath, and even through his pain there was pride, and tenderness. "You have a granddaughter. We named her Amy, after Mom. I'm going to find her, Dad. I'm going to find her and bring her home. If it takes the rest of my life."

Lester smiled and clasped his son's shoulder. "I know you will, Josh. That's what parents do."

A woman in a raincoat gripped his shoulder from behind, gesturing and shouting against the rain. "We have food and coffee at the inn," she said, pointing. "There are vans waiting to take you there just around the corner."

Lester smiled and thanked her and put an arm around his son's shoulder. "Come on," he said, "I have a lot to tell you, too."

The Hummingbird House began to fill with stranded travelers, muddied, bedraggled, some of them nursing minor wounds but most of them in need of nothing more than a place to shelter, a comforting touch, and a compassionate smile. Paul and Derrick hurried from group to group, offering clean towels and warm washcloths, while the servers moved through the crowd with platters of scallops and champagne. It would, after all, only go flat if it wasn't served.

Harmony stood at the front door, directing traffic with all the efficiency of a field medic doing triage. Telephones and e-mail to the right, hot coffee and blankets to the left, first aid straight ahead. Among the last to arrive was a pale woman in mud-streaked slacks with her dark curls plastered to her head by the rain, who just stood at the bottom of the steps, staring. Harmony, snatching up an umbrella with one hand and her long skirt with another, went out into the rain to get her.

"Honey, come inside," she urged, taking the woman's arm. "We've got hot food and blankets."

Megan tore her gaze from the wide stone steps to the view beyond, where misty clouds were just beginning to part around a deep violet mountain range. Somewhere within that range, she was sure, was a mountain formation which, when viewed from a certain angle, would look like a Tyrannosaurus Rex. She blinked away a mixture of raindrops and tears of wonder. "This is it," she said. "This is really it. How did I get here?"

Harmony peered at her with concern. "Are you okay? Did you hit your head?" Slipping an arm around her waist and holding the umbrella high, she urged her up the steps.

"Wait," Megan said, holding back. "I'm supposed to have my picture taken." She patted her pockets, and an expression of dismay came over her face. "I've lost my phone."

"It's okay, honey, we've got phones in the house. You can call anyone you want. Just come on in out of the rain."

She ushered Megan into the foyer, where Derrick was waiting with a stack of fluffy towels. He wrapped one around Megan's shoulders, and Harmony murmured meaningfully to him, "We're a little confused."

Megan looked around in bewilderment at the lights, the flowers, the silver trays, and liveried waiters. But when her eyes landed on the gallery wall, a slow and wondering smile began to curve her lips. "Not anymore," she said.

A laugh of sheer delight bubbled in the back of her throat as she went to stand in front of the primitive painting of a little girl in a red dress with a sailor collar sitting on the stone steps of the inn. Grinning, she whipped her head around. "Does anyone know where this painting came from?"

Derrick replied, "Why yes. We found it here, in our shed." He handed the stack of towels to Harmony and, edging his way between the bus driver and a woman on her cell phone who was saying, "No, we're fine, we're fine, really, the most wonderful people took us in, it's amazing really, we're fine," he came to stand beside Megan in front of the painting.

Megan dug into her pocket and brought out a slim zippered wallet. She opened it and took out the small sepia-toned photograph, handing it to Derrick. "Look," she said. "That's my grandmother. I think this painting is of her!"

Derrick looked at the photograph, and then at the painting. He looked again. "Well, my word. I think you may be right."

He returned the photograph and looked at the stranger with renewed interest. The joy on her face had transformed her from a wet and bedraggled victim to a beautiful woman radiating purpose. "What was your grandmother's name, dear?"

"Annabelle Stephens," replied Megan. "Of course, that was her married name."

Derrick said, "Annabelle? Are you sure?"

She laughed. "Of course I'm sure. Why?"

Derrick just kept looking at her, his expression tense and suspended, as though he hardly dared ask the next question. "I don't suppose you happen to know what *her* father's name was."

Megan's delight became tempered with puzzlement. "Jackson. I'm not sure if it was his first name or last, though. He never married my great-grandmother," she confided. "It was something of a family scandal."

Derrick looked a little stunned as he stepped forward and carefully removed the board painting from the wall. He handed it to Megan, and turned it over so that she could read the words written on the back in lead pencil.

Happy birthday to my darling Annabelle.
Love,
Daddy

She caught her breath, reading the words over and over again. "Oh my goodness," she said softly. "This is it. This is the birthday present she never got. This is what I came here to find." She looked up at him in amazement. "What are the odds? I can't believe the luck."

Derrick just stood there, staring at her, staring at the painting, and slowly he began to smile. "My dear," he said, "you have no idea."

Derrick heard someone calling his name and he turned to see the harried-looking chef in his spotless white jacket approaching with a very grim look on his face. "I have to apologize," he said without preamble. "I want you to know this is not the usual quality of service delivered by The Moveable Feast. I've done everything I can, been calling for hours, but the fact is we contracted out the desert course and the pastry chef is stuck in traffic with two gallons of crème fraiche and seventy chocolate hummingbirds painted with edible gold. Melting by now, of course." He took a deep breath. "All we have to serve is fruit from your garden, I'm afraid. I don't know what else to do."

Derrick was about to reply that melting hummingbirds were the least of their concerns at this point, but then the woman behind him stepped forward. "Maybe I can help," she said.

The chef stared at her. "Megan?"

Megan smiled, a little uncertainly, and thrust the painting into Derrick's hands. "Hi, Nick," she said, a little uncertain now. "I wasn't sure you'd want to see me."

He looked her up and down, slowly, and then more rapidly, as though trying to convince his brain of what his eyes were telling him. "I do," he said hoarsely at last. "I do want to see you."

Megan took a step toward him, and another, and as she felt her husband's arms wrap around her she knew what she had really come here to find.

Josh looked at his father in disbelief. "Do you mean she was coming here? To this place, to meet you? Leda was bringing Amy here? *Today*?"

"I had a private detective tracking her down for months," said Lester. "Not her, of course, but the baby. My granddaughter. We had no idea ..." He cleared his throat. "We didn't know if you were alive or dead, Josh, but I couldn't let that little girl grow up without a family. Of course, every time we'd get close, she'd move, and when my detective was finally able to talk to her, I think she thought we were trying to buy the baby. She wasn't going to let her go, Josh," Lester assured him quickly. "As hard as things were for her, she was determined to keep her promise to her sister, and to you. She's living with her mother about ten miles from here, and she finally agreed to bring the baby to meet with me, and give me a chance to prove who I was. That's why I was on the road when all this happened."

"Me too," Josh said. "I was on my way to find her too." And then a streak of panic crossed his face. "But we have to get out of here! They could be out there in that traffic! If she had Amy in the car—she could be hurt! We have to go look for her!"

He turned to barrel his way to the door, but his father caught his arm. "Maybe," he said, with an odd, quiet smile on his face, "we won't have to look very far."

Josh turned to follow the direction of his father's gaze and saw Leda standing only a few feet away, the hood pushed back on her yellow slicker, a flowered diaper bag over one shoulder, and on the other a bundle wrapped in a big teddy bear blanket that was speckled with raindrops. As she stared at him, her expression went from uncertainty to relief to joy, and the smile that finally came transformed her face from plain and weary to radiant.

"Josh!" she exclaimed. "Josh Whitman! Thank God! They didn't tell me you were going to be here. I've never been so glad to see anybody in all my life!"

But Josh barely heard her. He couldn't move, he couldn't breathe, and he couldn't take his eyes off the blanket-wrapped bundle in her arms.

"I almost didn't come out in the rain," Leda said, "and then Mama heard about the wreck on the highway and said I shouldn't try to make it. I figured she was right but something told me ... anyway I decided to give it a try on the back roads, and man, am I glad I did." She beamed at him and, letting the damp blanket fall away, shifted the weight in her arms so that the baby was turned toward him. "She just had her nap in the car," she said. "She's a sweet girl. No trouble at all."

She was plump and bright eyed and happy looking, sucking on her fingers as she surveyed all the lights and movement and people round her. She wore a pink teddy bear romper, and Leda had tied a pink bow in her curly honey-colored hair. Josh couldn't stop looking at her. The smile in his heart was so big it hurt his chest.

Leda put his little girl on the floor and said to her, "Can you walk to Daddy? Can you?"

Josh knelt on the floor and opened his arms. "Hi, sweetheart," he said. "Remember me?"

Leda let go of her hands, and his daughter, laughing, toddled across the floor to him. Josh laughed back and when she reached him he scooped her up, holding her, losing himself in the scent and the sweetness and the simple presence of her. Somehow, by the time he straightened up with Amy bouncing in his arms, the laughter had turned to something wet and warm on his cheeks and he had to blink his eyes to clear them. He felt his father's hand on his shoulder.

"She looks like your mother," he said softly.

Josh smiled, and Amy squealed happily in his arms. He kissed her cheek. "I know."

Then Josh's attention was caught by something across the room. He stared for a moment, and then grinned, lifting his hand in a wave to the ugly little man in the red plaid pants. Artie returned his grin, and raised his glass in a toast.

His father followed Josh's gaze. "Who's that?"

"A friend of mine," Josh replied, adjusting Amy's weight in the crook of his arm as she began to kick and squirm. "I'd introduce you, but I have a feeling he won't be staying long."

And sure enough, when Josh looked back, Artie was gone.

"Now this," declared Bridget, lifting her glass to the two hosts, "is what I call a party."

"We'll get the cleaners out for the Aubusson tomorrow," said Paul. He tried to sound cynical but it was hard to do with the pride of satisfaction shining in his eyes. He lifted his hand and called out across the room, "Hello, my darling! Marvelous to see you!"

A middle-aged woman in jeans with curls frizzed by the rain blew him a kiss and accepted the plate of risotto offered by the waiter. Lindsay said, "Who is that?"

"That's Eleanor Pakard," Derrick said, "she raises Bichons. Her mother used to oversee the entire science section of the University of Virginia library. Homebound now, poor thing, but sharp as a tack. Hello, Mrs. Bushnell," he called, and raised his glass to yet another lady who paused from her enjoyment of a corn fritter to return his wave. He answered Bridget's unspoken query with, "She runs the daycare for the Baptist church, has the most gorgeous petunias. I can't believe you don't know her. She was on her way to pick up her son from Little League practice when she got caught in the traffic jam."

Cici grinned. "I can't believe we were worried about you making friends."

Paul seemed to consider this as he looked around the room. "Everyone does seem to be having a good time."

Bridget wound her arm through his in a brief half-hug, pressing her face against his shoulder. "That's because, like I said, you don't know how to give a bad party."

"I can't believe," Lindsay said to Derrick, "that you're going to let that perfect stranger have a two-thousand-dollar painting."

Derrick took a sip of his wine, mostly to hide his wince. "Two thousand dollars?" he said. "I didn't want to say anything to her until I was sure, but unless I'm very much mistaken, her great-grandfather's name was Jackson Moncrief—also known by all and sundry as Hogpen Montana."

Lindsay breathed. "Holy cow."

Derrick nodded, his lips tight with resignation. "The last known Hogpen Montana original sold at Sotheby's for $263,000."

All three women immediately began to search the crowd for the mysterious traveler whose life was about to change in more ways than she could guess, but Derrick saved them the trouble. "She's in the kitchen," he said, "making dessert."

Harmony came up, beaming her magnificent smile, and inserted herself into the group. She slipped one arm through Paul's, and the other through Derrick's. "Fellows," she declared contentedly, "I'd say we are a smash."

Bridget raised an eyebrow as she relinquished her place at Paul's side, but smothered any protest she might have made in a sip of wine. Lindsay gave Harmony a crooked smile and stepped away from Derrick.

Paul said, "Who was that woman you were talking to in the Jimmy Choos? Striking looking, silver hair, white dress—and not a speck of mud, may I say, which was refreshing. I was going to come say hello, but then she went into the kitchen and I lost track."

"I thought you invited her," Harmony said. "She said she stayed here as a child. Fascinating woman. Her name was Annabelle, I think. She said her granddaughter was here, helping with dessert."

Derrick's face lost some of its color, and he stopped with his glass midway to his lips. "*What* did you say?"

But before Harmony could reply, there was a clatter and commotion from the foyer, followed by large men in black tee shirts rolling in big black crates of what looked very much like sound equipment. Paul looked at Derrick in utter bafflement, and they both started forward … then stopped dead.

Purline, dressed in skin tight jeans with a sequined butterfly on each back pocket, was followed by a cute blonde wearing a rhinestone studded cowboy hat, fringed snakeskin boots, and silver sequined mini-dress. She stopped every few feet to wave and shake hands and smile the smile that was known around the world. Everyone turned to stare, and a buzz went through the crowd. Those who had cell phones whipped them out and began snapping photos, others clutched each other and tried not to squeal like children. Derrick almost dropped his glass.

"Patty McClain," he said. He clutched Paul's arm, his voice growing higher. "That's *Patty McClain*!"

Purline, snapping her gum, made her way over to them through the crowd. "Hey," she said, "you should have seen the wreck that held us up. We ended up going around the back way." She glanced around. "Nice crowd, but I don't see anybody that looks even close to Ryan Seacrest. Where do you want the boys to set up?"

She turned and called over her shoulder, "Hey, Trish!" She waved her over and the blonde in the silver mini made her way through the crowd. "These are the guys I told you about," said Purline, gesturing. "This is Paul and this is Derrick."

Derrick said in a voice that was so high it was almost squeaking, "You're … you're …"

"Patty McClain," said Paul, stunned.

Purline frowned at them. "Of course she is."

Patty McClain leaned forward and pumped each of their hands in a firm, enthusiastic handshake. "Pleasure to meet you, gentlemen," she said in the lush, deeply Southern-accented voice that had won American Idol, launched three platinum albums, and sung to sold out audiences around the world. "I've got to say when cousin Purline first asked me to do this I wasn't all that wild about it. It didn't sound too much like my kind of crowd. But, boy, am I glad I changed my mind. These are my people!" She turned to the crowd and raised both arms to the air in a wide embrace. "Ladies and gentlemen," she cried. "I'm home and I want to sing! Are you ready to *party*?"

Basses thrummed, wine flowed, the crowd cheered, and melodies rang through the house. The Twittersphere lit up with snapshots and videos of the impromptu concert in the middle of the Shenandoah Valley at an unknown little place called The Hummingbird House. Lester Carson filed a story that would later win him one of the most prestigious journalism awards in his field. And as dusk fell and the rain stopped, Cici, Bridget, and Lindsay wandered on to the front porch, wine glasses in hand.

"I think," said Cici with a nod of satisfaction, "they are going to be all right."

Lindsay smiled. "I think they always were."

The door opened on Patty McClain's soulful rendering of *At Last* and Paul came out, followed in a moment by Derrick. "Roll your eyes all you want," Derrick was saying, "but the next time Harmony talks about spirits, I for one will be listening."

Paul groaned. "Oh my God, that's right. There will be a next time."

Bridget lifted her glass to them. "Congratulations," she said, "on an absolutely stellar success!"

"Patty McClain," said Derrick, and gave another amazed shake of his head. "Purline's cousin is Patty McClain."

Paul leaned on the rail beside them, wine glass dangling from his fingers, and adopted a philosophical air. "You know, it's amazing how sometimes what you've been looking for can be right under your nose all the time."

"It's just that sometimes," Bridget pointed out, "you have to stumble to see it."

Paul nodded thoughtfully, sipping his wine. "Of course, this whole thing is costing us a bloody fortune."

"I don't think the coverlet in the Indigo Room can be saved," Derrick confided.

"And the floors will have to be completely refinished," added Paul.

"We'll have to order all new towels."

"And, oh my God, did you *see* the sofa in the library?"

Cici started to laugh. So did Bridget. Lindsay raised her glass to them, grinning.

"Welcome home, boys," she said. "Welcome home."

READER'S DISCUSSION GUIDE

1. Personal responsibility is a theme that runs through *The Hummingbird House.* In what way was each character avoiding responsibility? How did the decision to accept responsibility affect his or her life?

2. Cici says that the difference between men and women is that men are accustomed to having things done for them and therefore expect life to be easy, while women expect life to be difficult and are accustomed to putting forth the effort to overcome hardship. Do you agree or disagree? How is Cici's theory proven or disproven throughout the book?

3. Despite their catastrophizing, Paul and Derrick seem to live charmed lives. Cici says they have "magic". Do you know anyone like that? Do you think this kind of luck is more likely to come to people with good hearts? Why or why not?

4. In the beginning, the ladies stage an intervention to discourage Paul and Derrick from their dependence on them. Were they successful? How do they continue to enable their friends' dependency throughout the book?

5. Bridget suggests that Paul and Derrick are masters of self-sabotage. In what ways do they prove her right?

6. Ida Mae says it's not the soil that caused the vegetables to grow so large at the Hummingbird House, but the place. Do you agree that some places have special qualities that can't be explained? In what ways does the Hummingbird House show its power throughout the book?

7. Who (or what) do you think Artie was? If he had a mission, what do you think it was? Why do you think Artie deserted Josh in Kansas City?

8. Someone once defined a miracle as "when God rescues us from the consequences of our choices". By this definition, which were the miracles in *The Hummingbird House,* and which were consequences of the characters' choices? How do you define miracle?

9. Megan eventually comes to understand that the reason that her grandmother kept taking her on adventures was to teach her courage. Why did Megan need courage on this particular adventure more than she ever had before? What do you think Annabelle really hoped to accomplish on this final journey?

10. Do you believe in coincidence? Or is everything, as this story suggests, simply a thread in the tapestry of destiny?

If you enjoyed ***THE HUMMINGBIRD HOUSE,*** you'll want to read how it all started with

The Ladybug Farm series

For every woman who ever had a dream... or a friend

A Year on Ladybug Farm
At Home on Ladybug Farm
Love Letters from Ladybug Farm
Christmas on Ladybug Farm
Recipes from Ladybug Farm
Vintage Ladybug Farm

Also by Donna Ball

The Raine Stockton Dog Mystery Series

SMOKY MOUNTAIN TRACKS
RAPID FIRE
GUN SHY
BONE YARD
SILENT NIGHT
THE DEAD SEASON
ALL THAT GLITTERS: A Holiday Short Story e book
HIGH IN TRIAL

Spine-chilling suspense by Donna Ball

SHATTERED
NIGHT FLIGHT
SANCTUARY
EXPOSURE
RENEGADE by Donna Boyd

About The Author....

Donna Ball is the author of over a hundred novels under several different pseudonyms in a variety of genres that include romance, mystery, suspense, paranormal, western adventure, historical and women's fiction. Recent popular series include the Ladybug Farm series by Berkley Books and the Raine Stockton Dog Mystery series. Donna is an avid dog lover and her dogs have won numerous titles for agility, obedience and canine musical freestyle. She divides her time between the Blue Ridge mountains and the beach, where she lives with a variety of four-footed companions. You can contact her at www.donnaball.net.

CPSIA information can be obtained at www.ICGtesting.com
Printed in the USA
BVOW08s1651310815

415714BV00001B/1/P